LARA'S HOUSE

The Letters From the Past Series
Book 1

TINA CLOUGH

He hadn't noticed Lara was in the restaurant but happened to look up and saw a slim woman with short dark hair getting up from a table for two on the far side and walking slowly towards him. Halfway to his table she made eye contact and he thought, 'It's Lara!' so he got to his feet and walked to meet her, and she started talking in a low voice as she approached.

'Hi, can you do me a favour, please?' she said. 'I need a bit of help. Would you please give me a big hug – as if you're really pleased to see me?'

For a fraction of a second, he was stunned, then he reached out, put his hands on her upper arms and pulled her into a hug. He could feel her body relax against his and thought that for some reason she really needed him, so he kissed her cheek and pulled her close to his side with an arm across her shoulders. Looking down at her he said, 'Does that guy you're with need a lesson? Or do you need rescuing?'

'I have to establish I don't belong to him exclusively,' she half whispered, her face turned up to his. 'Can I take you out for dinner next weekend on a pretend date? My treat – as a thank you.' There was a gurgle of amusement in her throat as she spoke.

'You're a dark horse, aren't you?' He gave her a little squeeze and grinned. 'Of course, you can take me out for dinner, I'll enjoy it. You have my number from when I tried to ask you out - just message me when and where.'

She giggled and stood on tiptoes with her hand on his shoulder and whispered close to his ear, as if she was telling him an intimate secret. He could feel her breath on his cheek. 'Can we do a medium-intense fond farewell now?'

He took her face between his hands and kissed her, and then she stepped back, smiled and went back to her table.

He resumed his seat among his friends, who had watched this performance with great interest and replied to their questions by saying she was a friend from long ago. Telling them he had only once met her before, and very briefly, would have created too much curiosity. He kept his gaze on Lara as the man at her table leaned forward, half-rising from his chair. His stance was aggressive, his raised voice carried across the room and Lara looked as if she was pushing her chair back, about to get to her feet again. A waiter approached their table and blocked the view for a couple of minutes, then Lara followed him to the desk, while the man she was with remained in his chair and reached for his glass.

Ignoring his friends' comments on the scene they had all watched, his eyes were on Lara as she paid and leaned forward to say something to the waiter. On her way out she turned in the doorway, looked in his direction and gave him a little salute before she disappeared out into the night.

———————————

Chapter 1

———————————

Returning to her aunt and uncle's big Edwardian villa in Stafford Street after her mother's funeral restores Lara's inner balance and she feels she can put a chapter of her life behind her without feeling guilty. While she and Aunt Bridget wait for Uncle Gordon to unlock the front door, she looks up at the tree-covered slope of Mt Victoria that starts only a couple of houses further up the street and thinks what a wonderful thing it is to have untamed nature as part of the city landscape. Since early childhood, this has been her haven of safety and calm, the place that formed her concept of what normality is, how parents who like each other interact, and how they deal with their children.

'Now then!' exclaims Gordon heading for the living room, pulling his jacket off and throwing it over the back of an armchair with one hand and loosening his tie with the other, a well-practiced move that makes Lara smile. He does that every night when he gets home from work, Lara thinks, and then a bit later Bridget comes along and picks up his jacket and tie and hangs them on the newel post at the bottom of the stairs. Isn't it amazing how such mundane gestures bring back good memories and make you feel all is well with the world?

'Let's have a drink and toast your poor mother!' Gordon runs his fingers though his thick wind-ruffled hair and heads for the tall Edwardian sideboard, flings open both doors and turns to Lara.

'What will you have? We've got nearly everything you can think of, and if you don't want a cocktail or a whisky you can always have wine – maybe that's more suitable at half past twelve?'

'For goodness sakes, Gordon! Of course, Lara won't drink whisky at this time of the day, if she ever drinks it at all – I put champagne in the fridge before we left. And we might as well sit in the kitchen so you can keep me company while I prepare lunch.'

Gordon winks at Lara and says meekly to Bridget's back, 'Quite right, darling – the perfect choice.'

The kitchen is large and square, still with the original glass-fronted cupboards above the work benches and a table and four wheel-backed chairs in the centre. The tabletop bears scars and stains from Bridget's forty years of using it for baking and preparing food and from various accidents involving hobby knives, protractors and coloured felt tip pens.

It's the heart of the family, thinks Lara, the place we gravitated to without thinking, where the twins did homework while Charlotte, Linda and I were drawing and colouring in. And when we got to the homework age, the twins were nearly at high school and sometimes worked in their room upstairs, but they kept dashing in to grab a snack and then disappeared again. She can clearly recall the day her aunt brought her back from Orchard Street to live here permanently, the feeling of calm that descended on her when she unpacked her clothes and put them away and knew that this was her home now.

She lifts her glass in a toast and smiles at her aunt and uncle, the most important people in her life, because this exact moment seems like the right time to acknowledge how important they are in her life and how much she loves them.

'If it hadn't been for you two, I can't imagine where I'd be today. You have been the anchors in my life forever, and I can't say how grateful I am. I was just sitting here thinking that you must never get rid of this table – it's a potted family history in code, the story of us all growing up.'

Gordon nods and drinks some of his wine trying to hide that he is feeling emotional. 'I'm sure you would have coped in your own quiet and self-sufficient way, Lara. And including you with our four was a pleasure – a pity none of them could come today, but it's the modern world, isn't it? To think that three of them live in different countries now and only Charlotte in New Zealand – and she with a new baby and not able to come. But you're right about the table – and it's still the centre of the house, look at us now. We didn't even think of sitting in the living room.'

'Who were those people who left first?' Bridget gives him a searching look. 'I didn't recognize them - and the way you thanked them, nearly rude!'

Lara, who had wondered the same thing, watches as Gordon's face takes on a look of intense displeasure. 'They were friends of Scott's from way back. Don't you remember them from his funeral? They made a real display of their grief then, wallowing in the reflected fame. I know it sounds harsh, but it made me sick today to listen to false sentiments from people who had studiously avoided Violet for decades.'

Lara nods. 'Me too,' she says quietly. 'After Dad left our lives changed, no more parties and very few visitors – after a while, none at all. I sat there this morning and thought of how different it was from Dad's funeral.' After a moment's hesitation she adds with a wry smile, 'But far less embarrassing, of course!'

Her father's funeral a few years ago was a true showbiz event with a packed St Paul's and flower tributes piled into high sloping banks of white and green with elaborate ribbons, and TV crews waiting outside. Her long-absent father had been transported by air from Los Angeles in a sealed coffin inside a large wooden crate to be buried in New Zealand as he had wished. People had come from the other side of the world to farewell him, and the newspapers had been reviewing his career and fame.

Her mother was drunk and made a scene that Lara will never be able to forget. Even now she cringes at the memory of how she had to get up in front of that huge crowd and try to subdue Violet's angry shouts and stormy tears, lead her back to their pew and try to calm her while the priest waited patiently. The picture is crisp in her mind with the shocked faces of the wealthy, influential and famous who had gathered to farewell her father, and the memory makes her shudder with distaste. Her inclination to step back, to become part of the landscape and avoid notice, makes this memory one of her worst ever, and that's saying something for a woman whose early life was punctuated by scenes of upheaval, anger and violence.

'I should have refused to take her, when I realised how drunk she was,' Lara says now and tries to smile at the two concerned faces watching her, 'but if I had, she would have taken a taxi, and I did think I'd be able to keep her calm. Thank goodness you were on hand to help me keep her seated after that.'

'You did a great job of the eulogy today,' says Bridget,

changing the subject. 'All those little childhood memories – such a good thing to concentrate on and Violet would have been pleased to hear you talking about happier times.'

'Thanks, Bridget – it was a balancing act, but I decided to concentrate on my early memories and just ignore the rest. They were the only things I could think of that were truly happy memories – after Dad left all that stopped. And today seemed like the right time to literally put the past behind me, or at least try to.'

She smiles at her aunt, grateful that someone has recognized how difficult it was to compose her eulogy, though she will never admit quite how long it took her to assemble enough good memories to make a decent job of it. Neither will she reveal how she had to exaggerate the good memories to flesh them out, make them brighter and better.

Bridget would understand how long Lara had hesitated over each memory, and how dark and painful recollections crept in and diverted her thoughts while she did it, but she is not going to talk about it. Bridget has lost her only sister and there is no point in dwelling on how few good memories Lara has of her mother.

That night she sleeps in the little bedroom where she spent uncountable nights after emergencies during her childhood, and where she lived permanently from the age of thirteen with her cousins Charlotte and Linda in the next room and the twins across the passage. The old wooden villa creaks as the timbers contract in the cold night air, and she listens to the wind in the trees on Mount Victoria and feels more thoroughly at home than she ever did in her mother's house. This house is full of memories that give her a feeling of permanence and security, and nothing has changed it in any dramatic way since she was a child apart from a bit of redecorating and a few new pieces of furniture. The feel of the house and the indefinable smell of home is exactly the same now as it always was, and she knows that even blindfolded, she would know where she was, the moment she walked through the front door.

The very first time she slept a whole night here she was four, the night after her parents had their first truly violent fight over her mother's drinking, when plates and glasses were flung, smashing against the walls downstairs while Lara cowered in her bed. Her mother alternately shrieking abuse and crying hysterically, her father growling like an angry bear and Lara under the covers with her hands over her ears. Then the night after, when Bridget picked her up after a call from her father asking for help.

I have spent many more nights here than I did at home, she thinks, so many times when she called and asked her aunt to pick her up after her father left and went to live in the US, when her mother was out of control drunk, and Bridget and Gordon simply came and took her away. And then fulltime after that terrible night when her mother pushed her out the backdoor into the freezing winter rain and refused to let her back in and threatened to set fire to the house, the day she was arrested, when Lara was thirteen. Were there ever two sisters as different as Bridget and her mother? They looked so alike, but their natures could not have been more different.

In her mind Lara pictures her mother; green eyes blazing and a mass of curly black hair, standing in the kitchen saying, 'I can't help it, Scott – it's my Irish blood. We're prone to strong emotions.' And the contrasting memory of Bridget tonight, standing in Lara's bedroom door, dark hair interwoven with grey and wrinkles around her hazel eyes, saying, 'I put a hot water bottle in your bed, darling – I know your feet never warm up when you get into a cold bed in winter. Just kick it to one side if it's too much.'

Chapter 2

The next morning, in a brisk Wellington wind, they pause just inside the gate to Lara's childhood home and contemplate its dilapidated state. 'Hmm,' says Gordon disapprovingly. 'I can't say I've had a close look at it lately, but it's gone downhill pretty damn fast! Look at the paint, hardly any left - and the guttering looks as if it needs replacing straight away. You don't want water to get in behind the bargeboards – that's a sure road to serious trouble. You might be better to sell it as a do-up and be rid of it.'

'It's terrible inside and it smells bad – brace yourselves.' Lara gets the key out of her bag and mounts the steps to the veranda outside the front door. 'I never interfered with Mum after she gave up drinking a couple of years ago, she got very stroppy if I suggested anything, so I just let her get on with it. She could easily have tidied it up, had it painted and re-carpeted and so on, but I don't think she could be bothered.'

'Well, let's face it,' says Bridget briskly as she follows Lara into the musty chill of the front hall. 'She lived in chaotic squalor for three decades, so she probably couldn't see how bad it was, got so used to it that it didn't register any longer. But I don't agree with selling it as a do-up – it's a fabulous old house with great potential. If you spent some money on it, you could sell it for a fortune - not that you need the money, probably. She can't have drunk all the money she so surprisingly got when your father died, can she? Fancy him leaving her all that money after all those years apart – you could have knocked me down with a feather.'

'It's in a trust, Bridget – remember?' says Gordon. 'Scott would never have left her in charge of that fortune, she could only use the income. Mind you, if she had wanted to fix up the house, we would have released capital for her to do it, but she never did. Perhaps I should have checked on her more often, but she resented advice and it was hard to deal with her – as you already know Lara.'

He walks into the dining room, and they follow and stop just inside the door, brought to a halt by the sight of the chaotic state of the room.

'Good Lord! I haven't been in here for years – what a disaster zone!' Bridget looks around the room and frowns. 'These towers of old cardboard and boxes – where on earth did it come from?'

'Internet shopping,' says Lara, 'and having everything delivered – years and years of it. She never went out if she could help it, anything that could possibly be delivered was ordered online. I've had a quick look through it and it's not just packaging and rubbish - some of the boxes haven't even been opened. I'll have to investigate them in case there's something good. And in the corner by the other window – those are the boxes I've found so far that she had opened but not unpacked – as if just looking at what she had bought was enough. I've only found one lot of things I'm keeping -

sets of lovely glasses, a dozen each of every type of glass you can imagine – really classy stuff, but never used.'

'Let's have a look at it later,' says Bridget studying the clutter with an assessing look. 'There could be real treasures here. Who knows, you might want to keep a few things to give away as presents – don't make any hasty decisions.'

'What amazed me more than his will was that they never divorced, just moved apart and lived on different sides of the world all those years - and never met even once,' says Gordon and shakes his head. He disappears through the door to the hall, and they hear him muttering as he continues into the kitchen.

The chairs around the dining table are heaped with clothing, piles of coats and jackets and on one of them what looks like a mound of clean laundry that has been left too long in the washing machine and dried all scrunched up and stiff. Under the table are piles of old newspapers and magazines, slowly sliding into one shapeless mass. A glacier of polystyrene packaging beads emerges from under the pile of boxes in the corner and Lara groans when she thinks of how hard they will be to tidy up, sticking to everything and having to be picked off one by one.

She stands beside Bridget and contemplates this scene for a moment longer, then they look at each other in near despair.

'I've never seen anything like it - a bit of a mission, darling, but I'll help you, we work so well together. We'll get it sorted,' says Bridget. 'I've watched a couple of those TV programmes about how they clear out the houses of super hoarders, you know where they have to go in with breathing gear and hazard overalls. This isn't so bad in comparison – at least it isn't full of dead rats and rotting rubbish sacks.'

'No, the mountain of rubbish sacks is outside the kitchen door, thank God – and I'm sure rats have been into them, they stink. I'm surprised the neighbours didn't complain to the council. I used to grab a couple each time I came and put them out for collection.'

She looks around the room and makes a face of disgust. 'She never hung anything up or put anything away– her bedroom is covered with piles of clothes and some of them I don't think she had worn for years - which probably accounts for the musty smell, I'm sure half of them were discarded years ago and never washed. Every time I visited, my fingers were itching to start sorting out the mess, but there was no way I dared to even offer - it made her furious. I wish I'd known about the untreated breast cancer and the brain tumour – it would have made it easier to tolerate her behaviour.'

'Come and look at this!' Gordon is standing at the kitchen window looking out into the back garden, shaking his head in disgust. 'It's a bloody wilderness – a child could get lost out there and never be found. Look at the size of those nightshade plants, they're like small trees – it's more a question of a chainsaw than secateurs. And the monster thistles! I don't think I ever saw a big, tall country thistle in the city before.'

Upstairs the four bedrooms are covered in dust and look as if they haven't been entered for years. Pale winter sunlight filters through the film of grime on the windows.

'See why we always stayed with you when we visited?' asks Lara. 'If I had dusted my old room, so we could sleep there without choking or cleaned the bathroom, Mum would have taken it as an insult, and we would have had another explosion of temper and tears and recriminations for hours on end. No way was I going to subject Roddy to one of her performances – and the fact that she liked him wouldn't have stopped her behaving like a madwoman in front of him. Since she went into care, I've only been here to do what was strictly necessary - tidy up dirty dishes, strip the bed and empty the fridge. It still seems unreal to think she moved into that place and then died within a few weeks. I hardly had time to get my head around it and then she was gone.'

'It's a pity that conspiracy mind of hers invented such dreadful stories about how evil we were,' says Gordon and shakes his head at the memory. 'Accusing us of stealing you from her and threatening to have me jailed for kidnapping. And saying Bridget had put a spell on you! So, we couldn't help her – she wouldn't let me in the last time I came to talk to her, just shouted abuse through an upstairs window.'

'A wasted life,' says Bridget. 'And when I think what a bright and clever girl she was, the life and soul of every party and so utterly beautiful – it doesn't seem like the same person.'

Chapter 3

Later, as Gordon drives them back to their place, Bridget says, 'You could do it up and live there. Watch that taxi, Gordon! I know you're supposed to go back to Hamilton tomorrow, but it is the school holidays, so you could stay a bit longer – go over the house properly with someone who understands renovations and get an idea what it would cost to do it up. It's a fabulous house and this part of Wadestown is lovely.'

In the back seat Lara unclenches her hands as Gordon manages to negotiate the taxi with millimetres to spare and lets out her breath. 'Mum's trustees might not let me,' she says tongue-in-cheek, knowing full well that Gordon is one trustee and the other is a partner in his law firm. 'And anyway, I've lived in Hamilton ever since I went to university there and I love my place, as you know. Why would I want to move to windy Wellington and take on that monster of a house?'

'I'm sure you don't, darling! It was only a random idea.' Bridget laughs at herself as she often does, and Lara thinks what an endearing habit it is, and how it had so often defused family situations in the past. 'It just seems a pity to let the house go out of the family – I still remember it as if it was yesterday, though it must be forty-odd years – how your father bought the house and then he found us one that was nearly its twin, but in a different part of town. It belonged to the parents of a camera man he worked with on a film he was either acting in or directing, and they were downsizing - not that anyone called it downsizing back then. We were lucky to have such a huge place seeing we ended up with four children, well five counting you.'

Gordon parks outside the front gate and speaks over his shoulder as he heads for the front door with the key in his hand.

'And what would she do there, Bridget? She'd rattle around in that house all on her own, only using a couple of rooms – or take in some others to share it, but do you really want to share a house at your age, Lara? Bet you prefer your convenient, modern home and having it all to yourself.'

Then he realises what he has just said and swings around with a flush darkening his face. He looks so stricken that Lara feels sorry for him and steps in to help before Bridget tells him off.

'You're quite right,' she says brightly, and hopes she sounds genuine. 'Since Roddy died, I've got used to having everything my way and I don't want to share a house with strangers. What if they turn out to be party animals and take drugs or play ghastly music late at night? I'd much rather be on my own.'

Bridget slips her coat off and her eyes crinkle in a smile. 'That's how I would feel too. Let's have coffee and then you can sit down and talk it over with Gordon while I make lunch – whether you want to sell as it is or do it up first, he'll know useful people who can help you, valuers and builders and whatever you need. He seems to have clients who can fill every requirement.'

After lunch while Lara sits at the kitchen table and watches Bridget make another round of coffee, the thought that maybe she should live in Wellington returns. It's only a fleeting idea that she dismisses nearly instantly, yet during the rest of the day it starts taking on a life of its own and develops by small increments into something that begins to resemble a plan. Perhaps it's the right time for a change, she thinks, she's only thirty-eight which is young enough to start afresh, make new friends, establish herself in a high school and get integrated into a couple of good book clubs.

Divide it, she thinks, turn the house into two flats, one on each floor, then let one flat and live in the other. It would easily make two two-bedroomed flats with plenty of room for a large open plan kitchen-cum-living area in each flat. It would pay the insurance and rates and there would be someone else in the house. And the back garden is such a suntrap – I could have a big wooden deck right across the width of the house at the back, big enough to share with the tenant, and I'd chop those huge trees down and let in more sun.

'I think I might take you up on that offer and stay a few days,' she says casually over a pre-dinner drink that night. 'It would be nice to spend some more time here and catch up with a few friends. I'm not in a rush to go home - it's two weeks until school goes back. And thinking about the house – you know how you said I would get the best price for the house by restoring it to its former glory? Do you think dividing it into two flats would work?'

She sees Gordon's hesitation and knows that if she were one of his own children, he would immediately have a strong opinion, for or against, but he has always been careful not to assume any parental rights over her. She smiles affectionately at him across the table.

'Feel free to say exactly what you would say to Charlotte or the others, you are in loco parentis after all - I really want to hear what you think. I mean, leave it in its original shape on the outside, fretwork and fancy verandah balustrade and all those lovely details – but turn each floor into a flat.'

'Possible, I suppose – let me think.' Gordon sips his whisky and gazes into the middle distance. 'Big enough for two decent sized flats, and that front hall is plenty big enough to divide off the half where the staircase is. Do you think you might get more for it if it's two flats? I'm not sure I agree – people are prepared to pay really big money for large old villas close to the CBD these days.'

'You'd have to do some serious alterations, so it would be expensive, re-plumbing for a kitchen upstairs and taking out a wall or two out to make a decent sized living space.' Bridget holds a bowl of salted peanuts out to Lara. 'Don't just take one, Lara, take a few - you're very thin. And you would need a bathroom downstairs, a full bathroom, but there's lot of room of course, plenty of scope.' She turns back to the stove. 'It's a pity Linda isn't in New Zealand - she would be useful to talk to, she does a lot of renovation design. People in the UK are buying old barns and windmills and all kinds of things and turning them into houses, even water towers – she's become a bit of a specialist in making the most out of what's already there.'

'How are the twins and their families – any news?' asks Lara. 'Did Oliver take the job in Canada? They have both got very lazy with Facebook in the last year or two – somehow Instagram isn't the same.'

'Everyone seems to be fine, for the moment at least. Linda's just found out she's expecting twins, did I tell you? Carrying on the family tradition of one set of twins in each generation on my mother's side. They are moving before the birth, their current house is one of those ancient narrow stone houses on three levels, one level half underground, York is full of them – and they can hardly fit in now with the two kids.'

'Covid changed everything, didn't it?' Gordon gives Lara a wry smile. 'First we've had nearly three years of various restrictions on travel and having to quarantine and be tested. And now Oliver and Juliet are going to live in Vancouver, and Linda's having twins of her own, so it's up to us to travel and do a world tour – we'll wait until Oliver and Co are settled in Canada first. And William is still doing nothing in particular, just plays in pub bands and refuses to take life seriously.'

'Don't knock it,' says Bridget placidly. 'At least he's not in jail or making money selling drugs.'

'But would we know?' Gordon has less faith in twin number two than Bridget has; he always did, and it occurs to Lara that maybe it explains William's refusal to compete with his more successful siblings.

Chapter 4

That night sleep evades Lara, and in her head a revolving stream of thoughts endlessly repeats without conclusion. Move to Wellington, divide the house, live in half of it, find a new school, sell the house in Hamilton – it somehow feels inviting, as if time and circumstance are right for a change, but there are negatives. What about all the friends she has made in Hamilton since she was nineteen and went to Waikato to study? And there's Roddy's mother, Davina and their weekly dinner when they talk about Roddy and look at photos and drink white wine, because Davina says her face gets red if she drinks red wine.

And I have some great friends among my colleagues at school, she thinks, and it's such a nice school – I would miss all that. Lara finally sleeps and dreams she is standing outside her mother's house in the dark in her PJs and with bare feet, and it's raining and freezing cold, but the door is locked. Desperate to get out of the cold, she bangs with her fists on the door and pleads with her mother to let her in. There are lights on inside, but she gets no response.

·   ·   ·

Waking up later than usual Lara lies still and listens to the quiet house and thinks maybe nobody is home, that maybe Bridget has gone to golf with Gordon, as she does sometimes, and if she did there will be a note on the fridge door, just as there always has been when something needs to be communicated. Standing at the top of the stairs she still hears no sound from below, but when she enters the kitchen to make breakfast, she finds Bridget at the table reading a recipe on her laptop.

'Chicken with cinnamon, dates and almonds,' she says and frowns at the screen. 'And Moroccan spices, on a bed of steamed jasmine rice. I think I've got what we need. Would you like that for dinner?'

She looks up over the top of her spectacles and it makes Lara laugh. 'Who could possibly say no? It sounds delicious. This is like time travel, Bridget. How many times did we come home from school and walk into the kitchen to raid the fridge and found you reading recipes and asking what we thought about this or that for dinner - we were so spoilt, and now you're spoiling me.'

'Nobody else around to spoil any more,' says Bridget briskly, and Lara hears the printer in the study next door whirring as it starts printing the recipe. 'Gordon always says the same thing when I ask him – "it sounds delicious, darling" - and goes off to read the paper. At least with you kids I got some feedback, someone was bound to say "Yay!" or "Oh no, not yucky dates".'

She gets up and walks towards the study saying over her shoulder, as if it were a casual afterthought, 'And did you think you might live in one of the flats yourself if you divide the house?'

It gives Lara the opportunity to collect herself before her aunt reappears, and maybe it is coincidence or maybe Bridget did it on purpose, thinks Lara, you never know with her, it's so easy to underestimate her, but she's so perceptive – she always picks up on the little cues most people would miss, and now she's given me the opportunity to think before I reply.

'I don't know, really,' she says when Bridget returns with a sheet of paper in her hand, reading as she goes. 'I might, but it's a big change. On the one hand it might be the right time for a change, to start something from scratch again – a new school, new friends, and all that. And pick up with all my old friends too, of course, I think lots of them are still here or have returned. But on the other hand, I would miss my Hamilton friends. And Roddy's mum Davina, who has lost her only child – I think she would miss me. She's a bit older than you and Gordon and her husband died a decade ago. She has two sisters and a brother and approximately four hundred nieces and nephews, most of them in Waikato, but I'm probably the only one who lets her talk about Roddy.'

Bridget picks up the electric jug. 'Coffee? And toast? But you can't live your life to please others – your friends will come and visit, and you can invite Davina to come for a weekend now and then or go to stay with her. And with those umpteen nieces and nephews living in the same town, or close by, it's not like you're abandoning her to sit alone at home, is it? I just wondered last night if you might feel tempted to have a real change?'

'Oh, I do – you're quite right. I'll think about it.'

On Monday morning, in the sunny dining room, which nobody seems to use these days, Lara turns on her laptop and thinks for a moment before she picks up her phone and texts Charlotte to ask when it would suit her to have a chat on Skype.

'Any time in the next three hours,' is the response. 'Thomas has just slurped, burped and pooped.'

'So,' she says a few minutes later and grins at Lara. 'What's this about? I can see you're in the parents' house – did you stay on after the funeral? I talked to you that morning, Friday wasn't it and I thought you said you were going back yesterday?'

'I was, but things got in the way and it's school holidays, so there's no hurry. I'll tell you a vague idea I have and see how you react – we've always been on the same wavelength about most things and you're such a good listener.'

There is a moment halfway through her story when she sees Charlotte's face changing from her listening look to a smile, though it's fleeting and by the time Lara gets to the end of her many reasons for and against moving to Wellington, the smile is gone.

'So, do you want me to reinforce your doubts or tell you what I would do if I were you?'

Lara frowns. 'For God's sake – of course I want to know what you think! It's the only reason I'm talking to you – well, not true, I also love talking to you. So?'

'Do it, of course,' says Charlotte quite casually and without any particular emphasis. 'It's perfect – just what you need. A complete change of scene, a huge project and some nice wet, windy Wellington weather. And you know the parents will be delighted to have you in the house until your mum's place is revamped, if it isn't done when you move – they really miss the visits now the other three are all overseas. Mum needs some semblance of family to worry about and cook for.'

Lara studies Charlotte's face, so like Bridget's, and wonders if she wishes she could move back herself, or have the cold, crisp Canterbury winters made Wellington's damp winters seem like a dismal ordeal in comparison? Lara feels a smile emerging. 'Oh, good! Not that I can't make up my own mind, but it's nice having somebody agree with me.'

'And if you do turn it into two flats, which I think is a great idea – you should live in the upstairs flat. Somebody noisy above you would be really annoying, don't you think?'

'I thought I'd be downstairs, that's how I've been picturing it in my mind. So, I can go out on the deck or into the garden whenever I feel like it. Not that there's a deck there now, but if I do this there will be a big deck on the sunny side.'

Charlotte makes a face and laughs. 'Oh God, it's leftover pregnancy hormones – my brain hasn't recovered yet. Of course, you want to be on the ground floor. Let the tenants drag their shopping and recycling up and down the stairs.'

Chapter 5

The assistant in the stationery shop is gazing out of the window with a vacant look on his face. 'Have you got graph paper?' asks Lara, and without turning directly towards her, he points. 'Aisle six, left hand side - about halfway along.'

This is getting very common, she thinks, as she walks down aisle six, scanning the shelves. A lot of kids who work in service jobs seem distracted. Is it that they wish you'd go away, so they can pull their phone out of their back pocket and check the action on social media?

With an A3 pad of graph paper she drives to the Orchard Street house in Bridget's car with Gordon's five-metre retractable metal measure and a pencil in her pocket. It is still raining lightly and the temperature inside the house is arctic, so she keeps her jacket and beanie on and spends two hours alternately measuring, drawing, and blowing on her fingers. Finally, she makes one last note, puts her gloves back on and studies the papers spread out on the kitchen bench. Rubbing her hands to warm her frozen fingers, she frowns. Will this be enough to use as a basis for some proper plans? I can't stay much longer or my fingers will develop frostbite, she thinks, and walks through the two floors one more time, adds a couple of clumsy notes with her gloves on, makes a few mental notes about her mother's furniture and appliances and finally leaves, chilled to her bones.

Four days later she stands in the hall of what used to be her mother's house with two men she only knows as Craig and Warren, because that's what Gordon calls them.

'No, no, no,' says Craig, the older of the two, and moves his bald head from side to side very slowly, as if he cannot believe anyone would suggest such a thing. 'Turning this lovely big hall into two separate entrances? It would ruin the house for sure – it would be a crime and the value would drop like a stone.'

His younger companion grins at Lara. 'Pay no attention to Mr Grumpy here – he'll just take a bit of time to come around to the idea. What you are describing seems perfectly do-able to me, but there are lots of details to be added to your plans, so we'll have to meet here again, perhaps next week when we've had time to go over your drawings? And if we could have a key, we can come back to check on things as we work on the plans so we get exact measurements.'

Lara smiles gratefully, relieved that at least one of them has a positive approach, something she suspects is going to be vital when renovating and dramatically altering a hundred-year-old wooden villa, full of unknown pitfalls and problems.

'The leadlight window above the door and the matching panels in the door must be preserved,' she says, 'and whichever way we achieve two separate entrances, the exterior must remain intact.'

'There's no hurry about that bit - we can put it on the back burner for now and map out the rest. Come on, Dad,' says the younger man and pushes the older one ahead of him. 'Let's spread out the plans Lara has drawn and talk though it.'

It takes three hours of looking at her plans and walking around, stepping over and around the clutter, checking details she hadn't thought of and discussing alternative solutions, because their experienced eyes see things from a very practical angle.

'No, we can't take out entire walls without having an expert look them over,' says Craig at one stage. 'One of these might be a loadbearing wall and we'd have to replace it with I-beams – steel, you know, or possibly laminated wood beams – which requires a permit and takes time. Proper plans and a lot more work.'

'So?' says his son. 'That's not a problem, is it? We'll get Sam in.' He turns to Lara. 'Sam's a structural engineer and we've worked with him several times before. He'll do some proper plans and we'll get a council inspection, and then we'll apply for the consent, if it turns out we need one.'

Craig shakes his head again. 'It means a lot more money, it all adds up – are you OK with that?'

Lara smiles at his discontented face and the way he seems to find something to object to at every turn. 'I have no idea what the revamp might cost until you tell me, so a bit more isn't going to make me say no at this stage, is it? I think selling my house in Hamilton will cover it.'

She is not about to start telling everyone she meets that she has inherited a trust fund with God knows how much invested which just keeps on making more money, because she knows without a doubt that the rumour would spread and change attitudes among both old and new friends.

She watches them walk away to their truck, amused by

how even from behind Craig looks as if he is continuing to make objections, and how Warren strides along with the rolled-up plans in one hand, probably laughing at his father's complaints. She gets into Bridget's car, reminding herself to tell her that the diff is making a slight grinding sound, and smiles at the entertaining relationship between Mr Grumpy and his son.

Over dinner that night Lara tries to describe to Bridget and Gordon how she is planning to have the two flats laid out and fails completely, so she runs upstairs and gets the first very rough draft she made and spreads it on the kitchen table. With a ballpoint pen she draws new lines in places and explains the changes suggested by the builders.

'So, you can see the two flats will be very similar, and we'll have the new kitchen upstairs directly above the one downstairs,' she says and leans back in her chair so she can see both their reactions, 'so the plumbing issues are minimised – and the same with the bathroom and toilet. Mr Grumpy is worried about how to create separate entrances – he thinks a dividing wall in the hall would ruin the house.'

Bridget looks at her in surprise. 'But why would you divide it? Surely it could be a shared space?' She takes the pen out of Lara's hand and points. 'Make a little wall this side of the staircase across to here with a door in it, which is your door into the kitchen-living area. And put a door at the top of the stairs and that's the tenant's front door so to speak – make sure there's a little landing up there for people to stand on to put their shopping down while they get the key out. Put locks on the downstairs doors into your flat, here and here, and one on this door, I suppose, though I can't remember what it is and it might not need a lock.'

She makes crosses in places on the plan of the ground floor as she speaks. 'So, you decide which door is your main one – either the new one here, that leads into the kitchen or this one that's already there, which takes you into the passage between the two bedrooms – where they are going to be, I mean. Or you have that one taken out, doesn't matter.'

'Ah,' says Lara. 'Very clever, thank you! So, we're left with the entire width of the entrance hall intact - the tenant goes up the stairs and unlocks their door, and I go to whichever door I decide is my front door on any given day and unlock it. Brilliant, because that big hall is such a feature with the stained glass in the door and the windows. And this door here.' She points at the third cross on the plan. 'That doesn't need a lock at all – it's a big walk-in wardrobe off the hall, and it can be a shared space to hang coats and leave umbrellas and things, maybe suitcases and big things - which will be useful. And then we install two doorbells outside the front door, I mean the main door – one for each flat.'

Gordon looks at Lara's nearly untouched wine glass, makes no comment on the plans and pours more wine for himself and Bridget.

'You were so lucky getting a builder,' he says. 'I still can't believe I happened to call Craig nearly the very moment he had put the phone down on someone cancelling the big job that was next on their list – incredible luck. Some people wait for a year to get someone to come and even look at a job. And I hope you don't call Craig Mr Grumpy to his face.'

'Of course not! It's Warren who calls his father Mr Grumpy – I wouldn't dare.'

When they tidy up after dinner, Lara says, 'I'll stay on for the rest of the holiday, if it's OK with you. I've got to get the place emptied out whether I divide it or not. I'll start on it tomorrow - and I'll get a skip delivered, or dumpster or whatever those things are officially called. And I'll hire a storage unit for the bits of furniture I want to keep.'

Chapter 6

Four days later Bridget stands at the upstairs hall window looking down at the giant skip. 'You know how I said I didn't think you'd need the biggest size skip?' she says. 'When the truck lifted it off and I stood beside it and realised how gigantic it is, I thought most of the contents of the house would fit inside. Now look at it, it's nearly full, even after all the useful stuff has been taken away.'

Lara joins her aunt, who like herself is dressed in several layers of clothes and covered in dust. They both look down into the skip.

'It's crazy, really,' says Lara, 'when you consider how much of the big furniture the Sallies picked up – that mess down there is mostly small stuff and junk. But I didn't know that the garage was crammed full of old rubbish. I hadn't been in there since Dad left home, I don't think, so I had no idea it was full to the brim.'

'It's good to know so much has gone to where it's needed instead of to the dump.' Bridget rubs her hands together before she tucks them into her armpits to warm them up.

'And the guy from the Sallies said they sell things to people who restore them and on-sell them – great idea!'

They do a tour of the upstairs rooms with Lara holding the first rough plan she made and try to imagine what it will be like when walls have been removed or repositioned.

'It will be lovely - light and sunny,' says Bridget standing in the doorway of a wall which will disappear and become the middle of the kitchen-cum-living area. 'Sun from late morning through the window over there and then a bit later in the day it will come around the corner and shine into this part here - provided you have those large elms and the pin-oak taken out. I can really imagine it now and it will be much more spacious than it looks on paper.'

She beckons to Lara who is looking down into the back garden. 'Come on, no daydreaming – we've got to finish the kitchen and then it's all done apart from the furniture they're taking to the storage unit.'

Lara surveys the collection in the hall and sighs. 'Who would have thought I will only be keeping four boxes of small things, and the photos from the roll-top desk, two artworks and three pieces of furniture? Apart from mum's jewellery and that stunning painting she had in the resthome, that will always remind me of her. I remember when Dad brought it home and she danced around the room, she was so delighted. Oh, and all those expensive glasses, and the pile of boxes with potential presents, but they're not for me, so I hardly count them. It doesn't seem much from such a big house, does it? I'll cancel the moving guys and the storage unit. This lot will fit easily in the cloak room now we've got rid of the junk that was there and if I stack things right. Let's finish emptying the last kitchen cupboards and then we're done.'

'What about the fridge? Do you think you and I can tip it into the bin?'

'God, no! We'd never get it over the edge, don't even think about it! We'd just hurt ourselves. I asked Warren and he said they'll have to get jumbo skips in for all the stuff they tear out, so they'll get rid of the fridge and the stove too – they are both far too old to be worth keeping.'

'No Gordon, we *will* take a taxi,' says Lara to her uncle a few hours later before she goes upstairs to shower and change. 'Tonight, dinner is on me, and I want us all to have champagne and a really good wine to celebrate what we've achieved. And because it's my treat, you have to do what I tell you.'

He pats the top of her head, like he always did when she was a little girl and says what he used to say then. 'OK, Lara Winstanley – you're the boss.'

'Very nice,' says Gordon an hour later when Lara and Bridget join him in the front hall to put their coats on. 'A great improvement on track pants and sweaters. That dress is pretty, Lara – is it new?'

Bridget stands back and looks critically at Lara's red dress. 'Suits you to a T. That bright red and the Chinese-style high collar - perfect with short black hair. But I've seen it before, I think.'

And Lara nods, but she doesn't say anything, because she knows exactly when Bridget last saw her wearing this dress, at the dinner Bridget put on for Roddy's forty-fifth birthday, a month before he died. She left it behind by mistake at the Stafford Street house that weekend and never picked it up on subsequent trips. Somehow the memory of when she wore it last made it seem unlikely that she would ever want to put it on again, but tonight for some reason it feels as if she is starting a new chapter.

'Great food – and what a nice place this is. I'd never heard of it before,' says Gordon appreciatively and looks around the Aubergine Café dining room. 'It's lovely how they use these old villas now without ruining the outside or tearing the nice details out.'

'Like what I'm doing with my house?' Lara laughs. 'But I promise it will look the same from the outside and as we know, the front hall will stay as one space. I asked a couple of friends for a tip of a good restaurant and they both mentioned this place – I'm glad you like it.'

'Someone at the mah-jong club told me we should try it,' says Bridget, 'and I agree, it's very nice and so pleasant being out of the business centre of town. I've always had a soft spot for Tinakori Road – you know, Katherine Mansfield and all that.'

Lara is just about to say something when Gordon's arm shoots up in the air and his hand waves vigorously. 'Tobias! Come and meet my niece!'

As Tobias comes across to their table, Gordon turns to Lara and says in a not quite sufficiently quiet aside, 'He's the oldest son of one of the senior partners in my firm – nice bloke, can't remember what he does – he's single again.'

Lara winces and Bridget's eyebrows pull together in disapproval, but before she can tell Gordon off, Tobias materialises beside their table. He is tall and blond and seems genuinely pleased to meet up with Gordon and Bridget. Lara notices the way his eyes rove over her when he is introduced and makes no effort to invite any particular attention. He is handsome and confident, asks how they are and tells them he is meeting a group of friends for dinner, and Lara takes a sip of her wine and contributes nothing to the conversation. And then, to Gordon's obvious disappointment, Tobias's friends arrive, and he leaves them.

'Nice bloke,' says Gordon again. 'No, don't frown, Bridget – I'm not trying to get Lara interested in him, I'm just saying.'

Bridget rolls her eyes. 'When you hear your uncle say "just saying" in that tone of voice, Lara, you'd better watch out. It means he is certainly not making an idle observation.'

Gordon laughs and raises his glass in a toast. 'Here's to the house!'

Chapter 7

The next morning Bridget calls up the stairs to Lara. 'Do you want me to answer your phone?'

'Yes, please – and I'm coming down!' Lara starts down the stairs just in time to hear her aunt say, 'This is Lara's assistant, can you hold please?'

Laughing she takes her phone out of Bridget's hand and glances at the screen, but it's just a number, not someone she has in her contacts list.

'Lara - was that Bridget?' asks a male voice she can't place. 'It's Tobias – I got your number from Gordon, just now – met him outside his office. Hope you don't mind but I thought we might get together for a drink or something. If you're not booked up this weekend?'

She pictures him in her mind; tall, big shoulders, thick neck, and imagines he plays rugby or spends a lot of time in the weight room at the gym. And very confident. She's not interested, because he seems self-assured in a way that probably means he regards himself as better than those around him. Snap judgement, yes, but why not, rather than risk a boring date?

'I'm pretty busy – I'm going back to Hamilton on Sunday, and I've already got a few things lined up. I think I'd better say 'no, thanks' or I won't have enough time with Gordon and Bridget.'

'OK, I just thought I'd ask. But perhaps another time when you're back in town?'

She puts the phone down and goes to find Bridget, who is doing yoga in front of a YouTube video on the TV in the living room and who instantly mutes the sound and sits up straight on her bright yellow yoga mat. 'Who was that? I thought I recognized the voice.'

'It was that Tobias chap we met at the restaurant last night. He was asking me out, but I haven't got time.'

Bridget snorts and gets to her feet. 'He'll be back! He likes a pretty face and he's probably running out of women to date. He's been married twice, and he has four or five kids and he's probably had more girlfriends than I've had hot dinners.'

'Ah, so not particularly desirable then? I thought Gordon seemed keen on him.'

'Gordon is, and this is God's truth, a marriage broker at heart! He was always on the lookout for some suitable man for our girls and now he's doing it for you. My advice is to ignore him, and if you don't like the look of Tobias, then don't go out with him. Being the son of one of Gordon's oldest friends is not a recommendation in itself. Not that there's anything wrong with James, but it doesn't mean his son is good husband material.'

'There she is - my precious little tootsie!' exclaims Julian that afternoon when Lara arrives at the café he chose for their afternoon coffee date. She looks with pretend horror at her old primary school friend, rotund and with a receding hairline, who stands there with his arms outstretched like a short, chubby version of Christ on the mountain top in Rio.

'I really wish you'd stop doing that! We only see each other every couple of years, and you always bring it up – can't you stop now?'

His beaming smile fades when her tone of voice registers and his arms drop. 'Oh, darling - I'm sorry! Your mother just died, didn't she, and of course you don't want to be reminded of her all the time.'

She instantly feels guilty at her bad-tempered outburst, not something she normally, if ever, indulges in, then suddenly she gets it and groans.

'Oh, God I'm so sorry – I shouldn't have snapped at you like that! You don't know the background. I apologize, Julian, I don't know what came over me, but it touched a raw nerve. I can't imagine why I thought you would know what sits behind that memory. I'll explain it to you when we've got our coffee.'

With their coffees ordered and an offer of cake declined by Lara, they find a table by a window and she reverts to the subject of the effusive greeting.

'Of course, you thought that over-the-top greeting from my mother when we came out of school every day was lovely, and so did a lot of others, adults included, but ...'

Julian interrupts, his chubby face creased with concern. 'But it was lovely, darling! Nobody else's mum was so delighted to see their child every single day. I can still picture how she would crouch down and open her arms wide and say that – and I would think how special you were to be so loved.'

'OK, Jules,' says Lara and decides to tell it as it was, no euphemisms. 'Just between you and me, this is the truth of how it was. The performance at the school gate was her public persona, the façade – playing the doting mother. She had probably limited herself to one bottle of wine up to that point of the day, so she'd be able to drive to the school and walk in a straight line. Even she could grasp that my father meant what he said – if she didn't pick me up from school every single day, he would be informed and claim custody of me.'

For some reason she can't quite identify, Lara pours it all out. 'And then when we got home, she would continue drinking, and by dinner time she was out-of-her-mind drunk and aggressive – and impossible to please. Any little thing would trigger a slap or screaming or being locked out of the house, rain or shine. My father had left, he couldn't take it any longer and my life was a balancing act - trying to avoid aggravating her, but not staying right out of her way, because that was just as bad. It was called sulking and resulted in more scenes, just a different kind.'

Julian's face takes on a look of deep distress, and he looks as if he might cry. 'Darling, I had no idea! I bet none of us kids knew. And I remember now, I can picture the scene - you never ran towards her, did you?'

Just then their order number is called, so Lara gets up, returns with their cups and smiles at Julian, who still looks upset.

'Please don't look so tragic – I don't normally agonize over it or even think about it. It's just that being back here and spending time clearing out the house and finding so much which reminds me – it's been a bit much. And I was rescued in the end.'

'Oh God, you poor darling, I don't know how you coped – at that age!' Julian's face is a mixture of pity and embarrassment, and Lara smiles to make him feel more comfortable.

'Don't worry, it's history and I'm not traumatised by it, this was just a temporary glitch. You've lived overseas for so many years so you probably missed some of the more mortifying milestones later on, there was plenty of gossip, I'm sure. My mother was an alcoholic and a chronic hoarder, and she had no control over her temper. I ended up living with my aunt and uncle – remember Charlotte's parents?'

She pauses while she drinks some coffee and decides to be totally frank for a change, to actually tell him about the most embarrassing moment in her life.

'But I can't believe you never heard about the debacle and drama of my dad's funeral. I really thought the whole world knew about that – the most mortifying moment of my life. It was all over the media, just ghastly.'

An hour later, they have covered most of what had happened since they last met. Glowing with pleasure, Julian tells her about his wedding in Queenstown and shows her a dozen pictures of his husband Harry, who seems to be a close clone of Julian.

'It's ridiculous!' says Lara and tries to resist laughing. 'I can't get over it - you could be brothers you're so alike, Tweedledum and Tweedledee. Are you sure he's not some long-lost sibling?'

'God forbid, darling – I don't think incest is my thing, and think of what my dear old dad would say. He can hardly bring himself to refer to Harry as my husband – well, now I think about it, he hasn't uttered the word once. He just refers to him as "your friend Harry" and says, "good thing your mother is dead and can't see this". But it isn't surprising, is it? A retired army man, a generation older than the parents of most of my friends – he's ninety-three now, so he'll never change.'

Before she can reply, Julian's attention has switched to somebody approaching from behind Lara and he gets to his feet, beaming with pleasure. 'Mark, mate! How amazing – I haven't seen you for years and years. And here I am with Lara - you know each other, I'm sure.'

'Of course, I remember you!' says Mark, who is very handsome and reminds her of Tom Cruise, though at high school he was just another good-looking older boy.

'I think I remember you.' She hopes she gives the appearance of trying to recall him. But of course, she remembers him, and how she once said something to him on the way out of assembly, and how he ignored her, so a cool approach seems a good way to start. 'I think you were a couple of years ahead of Charlotte and me.'

'Lara is just back in town for a funeral,' says Julian.

'I'm sorry to hear that.' Mark seems genuine and Lara hopes desperately Julian won't refer to anything she just told him about her mother. He's not renowned for his discretion, but he makes no further comment.

'And where do you live now?' asks Mark. 'Not another old school mate who's moved to the other side of the world, I hope?'

'I live in Hamilton – I went to uni there.'

'And are you enjoying your visit? Apart from the funeral, of course.'

'Her mother died – she only just got over the funeral,' says Julian firmly and frowns at Mark. 'It's not the easiest thing to get over, you only have one, after all.' He gives Lara a little conspiratorial smile as if to say, 'You and I know, but we don't have to tell everyone', and Lara returns the smile and thinks what a lovely guy he is, always has been, ever since they met at the age of five.

Mark's words of sympathy are interrupted by his order number being called and he returns to the counter to pick up his coffee, so Lara turns to Julian to continue their conversation. She is taken by surprise when Mark returns, pulls a chair over from the table beside theirs and joins them.

'So,' he says cheerfully, 'tell me what you're doing in Hamilton.'

'I'm a high school teacher – English, French and Spanish.'

'Wow! That's impressive, don't you think, Jules? I can barely speak English some days.'

'And how come you're not at work, Mark?" asks Julian in a tone of voice Lara knows well but suspects that Mark might not. 'Skiving off from the office like you used to at school? Got some lie ready to trot out?'

Julian, a kind man but given to occasional flashes of bitchiness, looks hard at Mark, who is clearly taken aback by this sudden interrogation.

'I had to come into the city to pick up some urgent papers from another firm, so I thought the traffic and parking could cop the blame for an extra hour. But I must go soon.'

When he leaves after leisurely finishing his coffee, Julian turns to Lara. 'See what I mean? Very tricky customer, always was.'

From the way Mark breaks his stride momentarily, Lara can tell he's heard the comment and she shakes her head at Julian. When they part after an affectionate hug and a promise to keep in touch, she walks back to where she parked the car and thinks that this visit has been surprisingly social, not at all what she expected. Tomorrow she is having lunch with a couple of old high school friends and then dinner with Bethany, who was one of her best friends in primary school, and who is on a short visit from Melbourne where she lives. Who would have thought the time after mum's funeral would turn into a kind of piecemeal reunion, she thinks, and how amazingly fast the word spreads on social media that people have met up with me and then others get in touch; it's a chain reaction and I had no idea that some I hadn't stayed in touch with are still here or have returned.

Chapter 8

On a Saturday in early August with a strong wind wildly tossing the trees on Mt Victoria, Lara is getting ready to meet a friend for lunch downtown.

'Take your storm jacket instead of that elegant coat!' says Bridget. 'You left it in the coat cupboard in the front hall last weekend – I found it after you'd gone. It's not going to get much warmer than this all day and heaven knows how far you'll have to walk and the forecast is for showers. Finding a parking spot at midday on a Saturday is pretty hopeless - you might be better to just walk.'

Twenty minutes later Lara pulls the zip up to her chin and tugs the hood down over her forehead, grateful for the orange jacket, and sets out to walk to Courtney Place where she is meeting Gabriella. Possibly the decision to walk the whole way rather than take Bridget's car is a mistake, but the jacket proves to be a wind and waterproof capsule, and inside it she is warm and dry, insulated by her favourite bright red merino jumper.

When she put it on, Bridget smiled at the sight. 'You look like something sent from heaven to brighten up the

Wellington scene on a day like today! I never understood why Wellingtonians insist on wearing black and grey in the winter, so depressing.'

The restaurant is like a separate universe of light, heat and noise. Lara stops just inside the door and scans the room until she sees Gabriella rise to her feet and wave vigorously. She weaves between the tables, smiles an apology at someone whose chair she nudges and breathes in the smells of Chinese food. Suddenly she is starving.

'How good is this?' Gabriella, who towers over Lara, hugs her tight and turns beaming to the six women around the table. 'She'll be back nearly every weekend – it will be just like when we were at high school. Sit yourself down, poppet – as you can see, I've organised a mini reunion.'

Lara drops her bag on the floor and shrugs out of her jacket. 'You're just the same, Gabs! You call me and say let's me and you get together for a little cosy catch-up and some gossip, and then it turns into a party. Exactly like when we were at high school.'

A waitress who looks like Sofia Vergara including the way her scoop-neck top seems to barely contain her abundant bosom, comes to take orders.

'Don't have the fish,' she says without lowering her voice. 'It's not fresh.'

Eight pairs of eyes look at her in surprise and then glance around the table at the others, and for a moment nobody says anything. Then Lara, trying unsuccessfully to hold back laughter, looks up at the waitress. 'You've just handed in your notice, haven't you?'

The girl giggles and points her pen at Lara. 'You're a sharp one – yep, resigned this morning as of this shift. Now – are you ready to order?'

After four hours, Gabriella suggests they move on to a tapas bar which has just opened and is supposed to be great.

'Not that I believe it till I've tried it myself – but let's go and have a glass of wine and check it out. How much change do we have between us? Nobody carries cash these days, but let's give that gorgeous girl a good tip.'

Having rustled up thirty-two dollars in coins and small notes for a tip, which Lara makes sure is put straight into the hand of the waitress, they stand outside in a freezing wind and discuss whether to walk or move their cars. After a couple of minutes of debate, Gabriella decides moving cars is ridiculous. 'It will be much quicker just walking - come on, you lot, get moving!'

The woman beside Lara, whose name she has tried to remember right through lunch, rolls her eyes and hooks her arm in Lara's. 'Let's huddle to preserve body heat – and doesn't it just remind you of Gabs at school? Absolutely no patience with dithering, so she just makes a decision for everybody, born bossy.'

'Yep, and we all follow her like a flock of sheep – just like we always did, she was always a leader.' Lara laughs. 'Look at her stalking ahead without even checking if we're following – no wonder she's CEO of that big tech company. Do you remember her younger sister, what was her name? Tiny blond girl, the absolute opposite of Gabriella.'

'Carina, I think – I didn't know her, but I remember those two walking to and from school together, always made me laugh to see them, so different.'

They walk the four blocks to the tapas bar and halfway Lara's phone pings with a message. 'No way!' she says to nobody in particular. 'I'm not taking my gloves off for anything, it can wait.'

The bar is rather excessively decorated with pictures of bullfights and matadors, but it's warm and they pull three extra chairs over to a semicircular banquette and ignore the look from the waiter, so they can sit at a round table. Lara gets her phone out to check who messaged her, sees a number she doesn't recognise and opens it to see who it is.

'Now, how did he get my number?' she says to herself and Gabriella, who is next to her, looks up from the wine menu. 'Who is it?'

'Mark what's his name – you know the guy a year or two older than us at school. Good looking guy – very popular. I met him when I had coffee with Julian a couple of weeks ago.'

'I don't remember him. What does he want?'

'Wants to take me out for dinner tonight.'

'Bad luck, Mark whoever you are, you're too late – we're not letting you go, Lara.'

'I won't be home in time for dinner – this is turning into a school reunion,' texts Lara to Bridget. 'I have my key.'

It is not until she takes a taxi back to Stafford Street after eleven that Lara's thoughts return to Mark and she wonders how he got her number. She texts back: 'Sorry, didn't see this message till now – just on my way home. Another time, maybe?'

Chapter 9

Charlotte appears on Lara's laptop screen for an early morning chat with baby Thomas draped over her shoulder. 'How's it going? How is Roddy's mum taking the news about you moving to Wellington? What's her name again?'

'Her name is Davina – please turn around,' says Lara. 'I want to see his face.'

Charlotte swivels in her chair and what Lara sees makes her laugh. 'He's sound asleep and blowing milk bubbles – so cute! Won't he wake up if we keep talking?'

'He's used to noise - he sleeps whatever is going on. I took a friend's advice early on - I even used the vacuum cleaner in the passage outside his room with the door wide open from the week he was born, never tried to keep the house any quieter than it would normally be, so he's used to it.' Charlotte smiles and jiggles Thomas who is deeply and floppily asleep and doesn't notice. 'I think people make a rod for their own backs by changing how they do everything because there's a baby in the house. I'm sure nobody whispered around the cradle back in the early farming days, when the baby slept in the kitchen because it was the warmest room in the house and where everyone spent their indoor time.'

'Amazing! But back to Roddy's mum – yes, she took it much better than I would have expected, very much better. She said she thinks it's the best thing I could do, have a new start and a big project, and she'll come for a weekend visit now and then when there's something she wants to do in Wellington. She's into art in a big way and often travels to see special exhibitions. It's a huge relief.'

'And what have you been up to, apart from travelling back and forth to Wellington every weekend?'

'Just the usual – but I handed in my notice this week and I put the house on the market.'

'Isn't it a bit early? But I suppose you could you put things in storage and stay with Davina?'

'Exactly what we decided – that it's a good idea to get rid of the house as soon as possible so I have time to sort things out now instead of at the last minute. And I told the school that I'll stay to the end of the year to give them time to find another Spanish teacher – French and English is easy, but there aren't so many people who teach Spanish. And because they've been able to offer it ever since I started there, we've built up a bit of a following – we now have Spanish classes from Year 9 to Year 13 and it seems to be quite trendy.'

Charlotte grins. 'Bet it's the same kids who take French. Kind of goes together in my mind – I know they're not at all the same, but it seems likely.'

'Quite a few of the same kids, yes, but I think it's because they enjoy learning languages generally. It would probably be the same if I taught Norwegian. How is Jonas's big new job?'

'He loves it – project managing a giant build like that is a real challenge, but he enjoys a challenge. And he says it makes him feel good working in the middle of town seeing how it's all coming together finally – the building he's on will be the final one in a whole block they tore down after the earthquake. He's playing squash this morning or he'd be hanging over my other shoulder to say hello.'

When they end their chat, Lara closes the laptop and goes to pack her bag for her trip to Wellington. Her flight leaves at quarter past eight and she is meeting Craig and Warren at the house at eleven, just enough time to go to Stafford Street, drop her bag and borrow Bridget's car, so she needs to be organised. And now that her Wellington social life far exceeds that in Hamilton, she is gradually moving clothes to the wardrobe at the Stafford Street house, things she has more use for there.

'Do you mind?' she asked Bridget last weekend. 'Word is spreading that I'm here every weekend and I suddenly find myself with a whole crowd of friends I haven't socialised with for a decade or more. Isn't it odd? Before Roddy died, we'd come to visit you, and briefly Violet, about once a month, but I never did anything more than meet the same old friend for coffee now and then. Time was always short.'

'Not odd at all,' said Bridget. 'Just the way things happen – people tell each other little bits of info, someone says "Did you know Lara's here every weekend now, let's get together and catch up" – and before you know it you have a buzzing social life. I think it's great.'

Now she stands beside her bed and studies what she has laid out to pack. Tonight, she is going out for dinner with Mark, and on Sunday she is having lunch with two of the old school friends she reconnected with when Gabriella organized the long lunch, before she flies back late that afternoon.

Chapter 10

When Lara arrives at the house, Warren is waiting in the hall with his dad. 'Well? What do you think about the plan? Could you open the attachment? And will it work?'

'More or less perfect, I think. What did the structural engineer guy say about the loadbearing walls?'

Warren leads the way into the kitchen, as yet hardly touched, pulls the paper out of his pocket and unfolds it.

'So – when this wall comes out here and then that one at right angles, we'll put up a few props to hold everything up while we install the beams. Sam suggested we get laminated beams rather than steel - seems nice in an old villa like this.' He points at the plan. 'Where the double lines are, here and here, that's where the beams will go, and they'll be in the same places upstairs. Nice and solid.'

'And will the council approve his plan?'

Craig grins, probably the first time Lara has seen any kind of smile on his face, and nods. 'It's pretty standard – there won't be a problem with the inspection. Sam was very relaxed about it, said the dimensions he's suggested are above what they demand, doesn't cost a lot more but it makes sure they approve it.'

After an hour and half, they have gone over the details that were impractical to discuss in emails, and Lara leaves with excitement fizzing in her head. Standing there today with Craig and Warren and hearing them describe the next step of the process has made the changes to the house real and immediate. It's as if something she has only thought of theoretically, but without much emotion, has abruptly taken on real life and it makes her feel unexpectedly happy.

Dinner with Mark is surprising on many levels, because Mark seems to genuinely enjoy her company and turns out to be attentive and charming, much more so than she had expected. While he talks to the wine waiter, she studies his face and thinks that she has let Julian's comments about him colour her thinking. The waiter leaves with their orders and Mark smiles across the table in a way which makes her feel special, as if she is appreciated.

'Someone said you're doing up a big old house in Wadestown which sounds interesting. Are you going to move here and live there yourself?'

'It was my parents' house, I used to live there when I was little, but it's deteriorated a bit, so I'm doing it up.'

Aware even as she speaks that she hasn't answered his question, she briefly wonders about her reluctance to commit herself publicly, and then the waiter arrives with their wine and Mark raises his glass in a toast.

'Here's to old villas! I love them myself, all the space and the high ceilings – and renovations have interested me ever since I was little and our neighbour tore the old wooden bungalow next door to bits and transformed it. Tell me what you're doing – I hope you managed to get someone good to do it.'

Over the meal she tells him a bit about the house and how she is dividing into two flats and elaborates on how convenient the front hall is with so much space and the staircase just off-centre. 'It really lends itself to being two flats,' she says and tastes her pasta chasseur. 'This is gorgeous! What's yours again?'

'Grain-fed Angus beef fillet steak, very nice. But tell me more about how you're dividing the house. Are you going to have to change the exterior? Some of those grand old Wadestown villas are so beautiful.'

She explains how the entrance hall is going to be left intact and what the main changes are. 'So, when a few interior walls have been taken out it will be light and spacious - and warm! All the wall linings are being pulled out and the walls and ceilings insulated. I can still remember the freezing cold bathroom and how I hated getting out of bed in the winter, the house was like a fridge.'

'I'd love to see it some time,' he says casually. 'When you have time.'

'Where are you parked?' He holds the restaurant door open for her. 'I'll walk you to your car – town can get a bit rowdy on a Saturday night. I could have picked you up, you know.'

'I'm right over there, so no need to escort me.' Lara points across the street. 'I drove up just as someone was leaving – perfect spot. I'd been to the City Art Gallery this afternoon with a friend and then we went back to her flat in Vivian Street and sat talking for ages, so I came straight here.'

They arrange to meet at the house at ten the next

morning, and he kisses her cheek. 'What number Orchard Street? I don't think you said.'

She tells him, crosses the street to her car and turns to watch him walk away. How surprising that was, she thinks, as she drives back towards Stafford Street. All those questions! Who would have thought he was so interested in renovating old villas? But it will be fun showing someone what she's doing, now that the work has started in earnest, and he might have some good ideas. And she must have mentioned the street, though she can't remember doing it.

'Watch your step,' says Lara the next morning and unlocks the front door. 'There are floorboards up in some places and pieces of wood lying around.'

They stand in the front hall while she explains how the two flats will work out. 'The upstairs flat will have a lockable front door at the top of the stairs and I'll have two doors I can use from here to get into my flat.' She leads the way through the demolished doorway into what used to be the dining room. 'So, I'll have an L-shaped flat and the upstairs will be nearly exactly the same, but with a bit of extra space above where the ground floor hall is.'

Mark studies the space and walks through the door to the kitchen. 'Wouldn't you rather have the bigger flat upstairs?'

Just what Charlotte said, thinks Lara, and one or two other people as well. Am I the only person who thinks of the access?

'Oh no, I want to be able to go directly out on the deck through what's going to be French doors over there – from what's going to be the living room.' She looks out into the jungle of the back garden and grins. 'I might have a herb garden and a couple of fruit trees. And I'll definitely have a big deck, maybe roofed - I might even get one of those patio heaters, knowing what Wellington summers can be like. But lugging shopping and recycling up and down the stairs – why would I?'

'You could have one of those louvred roofs over the deck – you know the ones that have a little motor and you open or shut them with a remote. Great idea, so you get sunlight into the house in the winter.'

She agrees that this sounds like a good idea and continues the tour, but in the back of her mind she dismisses the louvred roof idea as too modern. Her commitment not to ruin the exterior of the house can accommodate a deck with a roof that fits the age of the house, but not motor operated louvres.

'Two bedrooms?' asks Mark and studies the space through the kitchen to the living room. 'Small bedrooms and big living area?'

She walks ahead of him and points. 'One big bedroom with a walk-in dressing room over there, then a bathroom followed by a smaller bedroom, then the living area through here, right down the long side of the house – open plan with a large island counter separating the kitchen from the rest of the room.'

He thinks for a long moment and nods. 'That sounds good – I like the idea of the double glass doors to a deck, and this side will get the afternoon sun, I think.'

Lara remembers her thoughts last night and says, 'You really are interested in old villas – most people aren't so keen on all the details.'

'I often watch those TV shows about old houses being done up. Sometimes not as well as they could have been.' He leads the way out into the hall. 'Can we go upstairs and have a look there too?'

. . .

All through this visit to the house Lara has felt buried emotions circle in the back of her mind and wonders if it's to do with showing someone around, someone who isn't part of the family. She remembers her embarrassment the first time Roddy saw her mother drunk and abusive, ranting about how everyone thinks they know how she should live her life, because Lara made a suggestion about something minor. Once when Lara visited on her own and said she thought the big trees in the back garden needed pruning, her mother told her to leave if she couldn't mind her own business. But other memories float to the surface too, from happier times when she was very young and played hide-and-seek with her parents in this big house with dozens of cupboards and wardrobes to hide in. How she only understood as she got older that they had pretended they had to search for her, and that always hiding in the same place was a bad strategy.

Chapter 11

A few weeks later when Lara and Mark go out with some of his friends the evening starts out feeling entertaining and different, but she soon realises that his social life, and possibly also his lifestyle in general, is very unlike her own. Their group of six meets in a bar just off Courtenay Place, move to an Italian restaurant on the other side of the street and at eleven thirty, make yet another move to a new venue in Cuba Street with a band and dancing.

Lara, who has only been introduced to the others by first names, is slightly overwhelmed by the raucous banter and laughing and has ample time to listen and watch. There is something about the other two couples that is hard to define, but on a superficial level they have some characteristics in common and many similar mannerisms. They all gesticulate excessively when they talk, the men have identical designer stubble, the women have gigantic false eyelashes and intersperse their conversations with brand names.

By the time they cross the street to the restaurant, she has amused herself by allocating imaginary jobs to the others, some of them less than flattering, and she remains the quietest person in the group. A lot of wine is consumed and one of the women gets drunk and argumentative, which seems to amuse the others rather than embarrass them. Mark surprises Lara by egging the drunk woman on to become even more outrageous and rude, which makes the others roar with laughter. The whole situation is unlike most of her dinner dates with friends, and she can't help wondering about Mark. Until now he has been talkative, amusing and interested in everything about her, but tonight, he is as loud as the others and appears unfazed by the attention their table is getting from other diners.

When he drives her back to Stafford Street, she suppresses a gasp when he changes lanes without indicating and forces another car to take evasive action. She watches the car they nearly hit in the side mirror and thinks that it's a long time since she was in a car with a drunk driver.

'You should grow your hair longer,' says Mark abruptly, as he brakes outside Bridget and Gordon's house. 'You'd look nice with longer hair, short hair is a bit out of date, maybe shoulder length, put in some highlights.'

Lara starts to laugh, because this is the most unexpected comment she could imagine after a nearly silent ride. 'I don't think so – I like my hair short and I can't be bothered fussing around with curling tongs and whatever.'

Even in the half dark inside the car she can see that Mark is disconcerted by her laughter. 'Take me as I am or leave me,' she says in a light-hearted way, trying to revert to something less stressful. An argument is the last thing she needs, the evening has been a bit much on all fronts, and all she wants to do is go to bed. 'I'm a plain Jane – not the type to try to be glamorous.'

He takes this statement as the opening move in a discussion, leans in closer and slides his arm behind her shoulders. 'But don't you want to look a bit more … striking, a bit more trendy? You could make a lot more of your looks. It's not as if you aren't pretty.'

She opens the door and moves sideways, out from under this arm. 'Thanks for dropping me home, but I don't think I'm up to discussing my appearance at two in the morning.'

Mounting the steps to the front door she thinks how tiresome this evening has been, and how surprising that it culminated in unexpected style advice. And why now? He has seemed keen to get to know her better, happy to spend time with her and interested in her house, and now he suddenly offers personal criticism and wants her to change.

She lies in bed, puzzled by the sudden change, and tries to work out how she feels about him. An amusing and attentive companion, yes. But he is also a man who takes offence easily, and who was on one occasion naggingly argumentative about something that didn't matter. An uneven temperament, she thinks, and appearances seem to matter a lot to him. He compared her to those other two women who use every make-up trick to improve their appearance and probably spend a fortune on their hair. So, is he shallow or just keen to make her match his expectations? And why is he even going out with her if she doesn't? But on the other hand, it is nice to have someone to go out for dinner with, a male friend instead of one of her many women friends, and it's never going to be a romantic relationship, so Lara decides she can put up with the occasional snarl – at least he's fun to talk to and amusing most of the time.

. . .

'This is great!' exclaims Mark on a Saturday a few weeks later, after meeting Lara for lunch and asking her to show him how the renovations are progressing. He turns in a circle in the space which is going to be the open-plan kitchen and living room. 'This is going to be a lovely room. And how are they getting on with the bathroom?'

Lara leads the way and stops just inside the doorway. 'Walk-in shower here, toilet there and a wall-mounted vanity unit and basin against that wall. I'm having a super effective extractor fan over the shower and heated towel rails both sides of the basin.'

She can't help smiling as she stands there, because she can imagine exactly how it will look when the fittings are installed. Craig helped her measure everything, and they drew outlines with chalk on the floor so she could see how it would work out.

'Nothing worse than ending up with useless corners,' Craig had said. 'It's a big space for a bathroom, but you might as well do it to best effect. And if you want a bidet, we'll get the plumber to set it up – another fitting makes no difference and there's room for it.'

'Tiled floor, of course?' asks Mark now and looks around, as if he's trying to picture what it will be like.

'Hexagonal tiles, a deep terracotta colour – really nice, a friend of mine has them and I know where to get them. The colour will make the room feel warm even on a cold morning.'

'What you want is underfloor heating,' declares Mark decisively. 'Fabulous on cold mornings.'

'I can't, not without changing the level of the floor, or having a little step up from the passage, which I don't want. I think I'll have a heat pump in here too.'

'But it would be worth it,' he insists, 'and once the tiles

are in you can't add it - of course, you must have underfloor heating, such a lovely feel on a cold morning.'

His voice has taken on the irritated tone she associates with him trying to influence her to change her dress or her hair. To avoid a debate, she smiles and says calmly, 'You might be right —it's not a thing you can add later.' She catches the fleeting look of satisfaction on his face and knows he assumes he has made her change her mind.

In the main bedroom Lara stops and feels a smile come over her face; the framing for the wall behind the bed has already been installed though it was only a couple of days since she emailed Warren the sketch of how she wants it to be.

'Fast work,' she says. 'I only sent him the drawing on Thursday.' She walks around the framing, and Mark follows saying, 'Is this the dressing room? Why doesn't it go right into the corner at least on one side? It's going to look a bit odd, isn't it, like a box?'

'This freestanding wall is the right width for the bed with a bedside table on each side, and I can go in from either side - and there it is, my hanging space along the back of this new wall and shelving on the outer wall.' She doesn't say what she thought when she sent the sketch to Warren, that she'll be able to go in naked at one end and come out fully dressed at the other.

And Mark smiles and says, 'Plenty of room for two.' He puts his arm around her shoulders and taken by surprise she stands rigid under his arm for a moment, first confused and then hot with indignation. Does he think they will live here together? Surely not! They are not a couple, and she has given him no indication that she thinks they are. They go on dates, yes, but they don't have an emotional relationship, at least not in her mind. And she has always talked about herself in the singular when they talk about the house. Suddenly slightly alarmed she moves out from under his arm and walks around the framing and back through the doorway to the hall, and Mark follows.

When he leaves ten minutes later, she goes upstairs to inspect progress there. She stands at the window where her bedroom used to be, now incorporated into the living space, and her phone signals a text message from Mark: 'I can't wait to be able to be alone with you – hurry up builders!"

This is crazy, she thinks, how did this escalate in his mind to a point where he feels he can imply some kind of future for them as a couple. Or was he just joking and referring to how he hopes to get her into bed? At times she finds him hard to fathom, and it makes her slightly disconcerted and uneasy, as if she is dealing with two different people.

While she waits for Gordon and Bridget, who are coming to inspect progress after having lunch with friends in Eastbourne, she continues to dwell on the discrepancy between Mark's possible expectations and how she herself regards their friendship, which is not a relationship, and how uncomfortable his assumptions make her. But after a few minutes the tension drains out of her mind and she laughs; the solution is so obvious she can't believe she didn't see it right away. She will accept the next invitation she gets from another man to reinforce her unattached status, and perhaps it might be a good idea to find a tenant, never mind that it is a bit too soon. She won't mention to Mark that she plans to find someone to live upstairs until an agreement is in place, just in case he thinks he should live there if she won't let him move in with her. The way he said the dressing room was "big enough for two" and put his arm around her sits uncomfortably in her mind. She might have blown his comment up out of proportion because some of his behaviour unsettles her, though having a plan and taking some precautions won't do any harm. Better to be over-prepared than to suddenly find herself in some silly situation later

Chapter 12

On the Friday morning when Gordon calls, Lara is standing at her living room window looking out at the fog hanging over the Waikato river, thinking ahead to the weekend in Wellington.

'Just checking you still remember the alarm code,' he says. 'We're leaving for the South Island this afternoon, before you get here, so you'll have to let yourself in. I presume you bring your key every time you come?'

Lara stands at her living room window and looks out at the fog hanging over the Waikato river and tries to remember if she ever set the alarm at the Stafford Street house. 'No, I've got no idea what it is. I'll write it down so I don't forget.'

'No need to write it down – it's the date of Christmas Day – 2512.' Gordon chuckles. 'Simple, eh? We had to use something ridiculous when we had it installed, so the whole family would remember it – experts would say it's a bad PIN, but we're not changing it now. Any day now we'll get old and start forgetting new things. And how is it going up there in misty Hamilton?'

It makes Lara grin, the way he always refers to Hamilton as misty, which this morning is perfectly true. 'It is misty over the river today. I'm standing at the living room window looking down at the river – it looks like a valley full of clouds. Did Bridget tell you the house has sold already?'

'She did, but she said she was so impressed with how much it sold for that she forgot to ask when you have to move out. Have you resigned from the school?'

'The new owners take over in the middle of November and I'm leaving school at the end of the year. I'll stay with Roddy's mum the last month – all my furniture will go into storage at the removal company until it can be taken to Wellington.'

That night when she opens the door at Bridget and Gordon's place for Mark, he steps back from being poised to kiss her cheek and she can sense his mood turning unpleasant. 'Is that new?'

He is looking her up and down, and by now she knows this look, it means he's displeased with her appearance, which seems to happen regularly lately, but this time there is a note of overt displeasure in the way he looks at her which makes her uneasy, as if he is threatening her.

'No, I've had it for ages,' she lies and reaches for her bag on the table by the door, hoping this dismissive reply will stop any further talk about the lime green dress she bought on an impromptu shopping expedition with a colleague after school on Wednesday.

'What were you thinking? That style and the colour! It's for someone sophisticated - far too in-your-face for you, my dear.'

He sounds affectionately amused now, but she senses a hint of aggression behind the amusement, as she has a couple of time lately. This time she responds more firmly than she usually does to his criticisms, instead of passing it off with muted humour.

'Never mind – I've got it on now, so we might as well get going.'

But his voice hardens, and he frowns, takes a step closer. 'No, go and change – we still have time.'

But her decision is made and without a word she reaches over and enters the code into the alarm panel, walks past him through the doorway with the bag in her hand and stands holding the edge of the door, waiting to close it.

'Are we going? You've got another fifteen seconds and then the alarm goes off.'

For the first time in their dating history Mark meets a Lara he never suspected existed. She can see how surprised he is and tries to keep her face neutral, because common sense tells her she must stand her ground and not let any hesitation show, but neither must she seem triumphant, or he will turn nasty. She has long suspected that Mark is used to dominating women with his mood swings and the unvoiced threat of anger, and she needs to draw a line in the sand.

'Oh, OK then,' he says grumpily and turns to walk ahead of her. She locks the door and follows him to his car, and they say nothing more about it, but throughout the evening she senses resentment simmering behind his veneer of enjoyment. However normal and interested he seems to be in what she has to say, either to him or to the others around the long table, his eyes narrow a fraction when he looks at her. She knows he is furious with her for standing up to him, and tonight for some reason he can't totally conceal it; he has control over his voice and smile but not of his eyes.

When Mark gets involved in a discussion about property values with someone on his other side, Lara lets her eyes sweep around the table and wonders who organised this large group of people to celebrate someone's birthday. There were only one-sided introductions when they arrived, when Mark said, 'And this is Lara' and people smiled and nodded, but there was no mention of who they were. She recognises only one couple, a pair she met once when out with Mark and whose names she cannot remember. But as she studies the others, she realises that the woman at the extreme corner of the table from her seems familiar and after a moment, she puts a name to the face. It is Belinda, whom she hasn't seen since high school and just then Belinda meets her eyes and gets up from her seat at the end of the table. She comes around and leans down between Lara and Mark with her wineglass tilting dangerously just by Lara's shoulder.

'Can we please swap places for a little while, Mark? I haven't had a chance to talk to Lara for years.' She laughs and puts her hand on his shoulder. 'You can spare her for a few minutes, I'm sure.'

Without being rude there is nothing he can do, so he gets up and goes to sit in Belinda's chair.

'Goodness, he is possessive,' says Belinda. 'He didn't want to move, did he - but he couldn't very well say no. But he was like that at school too, always had to have things his way.'

'Never mind him! It's nice to see you,' says Lara and smiles at Belinda, who in high school used to ignore her, and who never had more than a two-minute conversation with her in her life. 'How are you and what are you doing these days?'

'To tell you the truth, nothing much – I've lead a very mundane life since my husband ran off with the nineteen-year-old from the fitness studio. This is the first time I've been out for a month. I presume you've heard?' Her voice is brittle, half sarcastic, half amused, but there is an undertone of deep hurt.

'I'm sorry! I had no idea – truly, I never heard about it. How long ago did this happen?'

Lara isn't sure how to handle this, apart from trying to be kind without probing. If she knew Belinda better it would be easy to provide some sympathy and maybe reach out to touch her hand, but they don't have a close relationship or any relationship at all.

But Belinda puts her hand on Lara's and says surprisingly, 'I just suddenly felt like talking to you – I hope you don't mind? I know you lost your husband, so you know about loss, and at school you were always so calm and self-contained – I used to admire your poise.'

Lara is surprised at this description of herself as a teenager and slightly alarmed at the way her hand is being gripped and suspects tears are dangerously close. Giving Belinda's hand a squeeze she smiles into the brown eyes that seem suspiciously shiny.

'You know what? I think you and I should go and sit somewhere else – just for a little while, some place where we can talk quietly away from all these people.' She looks around and adds, 'Not that anyone seems interested in what we're saying, but let's take our glasses and go and sit at one of those little tables by the bar.'

She ignores the strange look Mark sends her way as she pushes her chair back, picks up her glass and leads the way.

Chapter 13

They cross the dining space and sit down at a tiny table in the far corner by the bar, and Lara says, 'I know it's hard. And I know it's a platitude, but some platitudes are also true – things *do* get better, very gradually, over time. You think things haven't changed until you look back one day and notice that life is better, you feel different.'

Belinda takes a deep drink of her wine and puts the glass down with an expression of nearly desperate determination. 'I know – it probably will get better, but nobody will listen kind of unemotionally. They get too involved. When I saw you at the end of the table, I thought you might be the only person who could stand back and not hug me to death and make me cry, but just let me talk – and maybe say something I can relate to. People seem to want too much detail – when and how did I find out, how long had it been going on, have I met the girl, just endless. I simply can't cope with talking about it over and over.'

There is a question mark hanging in the air when she stops talking. She looks at Lara, and Lara knows without a doubt that this woman is deeply wounded and unhappy, and for some strange reason she, Lara, is the person she has chosen to help her, though she has no idea if she can.

But twenty minutes later, having moved her chair to avoid having to see Mark's repeated glances in their direction, Lara sees Belinda smile for the first time; a wry smile, but it is still a little smile, and she feels deeply relieved.

'You are right!' says Belinda and drinks the last of her wine. 'I just didn't want to admit it before – you know how friends are, they want to fix things for you and move on - or endlessly commiserate and I couldn't see what the middle ground was, but you've just pointed it out – in more ways than one. And I know you're right - a counsellor is what I need, someone to help me get through this stage. And what you said about being so angry at your husband for dying and leaving you alone – thank you for being so open, it made it possible for me to be frank too.'

Then she smiles more widely, a natural smile. 'And I will remember what you said about writing things down, little poems or stories, something creative and private. I'll try it, I promise. Writing isn't something I've ever tried, but it obviously worked as a diversion for you.'

'I'll send you one of my little stories,' says Lara. 'Not about Roddy or loss or anything at all, just a bit of nonsense. Somehow doing something small and creative gave me a degree of calm, as I said before. It kind of made me step aside from my pain. You don't want pain and bitterness to become the core of your inner self.'

When they return to their table, the party of fourteen seem to have hardly noticed their absence. Their desserts are on the table and the noise level has risen. Lara notices that Mark must have got up and switched plates and put Belinda's at his place, which tells her he is intending to stay where he is and their trip home will be fraught. But for once she doesn't mind, she has helped someone in a minor way and it is enough in itself.

As soon as they are in the car Mark bursts out, 'Who was that bloody woman? What cheek, coming over and demanding to talk to you! You must have known her sometime in the past – but really, how rude and selfish!'

'Oh, I don't think so – not selfish, she just wanted to catch up,' says Lara calmly. 'She was at high school with us, a year older than you, I think - and she's had some problems. Don't you remember her? Belinda - I can't remember her surname. She was very good at netball, and she used to hang out with Charlotte's friend Anna – I think they lived next-door to each other.'

'Well, what the hell was her problem and what's it got to do with you?' Mark's voice is rising as it has a couple of times lately, as if he is on the verge of losing his self-control like he did that night in the car when he said she should grow her hair longer. The hint of impatience or aggression behind some of his comments, even when his mood is supposedly amused, and that it might indicate of a potential escalation worries her. Having to always consider if she should deflect his mood by a semi-joking response or take a firm stand is an uncomfortable gamble.

'What were you talking about?' Now he's not asking, he's demanding an answer.

She doesn't reply straight away, because Mark is changing lanes without indicating, and she wonders if he has had too much to drink. A taxi honks his horn and Mark turns his head and stares angrily, and the car swerves sharply to the right.

'Watch out!' says Lara. 'You're creeping into the other lane.'

'Oh, for fuck's sake! I don't need driving lessons from you!'

He is back in the centre of his lane and Lara sits silent until he stops in Stafford Street.

'So, what were you and that Belinda woman talking about? Was she talking about me?'

Despite her discomfort with his mood, Lara nearly laughs. She turns her head and looks long and hard at him but keeps her voice calm. 'About you? Why on earth would she be talking about you?'

He doesn't reply and she wants to get out of the car before this conversation goes in some direction where another burst of anger will unsettle her.

'Thank you for dropping me home.' She opens her door before he can reach over to kiss her goodnight and gets out, but he is getting out too, and she hears the click of the car locking before he comes around to her side.

'If the olds are away I might come in – don't you think?' He takes her by her shoulders and tries to pull him towards him, his voice is soft and affectionate now. 'I've been waiting so long for a chance to be alone with you.'

She pulls away, too fast for him to retain his hold and shakes her head. 'No, I don't think so, Mark - not here and not tonight. Thank you again for dropping me home.'

For a moment he looks as if he is going to follow her through the gate, she can see out of the corner of her eye that he has taken a couple of steps after her, so she closes the gate behind her with a snap and walks to the front door. The key is in her hand and she weighs up if unlocking the door might be worse than staying outside talking to him. What if he pushes into the house and won't leave? But he takes the hint and returns to the car, calls out 'good night', so she goes inside and closes the door behind her.

Chapter 14

Sitting in the half-dark kitchen with an untouched cup of tea cooling in front of her, she tries to sort out her mixed feelings about Mark. He is possessive, sometimes critical, his mood tonight has twice swung quite abruptly from friendly to irritated or outright angry. She stares unseeing at the dark stain shaped like an avocado on the table in front of her, a long-ago accident with the ink bottle for Charlotte's calligraphy pen and tries to make up her mind about how it all fits together.

Sex was never an option, she thinks, because we're just friends going out for meals, it's not true dating as such, and with what I know now I'd never let him into my bed, no way! Aggressiveness mixed with sex, not my thing at all, so even if I were attracted to him in that way, I'd never let it happen. She is pleased that she has stuck to her normal habit of always paying for herself, so there's no need to feel she owes him anything. But she must go out with other guys to reposition herself in relation to him, and make excuses every second time he asks her out, perhaps. She can't have a relationship with him; she doesn't love him and it wouldn't work, he's too obsessive and she needs to draw a line in the sand, but carefully.

The word "carefully" seems to recur in her inner dialogues more and more often. Sometimes she even dreams she's telling herself to be careful, though there has been no hint of physical violence from Mark even at his most irritated and annoyed. She knows she could never mention this to anyone else, nobody would understand where this feeling of menace comes from, because she can't even explain it to herself. Worst of all, nobody would understand why she doesn't simply stop going out with him, why making a clean break now seems borderline dangerous, and a slow withdrawal feels like the only safe way out. She regrets having allowed this strange dating relationship to go on for so long, but now it has changed into something she feels certain must be managed with caution.

She wonders what Roddy would advise her to do, and she feels pretty sure he would reinforce her decision to slowly change things by going out with other men as the sensible option. She smiles at herself, sitting there in a nearly dark kitchen in the middle of the night, mentally checking what her dead husband might have thought about her dilemma.

When she finally goes to bed, she has made two decisions; she is going to avoid being picked up, she'll take Bridget's car or a taxi if she goes out with him again, and she will be very careful how she goes about things. The idea of talking to Charlotte about this is dismissed nearly instantly, because she knows she could never explain how complex the situation with Mark is. She enjoys his company, because he is funny and entertaining, often in a slightly sarcastic way that makes her laugh, but she doesn't like his friends and the way a less likeable side of his personality emerges in their company. And possibly the most problematic aspect is the feeling that has grown to near certainty, that he would try to get revenge if she simply told him she doesn't want to see him again. That he would see it as a slight to his self-esteem and react badly. Talking to Charlotte would only result in frustration.

The next morning a bouquet of pink and white roses is delivered by courier, and Lara stands by the kitchen bench and reads the card. "Please forgive me for being so temperamental last night! I shouldn't have taken my bad mood out on you. I'm falling in love with you, and we are never alone together, and I let my desire push me into being rude. Yours always, Mark."

She takes the elaborate bow and the cellophane off, puts the flowers on the edge of the sink and considers throwing them in the rubbish bin. There is nothing in his note that makes her feel any better, and his 'desire' didn't cause his rudeness. He had already been rude and bad tempered two or three times before she told him he couldn't come in. He has just changed the timeline to use it as an excuse, and now he hopes she won't see through it. He can be charming and entertaining, but she recalls her thoughts the previous night and knows that dating others is the only way she can separate herself from this image of them as a couple which she has allowed to develop.

She remains at the bench, staring down at the roses and knows even Charlotte wouldn't accept the logic of continuing to go out with Mark and at the same time trying to find someone else to be seen with. She would not accept that the option of setting a slow fuse to disengage herself and to re-establish herself as single, is the best way out. To Charlotte the obvious thing to do would be to break it off, to say "I'm not going out with you again", but every time she thinks of this option herself, she experiences a little shiver of apprehension.

I got myself into this, she thinks, because I thought having a male friend to go out for meals with was nice, and I was prepared to put up with the not so nice little things, because mostly Mark was and is amusing and charming and attentive. And then those flashes of real menace started happening, and now I have this ghastly feeling he might feel a need to extract some kind of revenge to soothe his injured pride, if I simply cut it off.

Chapter 15

Lara doesn't remember her promise to Belinda until she is back in Hamilton and finds the paper napkin with her email address scrawled on it, tucked into her bag. She spends an hour one evening going through all the little things she wrote in the year after Roddy died and decides to send her one which is hopefully light-hearted and amusing.

Hi Belinda,

As promised, I'm sending one of my little nonsense writings for you to hopefully smile about.

JANE NEEDS A CHANGE

Jane Eyre opened her book and walked along the Classics shelf to Pride and Prejudice. She knocked three times and Mr. Bennett appeared:

'Good morning, Jane, can I help you?'

'Is Mr. Darcy available?'

'I'm sorry – he is engaged.'

'Could he perhaps take a break and talk to me?' asked Jane politely.

'I mean he is engaged to be married – to my daughter.' He closed the door and left her standing on the doorstep.

'Oh, bugger! I was going to propose to him – I thought I had

managed to get into the story before she accepted him. I forgot that damn book is frozen in time,' muttered Jane and continued toward Sense and Sensibility.

'Perhaps I'll try Edward instead. They've been married for over 200 years - they must be sick of each other by now.'

But then she hesitated. 'No, Edward isn't sexy, he is actually quite boring – I won't bother with him and there's nobody else in there worth having.'

But as she turned to head back to her own book, she had a wonderful idea and strode off further down the shelf instead.

She knocked, put a smile on her face, and when the door opens, she was ready: 'Can I speak to Heathcliff, please?'

Hugs, Lara

The email reply from Belinda is in her Inbox the next morning.

Thank you - I love it! And I see what you mean, it must have taken you right away from dwelling on sorrow or letting bitterness poison your day. Please send another! Belinda xx

Lara replies straight away:

Here is one more, but it's your turn next …

The Bookshop Mystery

The woman picked up The Eyre Affair, scanned the blurb and started reading, intrigued.

"The idea! How wonderful it would be, to live inside a book. I know it's fiction, not real life, but think of being able to choose which book to live in – wonderful! I'll read some more, seeing the bookshop man isn't watching."

"Yes, she was here, but she isn't here now," said the bookshop man some hours later to the cops. "But of course, you're welcome to search the place."

They searched, more than once, and the man, who used to hurt her, was baffled: 'But how did she leave? I was waiting outside. And why would she leave?" he cried. "I just don't get it. She loves me!"

They never found her, because her life is fiction now, and she is happy in a book.

Cheers, Lara xx

When Mark calls her halfway through the week, she deliberately doesn't mention the flowers. She would rather be rude than appear to accept the excuse he wrote on the card, even by implication, and within a minute Mark picks up on her cool and neutral responses and changes his approach.

'Please forgive me, darling! I don't know what came over me - I've regretted it ever since and I'm mortified at myself. Please let me makes amends and prove I'm not really like that. I want to take you out on Saturday and give you a real treat, somewhere special – to compensate.'

Having had time to plan her strategy before he called, she accepts the invitation to dinner on the condition that she as usual pays for herself without any idea of how he will react, now that he has phrased it as a treat.

'Oh no, darling – no way! I know you always have before, but it wouldn't be much of a treat if you pay for yourself, would it?'

But she sticks to her plan and tells him she never lets men pay for her; it doesn't only apply to him.

'But why?'

Hoping she'll manage to deliver her response without making it sound as if it is directed at him in a personal way, she says, 'I don't like being indebted to anyone - I always pay for myself.'

Thoughtful, she ends the call a couple of minutes later, having agreed to meet Mark at Logan Brown on Saturday at seven. Knowing he would offer to pick her up, she has told him she is going for drinks at friends of her uncle's and she will come straight from there.

She is certain now her strategy is the right one. She will go out with Mark another couple of times, and she must somehow manage to be seen in public with at least one other man.

If she does nothing about dating another man, it could create just the kind of situation she most wants to avoid, where she goes out for dinner with friends and finds he is one of the group, which would mean either accepting his presumption that they are together or potentially creating a scene in public. She must distance herself by stages and with diversions. Despite the many times she has been through this in her mind, she finds it hard to justify even to herself this feeling that there is something behind Mark's mostly affectionate facade which frightens her a little. In the back of her mind, she wonders if he has the makings of a stalker or someone who might seek revenge if his pride is dented, an extreme idea that she tries to dismiss.

Chapter 16

On Saturday she arrives at Logan Brown quarter of an hour late and finds Mark waiting outside, affectionate and charming, and he makes no mention of how late she is or of the lime green dress she deliberately put on. She sees his eyes flick over her but he restrains himself, intent on being uncritical. And she thinks back to how she stood in front of the bathroom mirror after her shower and deliberately didn't ruffle up her short hair as she normally does but smoothed it down and formed it into sharp points around her forehead and temples, emphasising how short it is. And how when she came down, Bridget looked at her and grinned. 'Ah, here's the little girl with the urchin haircut I remember from long ago.'

Logan Brown, where Lara has never been before, is even more inviting and glamorous than she expected. She has always been aware of the stately building sitting like a reminder from the colonial past on its corner, but the inside is an eye-opener. The fantastic, sculpted ceiling, the shape of the dining room with the deep arched niches, and the pillars with ornamental capitals all contribute to the impression, and she instantly loves it.

The meal is delicious and Lara can't help thinking how odd it is to sit here genuinely enjoying herself and appreciating both the meal and how attentive and entertaining Mark is, and at the same time planning to slowly disengage from him. That underlying feeling of slight threat seems far away tonight, there is no sign of irritation or impatience, but she knows it is there, just better hidden than last time they went out.

When the waiter comes to take their dinner plates, she glances past him and sees Tobias seated with a group in the alcove on the opposite side of the room, and a wild and irresistible idea pops fully-fledged into her head.

'Excuse me,' she says to Mark. 'I won't be a moment.'

She knows he will assume she is going to the rest room, but she walks directly towards the table where Tobias is seated, and he spots her when she is halfway across the room. She makes eye contact with him, to make sure he knows she is coming to talk to him, and he gets to his feet and takes a step towards her. Nothing ventured, nothing won, she thinks, I'm going to use the poor guy, and maybe it won't work, but it's such a perfect opportunity – I hope it doesn't turn into a disaster. She starts talking in a low voice before she is quite up to him.

'Hi, can you do me a favour please? I need a bit of help. Would you please give me a big hug – as if you're really pleased to see me?'

The expression which flashes across his face and then instantly disappears is priceless, and she knows she will treasure this little scene for a long time. He takes a step closer, pulls her into a hug and kisses her cheek, then keeps her close to his side with his arm around her shoulders and asks in a low voice, 'Does that guy you're with need a lesson? Or do you need rescuing?'

'I need to establish that I don't belong to him exclusively,' she half whispers, looking up at him. 'Can I take you out for a tactical dinner next weekend, on a pretend date? My treat – as a thank you.'

'You're a dark horse, aren't you?' He gives her a little shake and grins. 'Of course, you can take me out for dinner, I'll enjoy it. You have my number from when I tried to ask you out - just message me when and where.'

She giggles and stands on tiptoes with a hand on his shoulder to whisper close to his ear, as if she is telling him an intimate secret. 'Can we do a medium-intense fond farewell now?'

He takes her face between his hands and kisses her, a short kiss, but a real kiss, before she turns and goes back to their table.

'Who the hell is that?' Mark's voice is furious, his eyes are narrowed and hard, and Lara slides into her seat and tries to sound casual and reasonable.

'Oh, it's just Tobias, he's the son of my uncle's partner – I've known him forever, and we got back in touch a little while ago. We've always been in touch at intervals, but he's single again.'

She lets this last statement stand for him to draw his own conclusions about what it implies, scared by the risk she is taking, but also convinced this is an opportunity not to be missed. Mark glares at her, half rises from his chair and leans forward over the table and nearly shouts, 'And what's that supposed to mean?'

Instinctively she pushes her chair back, away from him, as people around them turn to stare, and then a waiter appears beside them. "Do you require any assistance, madam?"

'No, thank you, but I want to leave now - alone. I just want to pay my half of the bill.'

At the desk she pays and says, 'Can you please make it a slow process for him to pay – perhaps take your time to work out how much he owes. It will give me time to reach my car.'

'Of course,' is all he says, but she can feel his concern and it makes her feel safe. She turns in the doorway to look in the direction of Tobias's table and sees him watching her, so she gives him a little salute and leaves. Walking quickly, she crosses Vivian Street, continues to where she parked Bridget's car and gets in with a sigh of relief.

'Morning, Bridget!' says Lara brightly the next morning when she comes down for breakfast. 'I hope Gordon hasn't gone out already?'

Bridget, who is standing by the toaster in her pink dressing gown, turns to stare at Lara. 'No, he's in the bathroom. Has something happened?'

'Heavens, no!' Lara checks how much water is in the jug and turns it on. 'Can you make two pieces of toast for me too, please? I've just got something I want to tell you both at the same time.'

She gets mugs and plates out and ignores Bridget's glances her way, until Gordon appears and has coffee and a plate of toast in front of him, then she says casually, 'Now – the news is that I'm going out for dinner with Tobias next weekend. I'm taking him out for a treat.'

'You what? Giving Tobias a treat? Why?' exclaims Bridget, while Gordon just looks at her with raised eyebrows.

'Sorry, that was evil, but I couldn't resist,' says Lara, thoroughly enjoying the situation. 'The things is, when I went out with Mark last night, I caught sight of Tobias and decided to use him. Mark is becoming very controlling, thinks he owns me and can dictate what I wear and how I do my hair, and he's a bit prone to being displeased with me, so I took the opportunity.'

She tells them the whole story in graphic detail, including the whisper in Tobias's ear and the farewell kiss, knowing how much they will enjoy it. Telling it as an amusing story, without showing how scared she was when Mark looked as if he wanted to hit her, requires self-control, but the temptation to see their reactions makes up for it.

'So, it's not that I'm interested in Tobias in any particular way – certainly not romantic, but we might become good friends based on how ready he was to take direction and stage that scene. Didn't hesitate for a moment, every move perfect. And he is precisely what I need to establish that I'm not Mark's property – another guy to go out with. And one who is willing to act the romantic part to perfection, he really does deserve a reward, he did it so well.'

'Good Lord, Lara – you do surprise me sometimes,' says Gordon and grins affectionately at her. 'I would never have guessed you'd be so strategic - and so ruthless. I'm proud of you!'

And Bridget pats Lara's hand. 'Very clever – and very quick thinking, and just what Mark needs from the sound of things. Telling you how to do your hair – I've never heard of anything like it!'

Chapter 17

When Lara and Tobias meet at the Highway Eatery the following weekend, a place he suggested when she messaged him, the first thing he says is, 'Did it work?'

'It's a work in progress. I'll fill you in when we've ordered.'

He has greeted her as affectionately as he farewelled her at Logan Brown. 'I'm really enjoying this, you know. Nobody's ever asked me to play a role before, it's a completely new experience. And we've got to keep up appearances, so a few more kisses won't do any harm. You haven't lived here for so long - you might not realise, but Cuba Street goes on and off the trendiness scale, here one year, gone the next. But this place is in at the moment, so I thought it would fit the strategy - I bet we'll see someone we know, someone who'll gossip about us.'

She smiles. 'It was the most inspired ad-hoc decision I've ever made, you know, last weekend. I never thought of engineering a stunt like that – and then, there you were, like a good fairy, ready to leap into action.'

'A bit less of the fairy if you don't mind! But seriously –

we're bound to see someone here who knows your friends and/or Mark. And we can take a photo to put on social media too. But it beats me why nobody else asks you out – or do they regard you as Mark's property?'

She hesitates for a moment before she replies. Their exchange of text messages was quite brief and she owes him an explanation, but the process which landed her in this situation is not easy to untangle.

'Let's say I was an idiot, I let him think he owned me, and didn't make things clear early enough, so it's partly my own fault. He's a difficult personality - he can be very controlling and possessive. I didn't understand it soon enough or that some people saw it as a developing relationship – something long term and serious. And it's not, definitely not, I never intended it to be more than causal dating. I can't understand why he wants to give that impression anyway because sometimes I feel he doesn't really like me at all.'

She looks seriously at Tobias, because now that they are friends, she wants him to understand her reasoning. 'It's really weird, because he gets annoyed with me quite a lot, and he wants me to change how I look and how I dress – he can't possibly be in love with me. And he has a temper.'

'OK, I only asked because I wanted to understand how you see it. I've done some quiet checking during the week, and it's a bit more involved than you think.' He reaches out and puts his hand on hers and looks carefully at her, as if he's trying to decide how much to say. 'He's actually telling people you're in a deep relationship, definitely long term – a couple of people told me they're expecting you to get engaged soon. They think you're moving in together when your house is ready.'

'What?! How ridiculous – I've never even been to bed with him!'

And then they both laugh when the couple at the next table turn to stare. 'Sorry!' says Lara in their direction. 'But I was so shocked at what I heard, it just popped out.'

'Don't mind us!' says the woman and raises her glass in a toast, and Lara turns back to Tobias, who picks up where he left off.

'I'll spread the word – I've already told a few mates I'm going out for dinner with you. It's sure to filter through to Mark eventually, this city is like a village at certain levels and I'm willing to bet some of my friends know him. But may I ask why you don't just ditch him? If he's a problem, just get rid of him. Wouldn't it be the most effective solution?'

It takes a considerable time to explain why she has felt obliged to develop a strategy of diversion, and how complicated her social life might become, seeing she and Mark knows so many of the same people. She doesn't say outright that she feels slightly worried by Mark's tendency to fits of temper; to someone else it might seem like a flimsy idea based on very little, but she can see Tobias begins to suspect it.

'Ah, I get it – you need someone to dilute the intensity, or what people see as intensity. Well, I'm up for it. We can play this out for an audience any time you like, I'm enjoying myself.' And then his focus shifts to someone over her shoulder to the right, and he laughs. 'Talk about the devil, the perfect people – we'll let them join us if they aren't waiting for someone. They will gossip about us, for sure.'

Before she can answer a couple appear beside her, introductions are made and a waiter is summoned to produce two additional chairs. The couple at the next table obligingly move a bit further over to give them room.

Tobias' friends seem to regard him as endlessly amusing and the kind of person you can safely give a lot of cheek without consequences, and the wife warns Lara about him in exaggerated terms.

'He's hopeless,' says the woman, whose name is either Laila or Delila, in a pretend aside. She slants a wicked glance at Tobias from under her false eyelashes and smirks. 'A bit like Henry the Eighth. Don't for God's sake get involved with him, he's already had a few wives and I doubt if he can remember how many kids he has.'

'Two wives, one live-in partner and five children,' says Tobias coolly, and surprises Lara by coming out with the same explanation she gave Mark a week ago. 'But Lara's uncle and my dad are senior partners in the same law firm, and we've known each other for years. We've just re-connected – Lara lived in Hamilton for years, but she's moving back here soon, which is lovely.'

He smiles at her the way a newly infatuated man might, so affectionate and sweet that Lara nearly chokes on her wine.

It's after midnight when they walk to Tobias's car and Lara takes his arm and smiles with satisfaction at how perfectly this new friendship is working out.

'Just message me whenever you need another date,' he says and breaks the speed limit by a good margin, barrelling down Taranaki Street, which he seems to think is the best route. 'And let me know what happens next anyway. And thanks for the dinner – the next one's on me, I haven't had so much fun for ages. They were completely taken in, don't you think?'

'I couldn't believe you came up with exactly the same explanation for how we know each other as I did with Mark.' Lara braces herself against the door as he goes around a corner too fast and with an alarming lack of control. 'And to think we never met before that night at the Aubergine Café. Serendipity is the only word for it!'

A text from Belinda appears on Lara's phone early on Sunday morning: 'Have you got time for a 5 min chat?' Lara is lying in bed vaguely thinking of getting up and having a shower before Gordon and Bridget get up, as this is still a one-bathroom house despite the five bedrooms.

'Of course,' she replies and her phone buzzes nearly instantly.

'Hi, how are you, Belinda?' Having no idea whether this call is going to be another morale boosting session or something else entirely, she decides to remain neutral until she knows a bit more. But there's no need to worry, Belinda is on a mission of a different kind.

'Someone said you're dividing your mum's house into two flats and I wonder if they've been taken? I have a friend who wants to find something smaller and without a big garden to maintain. He's totally reliable and honest, I've known him nearly all my life, but he's recently separated, and he's trying to find something suitable not too far from the centre of town, but not in an apartment building.'

'I'm having one of the flats myself,' says Lara and

arranges her pillow so she can sit up comfortably. 'And, no, I haven't done anything about letting the other one – but they won't be ready to move into until either just before or just after Christmas, probably after and the place is still full of builders and plumbers.'

'Oh, that won't matter – it's not urgent. So, is it OK if I pass on your name and phone number?'

'Of course, you can. And how are things with you?' This might be the wrong thing to bring up, she thinks, perhaps she should just pretend the chat in the restaurant never happened, Belinda might prefer to forget about it.

'Oh great – I've got a grip on my life and sanity since I saw you. I found a counsellor who is so constructive and sharp – she doesn't let me drift off topic and moan about things.' She laughs. 'She reminds me of my mother, actually – she sets me tasks and goals, things to tell myself at times to reinforce what we've discussed, ways to divert my mind away from depressing thoughts. Coping mechanisms and kind of confidence boosting things, very useful.'

'I'm so glad!' And Lara realises as she speaks the words, that she is genuinely glad Belinda is getting the help she needs. It makes her feel connected to Belinda, who is interesting and smart. 'I worried afterwards that I might have been a bit too prescriptive with my advice.'

'God, no! You said exactly the right thing, the best thing anyone could have done. And you know how I said my friends were driving me nuts? Well, now I just turn it off, divert them and don't let them dig in like I let them do before. So good for my confidence because it makes me feel I'm in control and not just at the mercy of everyone's curiosity. And another thing - but promise not to tell anyone – I took your advice and guess what, I'm writing little poems.'

When Lara gets back from her shower, her phone has a

message alert on the screen: 'I'm Belinda's friend, Weldon. You probably want to inspect me before you offer me the flat. I'm available nearly any time either this weekend or during the week.'

An instant tenant, thinks Lara, my God, this is perfect - and I don't have to do a thing because he comes with a personal recommendation which obviates the need for advertising and screening people. All I need to do is work out what I should ask in rent.

'Strike while the tenant is hot,' she says aloud, and sends a text back with a suggestion that they meet at half past ten in Enigma, which she has just discovered, and where they have an amazingly good walnut cake with yoghurt icing.

The reply is immediate, 'OK, great – see you there. How will I know you?'

'Short, dark, wearing a red jacket.'

At twenty-five past ten she is walking along Courtenay Place, only a couple of steps away from Enigma, when a voice behind her says, 'Lara?' and she turns to find a large and solid-looking male right behind her. 'Yes? Are you Weldon?'

He nods and walks around her to hold the door open. The place is busy with only a couple of tables unoccupied, which seems to surprise him.

'Must be a popular place,' he says while they wait at the counter, and Lara smiles. 'It's the weekend thing, isn't it? A late café breakfast or brunch. Don't you do it?'

'Never,' is the reply, and then it's their turn, and Lara orders a slice of walnut cake and a coffee and turns to Weldon. 'Try the walnut cake – it's possibly the world's best,' and to her surprise he does. She tries to work out why she felt so sure he wouldn't. Perhaps because he looks like the serious kind of man who doesn't order cake, she thinks, but she was obviously wrong.

'Tell me about yourself – like where do you work, and why are you moving? I'm completely new to this landlady role, so I'm not quite sure how it works. Stop me if I get too personal.'

He smiles. 'I have no secrets – none at all. No skeletons in the closet. I'm a scientist at the Innova Research Institute and I'm selling my house and I want to live in a flat, get away from distractions like lawn mowing and stuff. I do quite a bit of work at home, and I like to spend my free time differently and not have to worry about things like that.'

'What is the work? What kind of science?'

'Vaccines – mRNA vaccines, at the moment,' he says. 'This post-Covid phase is really important for my kind of research, we must take the next step and be prepared. It's not over, you know, and we need to understand more – how to make the effect last longer and maybe how to tweak things so one vaccine can protect against unforeseen future variants. Imagine if we had a vaccine to totally protect us against all versions of the corona virus - we could even prevent the common cold and practically eliminate Monday sick leave.'

She's not sure if he's joking, he is hard to read, but before she can reply their coffee arrives and he tastes the walnut cake. 'You are obviously a walnut cake connoisseur. Best ever. Anything else you or I need to tell each other?'

She looks thoughtfully out the window for a moment and tries to conceal the smile which threatens to break out, because she finds his total disregard for the formalities very entertaining.

'Maybe you would like to know where the flat is? Or how big it is? Or what the rent is?'

This is an Alice in Wonderland type of conversation, and not at all what she expected. She came armed with the relevant facts and a copy of the standard rental contract she found on the internet and printed out on Bridget's printer in the study, reluctant to involve Gordon in case it became too complicated. But Weldon seems to have little interest in the details.

'OK - can I get to the centre of town easily from wherever it is?'

'Yes.'

'And has it got a bedroom and a bathroom and a kitchen?'

'Yes.'

'Well, that's fine then – I'll take it. If you'll have me.'

Lara gets the contract out of her bag and unfolds it. 'Do you want a copy of a rental contract so you know I can't pull out?'

'No, thanks.'

She is half impatient and half amused. 'This is highly irregular, don't you think?'

He shakes his head. 'No, no - highly irregular is when you find a foot in the toaster oven, this is just a bit odd.'

'Fargo!' she exclaims and starts laughing and now he is laughing too. 'Exactly – best source of top class one-liners in the history of TV, at last season one was. I'm pleased you recognised it, it's a favourite line of mine. But I've got something to confess. Something else … a bit odd.'

Now he is looking at her in a way which makes her think he is going to say something significant, though she can't imagine what it might be. Don't tell me he has two large dogs, she thinks, because I already like this guy and I don't want to have to turn him down.

'I've got alarm clocks,' he says, 'three old-fashioned and very noisy alarm clocks, the kind with the dome-shaped bell on top - and they go off at different times. You might not like it - I mean, if you can hear them from your flat. So, if it seems too much just say and I'll find somewhere else.'

'I don't think I mind,' she says slowly, while she tries to make sense of this and not start laughing. More and more like Alice in Wonderland, this is definitely the most entertaining man she has met in a long time – unintentionally entertaining, perhaps, but who cares if it makes you smile.

'The entire house has been super insulated and as long as they don't go off in the middle of the night, I don't think it would matter. No worse than music or the TV, I wouldn't think.' And she cannot resist asking, 'Why do you have three alarm clocks set to go off at different times? And why the old-fashioned kind?'

The look he gives her is evaluating, as if he is assessing if she is going to understand or believe what he is about to tell her. His grey eyes stay fixed on hers and he leans forward by a couple of degrees. 'It seems mad to most people, but when I do some work at home – like in the evenings or the weekend, I tend to get so involved I forget the time now that I live on my own. And I'm a bit the same when I read for pleasure. One alarm is for getting up in the morning, one reminds me to make dinner at seven and one at eleven at night, so I don't forget to go to bed. And those old clocks are perfect - I have them all on the kitchen counter, so I've got to get up to turn them off – no way can I ignore them, they make a terrible racket and it goes on forever.'

He has not taken his eyes off her for a split second during this recital and again she represses the urge to giggle. It does sound a bit mad, but it is also intriguing.

'Don't worry about it. I'd far rather have your three alarms go off every day than someone who held all-night parties or played dreadful music. Though you might do that as well, I suppose. Do you?'

'God no!' he says with great emphasis and gives her a

wry smile. 'As my partner said when she left me – I'm so bloody quiet and boring it defies description.'

Then his forehead creases, as if this statement puzzles him. Perhaps he is surprised he told her such a personal thing, thinks Lara, but aloud she says, 'What a nasty thing to say. No, the alarm clocks don't worry me at all. I'll be back in Wellington next weekend, and I'll text you about which day I can show you the place.'

Chapter 19

A week later Lara is beginning to wonder if the Logan Brown episode registered with Mark as a breaking-off point, or if he's decided to pull back of his own accord, because she has heard nothing from him since. What a lucky break it would be if she doesn't need to do anything more to distance herself and the dating friendship simply peters out.

Getting an invitation for drinks with the woman she met with Tobias at the Highway Eatery surprises Lara, who initially can't figure out who Laila is. But the full message makes it clear, "Hi this is Laila, want to meet for a drink tonight? We'll to be at the Foxglove about 5, would love to see you. PS we met with Tobias, got your number from him."

Lara runs downstairs and finds Bridget in the kitchen doing something complicated with a chicken, a ball of cotton yarn and what looks like a long, curved darning needle. 'What on earth are you doing? Chicken surgery?'

'It's a labour of love,' says Bridget and swipes hair off her forehead with the back of her hand. 'Could you come over here and hold this stupid bird together so I can get the first stitch in? It's a lovely sounding recipe, but I think you need a chicken the size of a turkey to fit everything in – so many ingredients for the stuffing!'

Lara takes a firm grip on the chicken and presses it together while Bridget sews up the long slit in its belly with huge cross-stitches, which makes Lara laugh. 'God, it looks mad, like some weird kind of embroidery – maybe an exhibit for a modern art show?'

'It's apparently the way to do it,' says Bridget and ties a knot before she cuts the yarn. 'If the stitches are too close to the edge they just rip out – I might have made them it bit too big. I've never done this before and I didn't have any cotton string, just some yarn left over from when I learnt to crochet potholders last year.'

They wash their hands and stand back to admire the chicken which looks like a bizarre and badly put together parcel, full to bursting point. 'Is it for dinner?'

'No, it's for lunch tomorrow – remember I told you that Gordon's brother and his wife are in town this weekend? They're coming for lunch, so I hope you can join us.'

'Of course, I'd love to. And I know I said I wouldn't go out this weekend, just move between here and the house, but I might go for a drink tonight with the couple I met when I had dinner with Tobias last weekend. They kind of joined us halfway through the meal – interesting couple, she was very entertaining. They've asked me to join them for a drink at five, so I'll be back for dinner.'

Bridget leans against the bench and rubs cream into her hands. 'Don't hold back on the social life for our sake! I couldn't be more delighted – not that I don't want your company, but it's great to see you out and about again and having fun. Who are these new people?'

Lara considers and shakes her head. 'I can't remember – or perhaps nobody mentioned their surname. He's called

Derek and she's Laila. She was very funny, warned me about getting involved with Tobias.'

'As well she might,' says Bridget. 'When are you showing the flat to your potential tenant, was it before or after lunch today?'

'After – at half past one. Let me make something for lunch - I can cook, you know. Where is Gordon?'

'In the garden, swearing at the line-trimmer. Let's have a coffee before you make lunch, then. I need a reward for doing this damn chicken.'

Lara studies her aunt's placid face and wonders if she and Gordon have had an argument, but she's never heard them argue, or at least not in front of their children, so she needs to find out what this means. 'He's swearing at the line-trimmer? Why?'

'That's what he always does when he's trying to trim the edges along the path – he just can't get the angle right, and he keeps making V-shaped cuts into the grass and then he loses his temper. The neighbours are used to it. Go and look out the dining room window.'

Lara returns grinning. 'Yep – you're right! He's red in the face and muttering – I can't hear what he's saying but he looks frustrated.'

They have sweetcorn fritters on wholemeal toast with tomato chutney and fried haloumi for lunch. Lara is glad to see that Gordon's face has returned to its normal colour and says innocently, 'What a lovely day to spend a morning in the garden – I should have offered to help you.'

Gordon slants Bridget a suspicious glance and says, 'I'll tell you next time I have work to do out there and you can come and help me – Bridget refuses. She says she prefers to work alone.'

. . .

When Weldon pulls up outside the house in Orchard Street later that afternoon, Lara is sitting on the front step with the door open behind her looking at her phone, and she doesn't notice him until a shadow falls over her and she looks up.

'You cast a big shadow,' she says and smiles. 'Very useful, I had trouble seeing the screen.'

'I'm useful in a strong wind, too - you can shelter behind me.'

'Come inside and we'll do the tour.'

She gestures towards the stairs. 'The flat you can have is up those stairs. We'll share the hall down here including that room over there, which is a big walk-in coat cupboard kind of room, where we can both keep boots and jackets and stuff. There will be separate doorbells outside the front door. Shall we have a look?'

They do a tour of the flat and Weldon asks a few questions, but mostly he just looks and nods. Lara is beginning to think he doesn't like it, maybe thinks it's not big enough, but then he suddenly says, 'It's great, perfect - and much bigger than I thought it would be. I didn't realise what a huge footprint this place has. I'll be very happy to rent it. What do I need to get?'

'What do you mean, get? I presume you have furniture and things?'

He grins and gestures towards the kitchen. 'Of course, I do. I mean, what do I have to provide – like a stove perhaps, obviously a fridge. I need to know what to give away and what to keep – I've got a house full of stuff.'

She points at the floor. 'See those chalk marks – that's a map of what it will look like. This here's a cupboard with a louvred folding door with space for a washing machine and up-side-down drier above it and a tub with a cupboard underneath, all tidily hidden from sight. And the drier will be ducted to the outside so the place doesn't get damp. Then the pantry. And then a bench here, with cupboards and space for a dishwasher underneath. And over there the fridge and the stove separated by another little bit of bench.'

'Aha!' says Weldon. 'I've cracked the code inside the chalk lines, I can read the whole kitchen now.'

'And here there will be a big, wide freestanding island counter - on wheels that lock, so you can have it as close or as far from the fixed part of the kitchen as you like, it sort of makes a dividing line between the kitchen and the living space. And more drawers and cupboards in the body of it. Both kitchens will be exactly the same and installing a stove is my responsibility and so is the dishwasher.'

His casual approach is still puzzling her because he hasn't asked any of the questions she expected. 'Aren't you interested in what the rent is?'

The corners of his mouth twitch slightly, but all he says is, 'No, it doesn't matter, but you can tell me if you want to.'

'No, it doesn't worry me, it's just that I thought you'd ask. Never mind. But there's one thing I thought of, the keys. At first, I thought we'd have two keys each, one for the front door and then another for our apartment doors. But I so hate bunches of keys. If they are on my car key-thing they annoy me when I want to just put the car key in my pocket, and if I have a separate keyring for the house keys, I have to dig in my bag to find them. So ...' She pauses, thinks she is going too far, he'll think she is mad.

'And?' He looks amused, waiting for the rest of the sentence, and now she has to go through with it.

'I thought maybe - if you trust me - we could have all the locks key-ed the same, so one key fits everything – for convenience. And a single key attached to my car key would be OK.'

'I suppose your pockets are quite small compared to mine,' he says, deadpan for a moment before he grins. 'But seriously – of course I trust you, the question is why you trust me. You don't know me yet.'

This has not occurred to Lara, who just shakes her head. 'I've no idea – but I do.'

And in the back of her head, she hears Roddy's voice saying, as he often did, 'Honestly Lara, sometimes you do the whackiest things!' And then they'd both laugh.

'Well, OK then,' is all he says, and the subject is closed.

Chapter 20

On an impulse Lara deviates from her plan to walk along Jervois Quay and decides that at this time of the day in spring, there is nothing nicer than walking along the waterfront, past the rowing club basin and over the little bridges towards the playground with the lighthouse. The Len Lye Water Whirler is spraying thin jets of water, swirling and twisting like a live creature. She stops, looks out over the water, and thinks how beautiful Wellington is compared to many other cities and how nice it is to have such unrestricted access to views of the sea.

Approaching the Foxglove, she wonders why she has never walked right along to Queen's Wharf before. People of all ages are walking and biking, electric scooters appear with only a swish of wheels from behind her and seagulls ride the wind overhead.

Standing in front of the mirror in her bedroom before she left, she thought of the slightly over-the-top glitzy way Laila was dressed when she last saw her, and how much makeup she wore and decided to be the absolute opposite. Even as she pulled on jeans and a yellow sweatshirt and zipped up her white trainers, she wondered what made her feel impelled towards this gesture of dressing down. Maybe it was a reaction to Mark and his harping on about her appearance, though she wasn't going to meet him, or maybe it's because Laila is exactly the kind of woman, he has compared her to in the past. A high-maintenance woman who either earns a lot of money herself or needs to be married to someone who does.

Having looked for Laila and Derek at the tables on the terrace, she goes inside and finds that the place is more than she expected in many ways; larger and darker, with dark wood panelling, wide floorboards and lovely views through big windows. She looks around and tries to orientate herself, tries to guess where they might be expected to meet. And then she hears Laila's voice, 'Yoohoo!' and turns to see her and Derek coming in behind her.

'Lovely to see you!' exclaims Laila and air kisses Lara's cheeks. 'Perfect timing — let's go through to the upstairs terrace.'

Derek, who seems to be the kind of man who follows in the wake of his noisier and more exuberant partner, who nods at what she says, and who only really comes out of his shell with other men, smiles at Lara and gestures for her to walk ahead with his wife.

Before long they are joined by another couple and then by two men and a woman, whose relationship puzzles Lara until she discovers that the men are a couple, and the woman is a friend of Laila's who just happened to arrive at the same time.

She enjoys the next hour in a slightly muted way, which isn't surprising, she thinks, as she doesn't really know any of these people, who are all well known to each other. She has just made up her mind to leave, when Derek notices her stance changing next to him and says, 'Aren't you staying for dinner? We've booked a table inside.'

'No, I can't, thanks — I just came along for a pre-dinner drink. I'm expected elsewhere for dinner.'

'You must see this before you go,' says Laila decisively and gets to her feet. 'It's part of the unique charm of this place — I'll show you.'

Speaking over her shoulder as she precedes Lara inside, she adds, 'I hope you read The Lion, The Witch and The Wardrobe when you were a kid — or perhaps you've seen the film? Remember the magic wardrobe that you walked into and then through a door at the back into another world called Narnia?'

In the room on the far side of the bar is a free-standing, old-fashioned wardrobe with an oval mirror set into the door and Laila stops. 'Open it!'

The wardrobe is empty, but there is another door in the back and they walk through into a lovely corner room with large, multi-paned windows and long bench seats covered in blue velvet.

'Amazing!' says Lara. 'Who would have guessed? But I must go or I'll be late!'

She says goodbye and a minute later she is outside, walking briskly back towards Te Papa, when she hears a voice calling her name and turns around.

'Lara!'

Mark comes up to her and grips her shoulders, kisses her cheek and smiles, but she can tell he is worried. His eyes travel from her head to her feet and he says, 'Are you here for dinner?' which is a ridiculous thing to ask when she is obviously leaving. Aha, she thinks, the invitation for a drink was a ruse. Mark knows Derek and Laila, and they told him about her dinner with Tobias. She sees the exact moment when he realises he has made a mistake, revealed that what was supposed to be passed off as a coincidence, was planned.

'I've just had a drink with some people I met last weekend,' she says and hopes he won't realise she registered his gaffe and that she knows this was a set-up that failed. 'I've got a dinner date, so I'm on my way home to change.'

'We must get together, though. I haven't seen you for ages. You seem to have a very lively social life these days.' Now he is smoothly plastering over his bad mood, he smiles and takes her hand, runs his thumb over her knuckles. 'How about lunch tomorrow?'

'All booked up, sorry,' says Lara. 'Gordon and Bridget have relatives coming for lunch and I've promised to be there. Maybe next weekend?'

'Someone said they saw you having coffee with a giant – but I said it can't have been you, because I'm sure you don't know any giants.'

His tone is joking and friendly, but his eyes have a slightly narrowed look that she knows well, he is trying to find out who it was without actually asking.

'Giant? Oh, they must mean Weldon, yes, he is large - wide and tall.' She leaves it at that and waits to see if Mark is going to press her for details.

'I don't think I've heard you mention Weldon before,' he says innocently. 'Unusual name.'

'He's a friend of Charlotte's,' says Lara, not wanting to bring Belinda into the conversation. 'Nice guy, very interesting. Mark, I really must go or I'll be late.'

'I'll walk with you. Did you walk all the way? I can drive you home.'

'Oh, don't worry, I parked just a bit further on,' she says untruthfully and jogs away, and short of chasing her and making himself look ridiculous, he has no choice but to let her go.

. . .

Over the next couple of weeks Lara begins to think that her strategy is working. She has dinner with Tobias again in a popular place where two lots of his friends come up to their table, and he does his impersonation of love interest to perfection. The second time he waits until his friends have moved on and says, 'Are you getting interested in me, Lara. Feeling a bit of sexual attraction building up?'

'Sorry to dent your self-esteem, but no, not a smidgeon,' she replies and points her dessert spoon at him. 'I'm just acting out my part of this comedy. And admit it, neither are you attracted to me. We'll just settle for being mates and forget all that nonsense.'

And they laugh and talk about other things.

When she next sees Mark, it is with another couple for dinner and he seems to have accepted that they are slowly changing from seeing each other regularly, to going out now and then. She feels her worry about him begin to slowly ebb away. He has not pressed her for more frequent dates, neither has he made any hint at a supposed shared future.

Chapter 21

On a drizzly Saturday morning Lara and Bridget meet with a man from a landscaping company at the house in Orchard Street to discuss the changes.

'No thank you, I don't want anything elaborate,' says Lara decisively, when the man suggests herbaceous borders and roses to suit the era of the house. 'I want the three sides of this garden to have shrubs along the edges, evergreen shrubs of some kind that flower in spring perhaps? I'm sure you can suggest something. But no flower beds, just lawn. And these three tall trees have to come out, there's far too much shade here. The smaller tree in the far corner can stay, it doesn't shade the house - and I would like a light under it, a light that shines up into the canopy, but it's got to be positioned so it doesn't shine at the neighbour's house. And I want a lemon tree and an apricot tree, please, right at the back boundary.'

It's hard to say who looks most surprised at this definitive list of demands, the landscaping man or Bridget. Lara sees the glance they exchange and laughs. 'Sorry to disappoint you, but I've had a lot of time to think it through and I used to live here, so I know how important it is to have no shade trees on this side – it's where the winter afternoon sun comes in, and light and warmth are important in Wellington winters, I think.'

Bridget nods. 'True! Gardenias might be nice around the lawn, you know – it's nice shrub and not too big and the flowers have a lovely scent – they would do well here.'

'Fragrant Star is an excellent gardenia,' says the garden man, who has recovered his poise. 'And they would make a lovely border – dark green leaves, not overly tall, probably max six feet and they flower right through the summer, white flowers.'

'It sounds perfect, don't you think Bridget? Nice green leaves all the year round and white flowers - lovely! Do they give you hay fever?'

'Not that I've ever heard,' says the landscaping man and looks at Bridget, who shakes her head.

'And those things you have, the ones you always take in and put on the kitchen table.' Lara turns to her aunt. 'You know - those little bushes with masses of lovely, scented little whitish pink flowers?'

'Daphne!' says Bridget and smiles, happy to be able to have some input. 'They would look nice alternating with the gardenias and they flower from late winter into spring – evergreen and lovely to pick for inside. With those and the gardenias you'd have scented flowers for months. Pale flowers against dark shiny leaves, such a beautiful effect.'

On the way back to Stafford Street, Bridget glances across at Lara and grins. 'That poor man – he was dying to give you advice and draw up lovely, curved flower beds for the corners or a circular rose bed in the middle of the lawn. He was so disappointed.'

'He shouldn't be – I made it clear when I called the company that it was not so much about designing a garden as organizing the work, trees to take out, digging up various bushes and planting some new things. And I did ask about the light for the tree, and they said they do lighting, too.'

After dinner, when Lara is watching a rerun of Black Books on TV with Bridget, and Gordon is asleep in his recliner, Anna calls and asks if she has time for a chat. Lara gets up and walks into the kitchen to talk to her, expecting nothing more than a suggestion for lunch or dinner, but no, Anna has other things on her mind.

'I thought you should know that Mark is creating quite a bit of gossip by asking questions about you and who you've been seen with. Kate – you know, Crazy Shaun's sister - called the other day and asked if you two had broken up , she thought you were an item, as do most people. Mark asked her if she knew someone called Weldon, some big guy you've been seen with. And then he asked if she knows a Tobias, he had a surname for him, but I've forgotten what it was.'

'Oh God, I thought he'd lost interest!' says Lara. 'I was sure he had, but now he seems to be on some damn crusade. Anything more you've heard?'

'Yes – after I heard what Kate had to say, I made a point of asking a couple of people who might know what he's up to. I pretended he'd asked me too - and yes, he is asking around. Nothing too structured, just a casual question here and there. Have you broken off with him?'

Lara hesitates, but this is such a good opportunity and she trusts Anna. 'I've begun a process of distancing myself – without creating problems.'

Anna, as usual, is being practical and direct. 'What do you mean by problems? Is he being difficult?'

'Not yet, but let's say he has all the characteristics of

someone who might turn difficult if I drop him – prone to ownership fantasies, domineering, a few fits of sudden anger. All interspersed with shows of great affection.'

She waits to see how Anna will interpret this, because someone else's take on the situation would be valuable.

'Oh no, how ghastly! Stalker material for sure. Be careful how you go about this.'

'Don't worry, I'm being very careful, very slowly making sure he knows I have other people interested in me but without making comparisons or injuring his precious self-esteem. I hope to achieve a clean break soon.'

'You know he was saying you're a unit, don't you – like long term partners? Despite going around and asking about who you've been seen with? Maybe he's a fantasist.'

Lara ends the call with a thoughtful frown and stays in the kitchen for a few minutes, considering what she just heard. It was a relief to hear that the word 'stalker' instantly sprang to mind for Anna, too. She has sometimes wondered if she is being overly dramatic and making too much of the issue, but hearing sensible Anna use the word makes her feel she is right and that being slow and careful is the right strategy.

Late that night, when Bridget and Gordon are going to bed, Lara sits with her laptop at the kitchen table, preferring it to the dining room which never seems to get used, and starts researching "fantasist". There is no clear-cut definition, but the word appears to have morphed away from meaning a daydreamer or a visionary. In today's world it seems to mean a person who makes up stories to make themselves seem more important and desirable, but also someone who comes to believe the stories they make up. She pauses in her reading and wonders what the implications of this last twist might mean in real life. If Mark tells people they are a unit and in a long-term relationship, does that potentially mean he has come to believe this himself, genuinely thinks of it as reality? And if this is what is going on in his mind, then she really must be very careful how she goes about detaching herself from him. With his ego and his uneven temper, and if he feels she belongs to him, then she must orchestrate her exit with great care and in a way that does not make her a sitting duck for some kind of revenge, which he might imagine is his by right.

Chapter 22

The call from Bridget on a Friday afternoon, when Lara has just come home from school, is a surprise. 'Charlotte will be here this weekend, just for two days, isn't it lovely?' she says excitedly. 'You'll be able to show her the house. I had no idea she was planning a visit, and I hope you haven't made any plans for this weekend. She said she didn't want to call you during school hours, but she's sending us both an email with her plans, so I'll not bother to tell you now.'

'Oh, lovely!' Lara sits down on the edge of her bed where she was just about to start putting things into a suitcase. 'And what a surprise, it will be such fun to see her and talk face to face. I put my phone on mute this morning when we were having an impromptu talk from the Head - she hates phones going off while she's talking and then I forgot about it — it's been on mute all day. I'll check my emails now.'

'I'm dying to see Thomas again — they develop so fast these first few months and he'll have changed a lot since we flew down a few weeks ago. They're arriving on a flight mid-morning, but you'll see all that in her email, anyway.'

Lara opens her laptop and sits down at the dining table to read it with a cup of coffee beside her. She has never been able to figure out why she finds it more enjoyable to read emails on the laptop than on her phone, but she does. Charlotte's email is the only new one in her inbox:

"Hi, we're coming to see you and to check out the house renovations. Thomas and I will arrive midmorning Saturday and please cancel anything you have set up, because I've asked mum to babysit, so I can take you out for lunch (with Anna) and then perhaps go and see the house. Mum is cooking something nice for dinner and dad is sacrificing Sunday golf. I'll leave mid-afternoon on Sunday. See you tomorrow! C xx"

Lara closes the laptop and wonders what it means. If the message wasn't so cheerful, she would worry about trouble in Charlotte's marriage or an illness, because coming for just an overnight visit with the baby and without Jonas seems like a very unusual thing for her to do. She abandons the laptop, returns to her bedroom and starts thinking of what to take to Wellington. Over the last few weeks, she has left more and more clothes at the Stafford Street house, things she might need there more than in Hamilton, and with the thought that when she moves, it will be easier to take them to the house in her car, rather than pack them all up for the movers.

'I just got a text from Charlotte,' shouts Bridget up the stairs just after ten the next morning. 'Did you get it too?'

Lara reaches for her phone and sees a message alert and goes to the top of the stairs. 'Yes – I'm just about to read it.'

"Sorry, both of you - I'll be late, flight delayed by

possibly an hour, so here's a plan. I'll take a taxi from the airport, drop Thomas at home and continue in taxi to meet Lara and Anna at the Foxglove for lunch which is booked for midday. Can't make lunch later, Anna has to be away by 1.30 and don't know if flight will leave when they say, so don't wait for me at home, Lara. C xx"

'What a pity,' says Bridget, 'but needs must – whenever she gets here, I'll just grab Thomas and she can carry on, to meet you and Anna. Isn't it typical, such a short visit and then a flight delay! The fates are conspiring.'

At noon Lara stands outside the Foxglove and thinks what a coincidence it is that she is back at this place for a second time so soon, and with no connection between the people who set up the dates. Perhaps people have different orbits, she thinks, they habitually go between places within a certain area, and others hang out in a different area even though Wellington is a small city compared to most. And then Anna arrives and says, 'Did you check the flight?' and Lara has to admit she was daydreaming and didn't even think of checking.

Anna looks up from her phone. 'The flight took off half an hour ago, so you and I will have lunch and I'll see Charlotte tomorrow perhaps. God, I love that dress, very classy.'

Lara looks down at the lime green dress. 'I've had doubts about it, but I love the colour and lately I've been wearing it quite a bit, but the style is possibly a bit over the top. What do you think - honestly? I bought it on an impulse and I've never been quite sure if I made a good choice.'

'Looks great to me,' says Anna and looks critically at her. 'You're so slim, you lucky thing, you can wear that sort of figure hugging style. I'd look like a sack of potatoes.'

Lara makes no mention of why she asked, but as always,

asking Anna is a sure way to get an honest answer; she doesn't indulge people with kind euphemisms.

They part after lunch and on the way to where she parked the car, Lara's phone pings with a message from Charlotte: "Just arrived, waiting for you at home, having lunch with mum and dad."

Chapter 23

With Bridget and Gordon doing some work in the garden, Lara and Charlotte catch up over coffee in the kitchen, and Charlotte says, 'I totally agree with Mum about your dress, it's a gorgeous colour on you. I've never seen you in lime green before – it does wonderful things for your skin, emphasises that olive tone I've always envied.'

Thomas is slumped against her shoulder, half asleep after his feed. 'I'm so sorry I didn't make it for lunch, but there was no point rushing around to have a few minutes with Anna. Perhaps we can see her for coffee here in the morning. Has she and Paul made up their minds to stay in New Zealand now? I've been going to ask her, but we usually text or Facebook message and I never got around to it. It's only recently we have re-connected at all after years of no contact.'

'I think they are staying – you know he's found a good job? Very good, in fact, and she's looking around. I think there's something formal you have to do to practice law if you've lived away for so long. And isn't it funny that you and

Anna hadn't connected properly since they came back, until just recently – you used to be such good friends at school.'

Charlotte looks thoughtfully at Lara and says slowly, 'Do you know, I've never thought about it like that. Some old friends you stay close to and some you don't. And fifteen years in London is a long time, not that it's any excuse – I think we had grown apart long before. She went to Otago for uni and I stayed here – you know how it goes.'

'They're renting at the moment, and they could have had my upstairs flat, but I had just let it when I heard they were looking.'

'You've let it already?'

'All part of the master plan. I'll explain it to you in a minute.'

Charlotte interrupts, having scrutinised Lara for a moment as if she has never seen her before. 'You must tell me where you got your dress – it's gorgeous. Was it stupendously expensive?'

'Mm - let's say medium stupendously expensive,' says Lara. 'I went off it for a while after Mark gave me a hard time about it the first time I wore it. He said – well, never mind, but it wasn't flattering.'

Charlotte eyebrows pull together, and two perfectly parallel creases appear between her eyebrows and for a moment she looks just like Bridget. 'What's that got to do with anything? You must have bought it because you like it. And if you like it, you should wear it!'

And Lara says evasively, 'Oh, I do wear it now – quite often. I'm not going out with him so much now and I did actually wear it when I had dinner with him a while ago, just to show him he can't dictate what I wear. You know how I told you I've been out for drinks and dinner with Tobias a couple of times? And with Anna and a couple of her friends. Well, it's part of a slow process to detach myself from Mark.'

'Well! I know it's not my business, but …'

Lara gives her cousin a wry smile. 'That's never stopped you saying exactly what you think before, so don't start now. I can see you feel outraged, but you haven't heard the full story yet.'

'Not outraged, well – maybe outraged too, but mainly worried.' Charlotte moves the baby to her other shoulder, and he burps loudly and spits white dribble down her dark blue shirt. 'Oh, bugger! Now I have to change and soak this blouse in cold water, or it will smell of sour milk forever. I'll put him down for a nap and come straight back down – and this topic is not closed.'

She walks away and Lara studies the baby's half-asleep face bouncing gently on Charlotte's shoulder and thinks how relaxed and calm she is with the baby. Maybe some women have an inbuilt ability to deal with babies as opposed to several of her friends who seem to find it difficult and tiring and say they're exhausted all the time.

When Charlotte returns five minutes later, Lara says, 'You are so competent, no fuss at all. Some of my friends who had babies spent months complaining they were exhausted and never had time to put make-up on and their house hadn't been dusted for weeks – or their partner wasn't helping enough. How do you do it?'

Charlotte shrugs and picks up her now cold coffee, takes a sip and makes a disgusted face. 'I'm tough – or maybe I'm more like mothers were before bringing up babies became a job for two people to endlessly fret about. I have no patience with the endless agonizing people do. Thomas has a regular schedule – none of this demand feeding nonsense and random screams in the night for me, thank you. And so long as he's fed and clean, he is happy to have a nap after every meal, even though he's nearly six months old now. It might change when he starts getting his molars, but I'll deal with it when it happens.'

'I'll make us another cup of coffee.' Lara reaches for Charlotte's cup. 'You need a fresh cup to have with the cake I bought on the way back, the one you used to love - and I'd like one too.'

'OK, thanks. But don't think I've forgotten what we were talking about earlier. I do worry about you sometimes, you know. You and Roddy had a lovely marriage, and he was such a good man – but I'm worried about your relationship with Mark. I hope you aren't slipping back into your old way of appeasing and trying to please, because then you might end up never getting around to ditching him.'

Lara turns from the bench where the electric kettle is starting to boil behind her and gives Charlotte a little smile. 'I got myself into it and I'll get myself out of it, but if I explain how it developed, you might see the sense of my plan.'

She starts the story about Mark's temper and his controlling nature and explains the plan to slowly disengage from him by re-establishing herself as unattached again. When she relates the scene in Logan Brown Charlotte is fascinated and insists on hearing every single little detail. At the end of story she laughs, delighted and surprised. 'What an amazing thing to do – you really are deceptive, you know. So demure looking and such a schemer underneath! You can't imagine how worried I've been. I picked up on the little hints of what Mark is really like behind the smooth veneer, just from various things you've said when we've been on Skype. Because I hear about him on social media now and then and the comments often seem to have a slight edge to them, as if there's something hinted at that others might or might not know. And I also worried because I remembered how non-assertive you were when you were little. You crept about like a mouse when you stayed with us, you always retreated when the rest of us squabbled or fought. When we were teenagers, you would often give up on stating an opinion or taking sides rather than risk getting into any kind of debate.'

She frowns and shakes her head. 'I sound like I'm being critical, I know – and I don't mean it that way. You are my very closest friend and I love you - and it hurt me to think that Mark was taking advantage, and how he got angry about things. I didn't know him at school, but I knew who he was, of course, everyone did - I didn't like his attitude then and I don't like the sound of him now.'

She picks up her piece of caramel slice and looks suspiciously at it. 'Probably a thousand calories! Never mind, I haven't had one of these for years – thank you!' She takes a bite and smiles at Lara. 'But seriously, darling – you know I love you as much, if not more than I love my siblings, and it really worries me that you're still going out with Mark, even now when I know you have an exit strategy. I haven't seen him for years, but I'm sure he is still a little shit under the sophisticated veneer. As I said, I have friends on social media who socialize with him, and I've picked up quite a bit of gossip – I think he's bad, Lara, plain bad. I don't think you should go out with him at all, just keep your distance.'

She watches Lara for a moment, as if she is trying to work out what feelings hide behind her neutral expression, but Lara manages to keep her expression calm. They are cousins and have been best friends for decades, but Lara knows that until this moment Charlotte probably never thought that Lara could hide from her and it has clearly surprised her.

'I'm going to tell you why I think it's important you stop seeing him - and I'm leaving tomorrow, so we don't have much time. I have to be back for a barbeque at Jonas's boss's place at six – I missed the last one and it was commented on. Now that he's in this new role and heading for management, all this stuff has become important.'

Lara waits without comments and her expression doesn't change, so Charlotte continues. 'You should get rid of Mark - now! He's not up to your standards and there are things about him you're probably not aware of.'

Lara knows she means it, that she's seriously worried because otherwise she would never go out on a limb like this and risk alienating her.

'I think you should say what's on your mind – I can take it.' She gives Charlotte a little smile and waits, but now she is quite apprehensive; there must be something serious behind this increasingly intense conversation.

'You know Mark didn't finish his law degree? Did he tell you?'

Lara shakes her head and thinks, this can't be it, it's not enough – she knows something more, and I don't think I've ever known Charlotte not to come straight out with it.

'Gordon told me – he said Mark works in a law firm, but not as a lawyer. I thought he was a lawyer, so it was a surprise. When I asked how he knew about a much younger guy in a smaller firm – and one who isn't a lawyer - he said he'd heard his name mentioned, that's all. What are you hinting at?'

'Did Dad know why Mark never got his degree?' Charlotte is leading with questions and not volunteering anything, and it can only mean one thing; she has heard something really bad about Mark. She is approaching whatever this is step by step, as if she's trying to find out exactly what Lara already knows, maybe trying to soften the blow of what is to come.

She shakes her head. 'He didn't say anything about

why, he just said he knew the name and had asked someone when I started going out with him, because he couldn't remember where he'd come across the name. Please tell me what this is about! You're driving me crazy, Charlotte – just tell me if there's something I should know!'

'Mark was at Vic, in his third year of law and he got expelled or whatever universities call it.' Her eyes are on Lara's face, steady and concerned. 'I never knew him there, but I remembered him from high school of course, so I was interested when I heard about it from someone who was on the union board. Mark stole from the Student Union – he was the treasurer. It was discovered, but because he paid the money back straight away, they didn't prosecute, so he has no record - but he was barred from continuing, so he never got his degree.'

Lara looks at the branches of the apple tree bending in the wind outside the kitchen window and thinks for a few moments. 'A lot?'

'I don't know, but enough that it was regarded as very serious. I have no idea if his current employer knows about it, but he has applied for a new job, a good job with big responsibilities in a construction company - just recently. A guy I knew at uni works at the placement agency that's screening the applicants for the job. He sent me a message last week, just to check that his recollections of the debacle at uni was as he remembered it.'

Charlotte frowns down at the last piece of cake on her plate as if she is contemplating leaving it as a token gesture, to demonstrate that she isn't greedy.

'He wasn't sure what to do about it, which surprised me – of course he should mention it, but he just said he was concerned. Later he found out the amount involved, which I never did, and he messaged me and said it was 'significant'. I think he was really trying to find out if I was in touch with Mark.'

'Was he wondering if you knew anything new about him – like some further problem?'

Charlotte nods. 'I think there's more to it than meets the eye. He didn't say, but people who work for those agencies pick up a lot of corporate gossip, and they know people all over the commercial and political landscape so to speak. Obviously, he's read Mark's CV and maybe he has heard something and was trying to get it confirmed.'

'God - Wellington!' says Lara with great emphasis. 'It's like a village in some respects, isn't it? What with thousands of civil servants and lawyers and all the connections – who needs a village pump?'

Charlotte picks up the last piece of caramel slice from her plate and sighs. 'Bliss! Did you get it from the place Mum used to get it from, the coffee roasting place? Anyway, to get back to Mark. This is my theory – I think the guy who asked me about Mark has heard some rumour about why he is leaving his current job. Perhaps his bosses have found out about the theft at uni and he never told them when they interviewed him, or he's done something else, maybe in this current job. I don't know which but reading between the lines that's what I took from our conversation.'

Questions crowd into Lara's mind and she finds it hard to know where to start. 'God, Charlotte! This is awful – this is even worse than the reason I decided on my exit strategy, as you call it. That's mainly because of how controlling he is and how he loses his temper - and I don't like the vanity – I've been beginning to wonder if he is a narcissist. I mean, not just with a tendency that way, but a true textbook narcissist. Maybe I should just end it before anything worse crops up?'

'And there is another thing,' continues Charlotte without

responding to Lara's confession. 'I haven't finished, it gets worse. And it was kind of weird how I got this final bit of info in a round-about way. I was on WhatsApp with Kate and she was running through a few people she met up with at some informal fifteen-year graduation reunion a month or so ago – just catching me up with the latest gossip, like who got married or divorced or had a baby, well let's face it, for most of them it's another baby, I'm the late starter.'

She squashes the crumbs of the caramel slice with her fingertips, licks them off and sighs again. 'This was so lovely! Anyway, someone told her Mark has snared an heiress – Kate had no idea it was you he was going out with, and neither does she know anything about the money held by the trust. She just mentioned it in passing and laughed and said, "good luck to him, and he's going for a good job too, so maybe finally he'll be able to afford his expensive habits". The person who told Kate is a close friend of Mark's, and she has met you, but she didn't tell Kate your name so Kate didn't make the connection – and I didn't tell her it's you.'

She looks carefully at Lara's face to see what her reaction is, but Lara keeps her expression neutral, a defensive knack from childhood when her mother was looking for an excuse to start screaming at her or maybe lashing out, so now she just waits.

Charlotte carries on, having seen no signs of imminent emotional turmoil about to break out. 'And I know you're an adult and much cleverer than I am in all sorts of ways, but it made me feel very concerned about you. In case it's all a clever plan of Mark's to get a free ride. And now I'm so relieved to hear you say you're already distancing yourself. I mean, you're lovely, and anyone could fall in love with you, but maybe he is doing it for mercenary reasons more than love?'

'Heiress? Really?' The word seems over the top and old-fashioned to Lara. Is she an heiress? How much do you have to inherit to be classed as an heiress? She wonders if people are gossiping about the actual amount, but how would they know?

'You're probably right,' she says slowly after a pause to let the implication sink in. 'And it would explain why he seems to find me lacking in so many respects, but he's still keen to date me - he's after the money. And he probably doesn't know the way Dad left it, so Violet wouldn't be able to squander it all but just use the income. And the trust remains the same - I have to apply to the trustees to spend any of the capital.'

She isn't sure if Charlotte knows that Gordon is one of the two trustees and feels disinclined to discuss it, but she need not have worried.

'Oh, I know,' says Charlotte casually. 'Dad talked about it when your father died and left all his loot to Violet, and I assumed you would inherit the trust on the same terms – but as you say, does Mark know this? I mean, that Gordon could theoretically stop you using the capital – not that he would. And don't forget the house, another nice asset to consider. And I just thought of this, there's also Roddy's life insurance – I remember you telling me the production company had him covered. You're a real catch, Lara!'

They sit silently looking at each other across the table, and then Bridget comes in, and interrupts the conversation.

'Are you two going over to the house now or later? I'm happy to look after Thomas, I think I remember how to deal with babies. And where is he? Did you put him down for a nap?'

Looking round the big open space that is going to be the kitchen-cum-living room, Charlotte says, 'I can't believe it! It's amazing – much, much bigger than I expected. I haven't been inside this house since I was a toddler, I think - I had no idea how large it is. As big as mum and dad's place. Are all these outlines where the appliances and benches will be?'

They discuss the layout of the kitchen and continue to the bedrooms. 'I'll have this big one, of course,' says Lara. 'And here is the dressing room – I can go in naked from one side and emerge fully dressed at the other end.'

And then her mind plays back the scene of her standing here with Mark's arm over her shoulders and she hears his voice saying, 'Plenty of room for two.' She shivers briefly and leads the way to the bathroom and the smaller bedroom.

'Is this for visitors or like a study? Or both?' Charlotte studies the second bedroom. 'And you said it was small, but it isn't – it's a perfectly normal sized bedroom. It's just that yours is so big, it's the comparison.'

'Guest room, I think. I don't need a study, and if I did, I wouldn't lock myself away on the shady side, I would sit in the living area – like, if I suddenly turned into a writer or something. Davina will come and stay now and then, so I must have a spare room.'

They do a quick tour upstairs and Charlotte remembers Lara's promise to tell her more about her tenant. They sit down on a pile of boards outside, shaded from the sun by the trees which will soon be cut down, and Lara says, 'Belinda, remember her – she was friends with Anna, but a couple of years ahead of us at school? I've connected with her recently – she asked if she could give my name to a close friend of hers, who is looking for a flat. So, it happened very fast. We went out for coffee, that's Weldon and I, and I like him and he likes the flat. And I don't need to advertise or have some rental agent screen and interview applicants or anything.'

'And who is he? Apart from a friend of Belinda's?'

'He's a scientist, works at the Innova Research Institute, you know the privately funded one. He's selling his house after a relationship broke up, says he can't be bothered keeping a big garden in trim. He's very funny in a dead-pan kind of way, a man of relatively few words, but entertaining. I like him.'

'Oh good,' says Charlotte. 'It's good that you'll have someone reliable living here. I thought about it the other day and wondered if you'd be able to get rid of an unruly tenant once they were in – like someone who had parties every weekend or practiced the tuba at four in the morning or whatever, something really intrusive and irritating.'

'God, no – Weldon isn't the type to have parties or be obnoxious at all. But he does have three very loud alarm clocks set to go off at different times.'

'You're kidding, right?'

'No, it's true, it was so funny when he told me, he thought I would say I didn't want him as a tenant when I heard. The look on his face! As if he was about to confess that in his free time, he was actually a serial killer.'

That night they have an extravagant three-course dinner with a wine which Gordon says he has saved for a special occasion, which Bridget says means he bought a dozen for twelve special occasions and they need a new space to store all the wine he keeps buying for those occasions.

The conversation with Charlotte stays in Lara's mind for a couple of days, and she begins to wonder if there is something wrong with her perceptions and her ability to assess people. Why has it never occurred to her that it might be her famous father's money which attracted Mark? She should have thought about it earlier, and from what she has heard, she is not in the least like his former women friends. Right from the start he was never satisfied with how she dressed and all the nagging about growing her hair longer, and how he always wanted her to wear very high heels. He is used to having women friends who attract attention, status symbols, so she never measured up, but he was attracted enough to her money to overlook her shortcomings.

God, I'm stupid, she thinks, I should have thought of this earlier. Probably Charlotte's sudden decision to visit was because she was worried about me and she felt she felt she must tell me what she knew face to face. Bridget was certainly surprised that she came for such a short visit and without Jonas.

Considering what she knows now and taking into account the contradictory signals Mark gives out, everything from aggressive criticism to endearments, often in close succession, there is only one conclusion. There's something wrong with him, she thinks, even apart from the mood swings and the passive or not so passive aggression. I must make a clean break.

Chapter 25

Having considered carefully, Lara accepts an invitation from Mark to have lunch on a Saturday a couple of weeks before Christmas. In her mind is a mental map, a timeline of how she is going to end this disastrous dating connection with him. She refuses to dignify it by calling it a relationship even to herself, because it is only friends dating; she has never had sex with him and she is not in love with him.

The plan, as she outlined it to Charlotte on Skype the previous day, is to see him only once or possible twice more, and she has a raft of excuses waiting to be used, mostly involving family events and other occasions which he can't possibly muscle in on. The final date for this prolonged and exhausting saga is the beginning of January, because she wants to be installed in the house with the tenant living upstairs before she cuts it off completely. When Charlotte asks why, Lara is unable to explain why this matters, and though there is no logical reason for it she feels very strongly that living in the house represents safety of a specific kind.

She hasn't mentioned her feeling of fear to anyone,

because there is no direct evidence that Mark would be violent towards her, and it seems over-dramatic to speculate about it, but she wonders if he not only has the hallmarks of a stalker, but that he might even become violent. His fits of anger have once or twice been out of proportion to what upset him, as if having initially lost his temper the anger flares into something close to rage.

Once she is in the house, she'll feel safe because Weldon will be upstairs and she won't have to wait for flights, arrive at the airport, or catch the shuttle into town, or in any way expose herself to harassment. This scenario is so extreme that she can't mention it to anyone, as if even talking about it might make it happen, but it sits in the back of her mind like a dark shadow.

So, here she is in a lovely restaurant which has just opened, for a final date with Mark, who is attentive and cheerful, and she thinks what a mad situation it is. They have a delicious lunch and Lara is studying the dessert menu, when Mark takes her by surprise by asking if she wants some advice about curtains. He hasn't mentioned the house once since they sat down and bringing up curtains seems madly inappropriate.

'Advice?' she says, genuinely confused. 'About curtains?'

He smiles his most caring smile, the one that often signals a criticism. 'I mean colours and so on,' he says lightly. 'I know you're not so good with colours, so I thought I might be of help.'

Aha, she thinks, he is referring to the lime green dress again and he has, of course, no idea that the curtains are already made and going up straight after this weekend. She has deliberately lied about delays and slight problems, making it appear unlikely that she will be moving in before the New Year.

Now she smiles back and says casually, 'I've already chosen the curtains, they were ordered just last week, but thanks for the offer.'

'Maybe I can be of help with advice about the deck and the garden?' He lifts his wine glass and studies her face, and his expression belies the casual tone of the question. She can see he is angry now and tries to keep her expression calm. 'I have a really good idea for a deck design.'

'The deck is completed,' she says, suddenly unwilling to lie about it or be evasive, wanting to draw one line in the sand at least. 'And the landscaping man was there with the arborist this week.' And she waits for the storm to break because his eyes are narrowed in anger and he stares across the table as if she is an enemy. Which I probably am, she thinks, but he doesn't know that yet.

'I'm really pleased I decided to have those big elms taken out,' she continues, as if she has not noticed the anger building. 'They cast so much shadow and with only the lovely gnarly tree in the corner left, it's as if the garden has ballooned out to twice the size. I'm going to have a light on the ground shining up into it – it's got a lovely structure.'

'OK,' he says in a tight, clipped way. 'I can see it's proceeding well without any input from me.'

And once again she wonders if he really does think he is going to live there. It seems unlikely that he could still imagine such a thing, but maybe he is a fantasist of the kind Anna suggested and believes his own script even in the face of the evidence to the contrary.

But he has controlled his expression again and gives her a smile as if he is forgiving her for making all those decisions without involving him.

'So, you'll be looking for a tenant for upstairs soon?' His

voice is playful and she can tell this is intended as a joke, and she suddenly understands he thinks he will live there and that there is no need to find a tenant. His implied understanding that they would live together seems to have transformed into a belief that he is going to live upstairs.

'Oh, it's all settled,' she says and tries to sound calm but worried now about a scene in public. 'I got a tenant signed up a little while ago, a friend of a friend.'

'What?! You did what? How dare you?'

People at other tables are staring in their direction and a waiter moves hastily towards them, alerted by Mark's raised voice.

Lara says, 'If you can't control your temper I am leaving - right now. I mean it, Mark. This is the second time you've embarrassed me in public and I won't have it!'

He makes a visible effort to appear calm and says nothing for a moment, while Lara waits to see what will happen next. The waiter pauses a few steps behind Mark and continues to watch them. At least he can't assault me in a restaurant, she thinks, and if it looks like turning nasty, I can ask the waiter to call a taxi and accompany me outside.

But disconcertingly Mark performs one of his lightning-fast changes of mood and temper, and says in a normal voice, with no sign of fury, 'I'm sorry, darling, that was uncalled for, please forgive me. I had thought I would have the flat upstairs.'

'Oh, no – did you?' She tries her very hardest to sound surprised in a laid-back way. 'You never said – I had no idea! But it's too late now, he signed the contract a few weeks ago and I have no legal reason not to fulfil my part of it.'

'Him? Is it a man? Someone I know?'

He thinks it might be Tobias perhaps, not that he knows him, she thinks, but he has seen him, and he knows I've been going out with him.

Aloud she says, 'No, it's probably not someone you know, I'd never heard of him before, he's some kind of scientist. Very quiet.'

'And you didn't think you should have told me?' And there is the edginess again, the little whiff of anger.

'No,' she says honestly. Because now she feels like being honest and this lunch can't get any more embarrassing than it already is. 'I didn't think it had anything to do with you. If you thought it did, I'm sorry, but it's done now.'

She excuses herself to go to the restroom, but it is part of the ad hoc escape plan which has formed in her mind and on her way past the desk she pauses, hands over her credit card and says, 'Charge me half the bill for our table – I'll be back in a moment. And could you call a taxi for me, please?'

The man behind the desk is the same waiter who nearly intervened when Mark raised his voice, and he nods and gives her an understanding little smile. On the way back to their table a few minutes later, she keys in her credit card pin and picks up the receipt and her card.

She walks slowly back to the table, very slowly, and sighs with relief when she sees a taxi pull up outside and thinks, God, that was quick, saves me sitting down, now I can go straight away. She stops for a moment on her side of the table and says quietly, 'I'm leaving now. I've paid my share of the bill. And don't ask me out again, we're done.'

This is it, she thinks, I've done it and I'll never have to deal with him again.

She walks away, safe in the knowledge that he can't follow her outside; he must pay and by the time he has, she will be in the taxi taking her around the block to where she parked Bridget's car.

. . .

'Do you still dream a lot?' asks Bridget casually the next day with her back turned to check on something in the oven.

She is being kind, thinks Lara, she doesn't want to pry, but something about me must have made her wonder, I can't think what it would be. Aloud she says, 'Not nearly as much as I used to – thank goodness. Have I been talking in my sleep?'

'I heard you say something when I got up to go to the loo last night and I thought you were talking to me, but you were asleep.'

She gets a bowl from a cupboard and puts it in front of Lara, adds a chopping board and a knife followed by three carrots and a kumara. 'Could you peel and chop those into large chunks, please, and put a bit of oil and salt on them – I'm doing a roasted vegetable salad when this cake comes out of the oven.'

With the school year ended, Lara is staying until Monday night and Bridget is delighted – another day with someone in the house. Lara has gradually realised that her presence has made Bridget's life better in some way, perhaps it's having someone to look after in addition to Gordon, or just having company on and off during the day.

'What's the plan for this coming week? What do you need help with? Would it be useful if I come with you to Hamilton?'

'Thanks, but there's really nothing to be done. Because I've been living in Davina's spare room since the new owners took possession of the house, I have very little left to pack. Just clothes and my laptop and things, the rest is in storage at the moving company's yard until they bring it down here on Thursday.'

Bridget turns from the bench to look at her. 'Two days early! Or did I get it wrong? I thought you were moving in on Saturday.'

'Oh God, I'm sorry! I forgot to tell you. I had a call from Warren just as I was boarding the flight to come here – the tiler will come and do the grouting on the kitchen floor this morning instead of Tuesday or Wednesday because he had a cancellation for another job - and it was the last thing I was waiting for. So, I asked Warren if he could get the commercial cleaners in as soon as possible and they're coming on Wednesday.' She smiles at the memory. 'And then I had to be very persuasive with the movers, but in the end, they agreed that if they got a couple of reserve guys in, they could move my stuff early – they had a truck free, just not the manpower that day. I really want to be in and settled before Christmas – I know we're having Christmas Day here, but I was thinking of having you over for dinner with Charlotte and Jonas on Boxing Day if you're not doing anything else. It's time I cook for you for a change.'

'Won't it be lovely – your first Christmas in the house. Well, the first one since it was re-modelled,' says Bridget. 'Luck has really been on your side right from the start with this rebuild – not like most stories I've heard about things always being later than scheduled, sometimes by weeks, or not going to plan. A woman at the mahjong club said her son has waited eighteen months for someone to come and remodel their kitchen.'

It is not until she is in bed that Lara remembers fragments of her dream from the previous night. She was standing on a grassy river bank at dusk, and someone was swimming towards her. She saw the swimmer's face and it was Roddy with his goggles on and she was holding a big, striped towel, waiting for him to come out of the freezing Waikato River. And then his face changed, and it wasn't Roddy, it was a faceless man, but she knew he was dangerous and she dropped the towel and ran.

'Excellent!' says Weldon when Lara calls him the next morning. 'I'll have all the time in the world over the Christmas break to get my belongings organised, if I can move things in before the holiday. How lucky that they finished the job early, very unusual.'

When she asks if he will be able to get movers to shift his furniture at this busy time of the year, he laughs. 'Movers? You think I need movers? I'll do it with a rented truck and my brother, we're both big and strong. Is it OK with you if I get the key and move in one evening this week?'

'Of course – I'm coming back from Hamilton on Thursday, I'll leave at the crack of dawn, and the truck with my stuff should arrive after lunch. What's the most convenient way to get the key to you? Oh no, wait - I'll get Warren, he's one of the builders, to put the key in some safe place when he goes to check that the cleaners have done a good job, and I'll text you and tell you where to find it.'

'And the power is on?'

'Yes, separate accounts for both flats, but until now both are in my name. We'll change it after we move in.'

Chapter 26

The farewell party in Hamilton, which Lara thought would be a low-key affair with finger food and wine on Wednesday night, turns out to be a major event in the large garden at Davina's younger brother Tim's house just outside town. Lara parks on the grass beside the long drive where at least a dozen cars are already parked at various angles, and takes care not to get boxed in.

She turns to her mother-in-law with raised eyebrows. 'Did you know about this? It looks huge!'

Davina shakes her head and denies any prior knowledge. 'They might have combined it with a Christmas party for their friends. You know how they like big parties – they're the perfect match those two, they've partied in one way or another since they met in high school.'

When they walk around the side of the house to the big lawn at the back, they find three barbeques set up at one end of the terrace, and a crowd of people with drinks in their hands scattered over the lawn.

'Cripes,' says Davina and starts to laugh. 'As far as I can

see, I think it's just family - and look at all the children, it's a swarm.'

'It is just family,' says Tim who has come up behind them. 'We've multiplied over the last few years, ours and Suze's sisters' kids plus all their partners and then their kids, who will have partners of their own any day now. I think we're nearly eighty all up, which is why I hired a couple of extra barbeques.'

After a late night of noise and laughter, with coloured lanterns suspended from the trees, over-tired children falling asleep in unlikely places and teenagers disappearing on mysterious errands and then reappearing again, Lara and Davina drive home exhausted.

'Cripes,' says Davina again and Lara smiles; Davina only has one word for anything surprising. 'What a crowd - and how noisy they all are. When you live on your own and have a quiet life, this sort of evening is nearly overwhelming.'

Lara smiles in the dark when she thinks of Davina's so-called book club girls who meet at her place; a dozen women ranging from mid-fifties to mid-seventies, who drink copious quantities of wine and gin, constantly talk over each other, laugh a lot and make as much noise as a popular pub on a Friday night.

'I know,' she says with a straight face. 'It's a quite a culture shock.'

Setting out early on the same morning as the movers' truck had seemed like a good plan when she discussed it with the man at the moving company, but getting up at half past five the next morning doesn't feel quite so clever. She wants to be ahead of the truck, which is due to leave at seven, and she knows she will need a pit stop on the way. The truck guys will probably buy pies at a service station, she thinks, they can eat on the run, there's two of them to share the driving, but that might be an old-fashioned idea. These days they probably stop and sit down at a table in a café and order smashed avocado on toast. She stops at Turangi for a coffee and a short walk, tops up with petrol and continues.

All goes well until she is nearly at Mangaweka, where the engine temperature warning light comes on and she stops on the side of the road. At the front of the car, she can feel heat before she even touches the bonnet and thinks, it's certainly overheated, but why? It was serviced only a couple of weeks ago. There isn't anything she can do until the engine cools, but she knows that at best she is going to need water, or at worst a break-down truck. She opens the bonnet to help the cooling process and prepares herself for a considerable delay.

After flagging down half a dozen cars to no avail with none of the drivers having water or any specific ideas that might help, a truck stops and the driver brings a thick glove from his cab and carefully takes the lid off the radiator, checks the overflow tank and finds it dry. He mutters something about the radiator plug, gets down on the ground and squirms his upper body in under the front of the car, confirms it's leaking and tightens it up as much as he can. Not only does he have gloves and a toolkit; he also has a large plastic tank of water that he keeps behind his seat.

'Can you imagine anything worse than being caught in some remote place without water? Like right here,' he asks with not unkind irony and lifts what looks like a ten litre tank of water out from behind his seat and brings it over to the car.

'I've carried one of these for years, but not many need it these days, I think leaking radiators are on the way out. I'll fill the radiator and then you start the engine and we wait a few minutes. Have you got some paper?'

Lara finds a copy of The Listener on the back seat and he puts it under the front of the car. They stand there with the engine idling, intermittent traffic passing and people's head turning to stare at them until her rescuer decides enough time has passed and pulls the magazine out. 'Not a drop,' he says, satisfied that the problem is solved. They part the best of friends, and she promises to check there is still no leakage next time she stops.

Chapter 27

When Lara turns into Orchard Street at quarter past two, the first thing she sees is the front half of the large furniture truck sticking out over the pavement from her short driveway. Standing on the opposite side of the street she can see that they have just managed to squeeze in between the gateposts. She slides through the gap and hears men's voices and someone says, 'Watch the corner!'

The metal ramp which spans the gap between the truck and the front veranda is vibrating as she walks past it and a flatbed trolley appears loaded with boxes. She glances up and says, "Hi!' to the man pushing it and he looks down and grins. 'I thought you were supposed to be here before us – did you get lost?'

'No, breakdown – you must have passed me when I stopped and bought something to eat.' They can't possibly have got here so fast without breaking the speed limit most of the way, she thinks and manages to get up the steps beside the ramp and into the hall.

A man with a handcart comes towards her. 'Your friend's in the bedroom – good thing he was here to let us in.'

In the door to her bedroom, she meets Weldon coming out carrying a box with 'Bedroom 2' written on the side, and he smiles and says, 'Move over so I can put this in the other bedroom.' She drops her bag and car keys in the corner and starts working.

Just after seven they call it quits. The truck has long gone and Weldon, who offered to help move things around in a way that left it open for her to refuse without giving offence, has carried boxes, shifted furniture and assembled her bed.

'OK,' says Lara, 'the pizza will be here any minute. Now we'll have a drink, you really deserve it, you've been marvellous - thank you! I never expected to have everything unpacked and put away today – it feels like home already.'

She opens the fridge which she turned on the moment the movers put it in place, gets a bottle of champagne out, hands it to Weldon and turns to get glasses out of the cupboard where she put them away no more than an hour ago. 'I ordered two pizza Margherita forty minutes ago, so they shouldn't be long. You must be starving.'

'I've had three nutbars and a lot of water,' he says and lifts his glass in a toast. 'But I'm starving, so I hope you ordered big pizzas. Here's to the house!'

'When did you move in?' She suddenly feels guilty that she hasn't asked him earlier. 'God, I hope you haven't ignored your place because you felt you had to help with mine!'

'No, not at all – I've got plenty of time to unpack boxes, but it's pretty civilised already. Come upstairs and I'll show you.'

They take their glasses and climb the stairs; Weldon takes two steps at a time and waits at the top for Lara to catch up. 'You first, see what you've given me – the perfect space. And it's much better than my house was, everything better laid out. I like the kitchen-cum-living room, it's great.'

When Lara finally has a shower in her lovely bathroom, it is nearly midnight, the very last things have been sorted out in her dressing room and she is so tired her whole body aches, but she doesn't fall asleep straight away. A bubble of excitement is expanding in her chest and she knows this is going to be a happy place. There is no remnant of the unhappy environment she grew up in until Bridget and Gordon rescued her, no lingering ghosts of raised voices, slammed doors or smashing crockery; the house feels calm and safe, like a haven.

The next day, a text arrives from Mark: 'Are you in town? Missing you!' and it puts her in a problematic spot. He doesn't know yet that she has moved in, and she'll do anything to avoid him finding out and simply turning up at the house. She knows without a doubt that he is going to push, try to re-establish their so-called relationship; he hasn't given up.

Since the disastrous lunch date, he has sent three texts with little loving messages about how he knows she must be busy in Hamilton, and how much he is missing her and she has not replied to any of them. All signed with kisses and she finds them scary, because she doesn't know if he really believes they still have something going, or if he is just pretending or deluding himself. The word "fantasist" has stuck in her mind and she thinks it is probably the most accurate label for Mark, and he is denying the reality of her breaking off with him in the restaurant. She doesn't reply to his text, just turns the phone off and puts it in her pocket.

Chapter 28

On the Saturday morning, Lara has just returned from a major shopping expedition at the supermarket, where she went very early in the hope that going early would be a good idea so close to the pre-Christmas frenzy. But hundreds of others have had the same idea and she returns to Orchard Street, frazzled and out of patience with the bad trolley manners of stressed shoppers. It's a week to Christmas, she thinks, and who would have thought so many would be out this early. She is unloading the first bags when she hears Mark's voice behind her. 'You moved in! What a surprise!'

Even as she swings around, she has time to think that he has obviously found out she has moved in, and why is he here when she told him she wasn't going to see him again?

'Hi,' she says and stays where she is, trying to think of how she can prevent him trying to follow her in. If she goes inside, he might follow and then she'll be forced to waste time on showing him around. Telling him it's truly over, here and now, is not ideal; too impromptu and she doesn't feel composed enough.

'I heard on the grapevine you'd moved in,' he says casually. 'Let me help you with those.' Without waiting for her to reply he picks up three shopping bags from the boot of her car and heads up the steps to the front door.

Putting the bags on the kitchen counter, Mark wanders down the length of the living room and stops to look out the French doors to the garden.

'Very nice,' he says, but his voice has an edge to it and Lara thinks, surely, he's not going to start criticising how she has done it, but no, he turns. 'Aren't you going to show me the rest?' Without waiting for a reply, he turns and walks toward the bedrooms.

She blesses the fact that she made the bed, despite her urge to do the shopping as early as possible. Somehow, she knows that having Mark look at her unmade bed would feel like an invasion of her privacy.

In the bathroom he frowns. 'You didn't have the underfloor heating put in, did you? The floor is the same level as in the passage. And I told you!'

She can't imagine what this strange comment, which sounds like an accusation, could possibly mean. Several things come to mind, none of them good. So instead of replying she simply turns on her heel and goes back through the living area to the kitchen, and he follows.

'I have to get the last bag out of the car,' she says, and Mark follows her through the shared front hall and outside. There is a man standing beside her car, so she walks around the front of the car, concerned that he might have taken something and comes to an abrupt stop when she sees the knife in his hand.

For a long moment they stare at each other, then his face contorts with anger and he says, 'I want money - cash!'

She backs slowly away from him, step by step until she can turn and run towards the veranda, where Mark is still standing on the top step watching them but making no move to come to her aid. The man's footsteps are close behind her now and she turns to face him, unwilling to have him catch her from behind. Mark shouts, 'Fuck off, you loser!'

Lara feels certain she is about to be stabbed, in broad daylight in a respectable suburb, but hands grasp her upper arms firmly from behind, and she is lifted aside and deposited on the second to bottom step.

'Inside - now!' says a voice she knows must be Weldon's, though she didn't hear him coming. Her eyes are still fixed on the man in the camo jacket, who stands swaying with the knife held in an underhand grip which makes it look as if he is getting ready to stab someone with an upward motion. He looks scared and desperate at the same time, and she thinks what a dangerous cocktail of emotions this is, so likely to erupt into violence.

For a moment she is incapable of moving. Weldon advances on the drunk and Lara turns and leaps up the last two steps, but she stops beside Mark and turns. The man is on the ground now, shouting incoherent abuse and Weldon picks him up by the collar of his jacket and sets him on his feet. 'Now, fuck off! Don't ever come near this house again or you'll regret it.'

The man tears free and runs stumbling away up the street and she watches him cross to the other side and disappear around the corner. Weldon picks up the knife and mounts the steps in two bounds and scans her carefully. 'You're OK?'

'Yes – no damage. Thank you!'

'Don't mention it.' He disappears up the stairs and leaves her staring after him.

'For God's sake, come inside and close the door,' says Mark, irritated and flustered. 'Maybe even this part of town isn't safe these days.'

'Don't be silly – it's no less safe than anywhere, it was just a random crazy guy.' Though despite her calm words, Lara is shaking. 'Thank God Weldon heard him and came down or I could have been in real trouble.'

'I suppose it's the only advantage of having a brute like him in the house.'

'He is not a brute, Mark!'

'No? Well, he looks like one and he acts like one.'

Well, you were no use at all, she thinks, so maybe a bit of brute strength is a good thing to have in an emergency.

Aloud she says, 'He's a scientist. I want you to leave now Mark!'

An hour later she calls Weldon. 'Hi, it's Lara,' she says and feels slightly ridiculous, picturing him standing just above her head in his kitchen, perhaps leaning against the bench and waiting for the water to boil, like she is doing. 'I just wanted to thank you for possibly saving my life – I can't imagine what would have happened if you hadn't come down. Have you got time for a coffee? I've just turned the jug on.'

Ten minutes later they're sitting in her living room and he takes a shortbread biscuit and looks seriously at her. 'Did you report it?'

'No, I didn't,' she says. 'There didn't seem much point when it's over and that guy's run away. It's not as if I had a photo of him or anything concrete to tell them.'

'But I have the knife, and I haven't touched the handle. I'll go and hand it in and tell the cops what happened after we've had coffee.'

And then he shakes his head with a rueful smile. 'I hardly ever get around to having a cup of coffee now – it's weird, I used to always have a cup mid-morning in the weekends.'

His eyebrows draw together in a frown, he looks away from her, and she knows what he is thinking of; those lost pieces of the couple routine, the little things that don't feel the same when you suddenly find yourself living alone.

'I was like that too,' she says and tries to sound casual even as she doubts she should say this. 'When my husband died in an accident, I just stopped doing a lot of little things we used to do together. Not on purpose, they just kind of disappeared somehow. And sometimes I wondered if I would ever again have a life full of pleasant little things, those unimportant rituals that rounds out your life. It felt as if without Roddy there wasn't much point doing them. But time changes things.'

The next morning Lara is just about to pour milk into her second cup of coffee and looks forward to sitting in her favourite armchair with the big sliding doors to the deck open. But before she has time to add the milk, her phone buzzes at her from the living area and she closes the fridge door and runs to pick up her phone

'Brian! How nice to hear from you – are you in Wellington?' She smiles to herself as she pictures him, tall and skinny and usually with an intense frown on his face, standing on a film set somewhere waving his arms and shouting orders at actors and technical staff, never still for a moment and constantly talking. They're old friends after meeting on various sets where Roddy was working and Brian was the director.

'I need help! And fast as hell! We're in a real mess here with streets closed off and our usual guy cancelling in the last bloody second. If I text you the address, could you come right away?'

She understands the urgency and doesn't waste any

time. 'You're lucky – I just moved down here and I'm not doing anything. Send me the directions and I'll leave in five.'

When Lara gets out of her car in Glenville Road, which she had to look up on Google maps, she stands for a moment taking in the scene in front of her and something stirs inside her. Since Roddy died, she has only twice been asked to work on a film set, and both times she sensed a degree of unease among the crew, as if having her there might bring bad luck or maybe create an embarrassing scene. As a confidence booster in the face of a possibly emotional atmosphere, she has dressed in clothes that will give her confidence.

She stands here in the old jeans with the oil stain on the thigh which will never come out, the jeans she used to wear when practicing with Roddy, and the old hard soled sneakers she wore when she learnt to do heel-and-toe changes. But this time the slightly unnerving feeling doesn't materialise, and she is not sure if something has changed or if she imagined it. Perhaps the crew never did feel awkward around her, perhaps she transferred her own feeling to them. She waves to a couple of familiar faces, ducks under the tape that blocks access to the street and threads her way between trailers and technical people until she reaches Smidge, the key grip.

'Lara!' he says and claps her on the shoulder. 'My God, it's good to see you again! I heard you were helping us out. Brian's over there - he wants to have a chat to you about an idea he has for one of your famous handbrake turns. And we've laid down a big speed bump for you too.'

'Over here!' shouts Brian and waves from where he stands in a cluster of men beside a white Toyota Corolla. 'How are you, girl? You look great! Have a look at this – we haven't got much time.'

'What happened to the guy you booked?'

'Broke his wrist, the silly bugger – showing off for his nieces and fell off a trampoline. Thank God you're on the spot, we've only got this street for three hours and they'll only let us have it on a Sunday and we can't wait another week. But there's only one scene left now, and we've got an hour forty before we've got to be out of here. Sorry about the late notice, but the guy only called half an hour before he was supposed to be here – and I want it done properly. Lucky that one of the crew remembered you'd moved to Wellington, or we'd be up shit creek without a driver.'

He laughs and gestures at the two men beside him. 'These guys offered, but I want this to be done just the way I want it. Now here's the plan.'

He spreads a sheet of paper on the boot of the car and uses a pen to point. 'We're filming this both from the ground and from a drone, cameras here and here and here. The drone will follow the car which speeds down to this corner, does a drift turn into the street on the right, see – down there, second corner.' He points with the pen. 'By the house with the pointy roof. Lots of squealing rubber and smoke, you know the drill. Then one block further down a left turn into the cul-de-sac. Same thing – squeal and smoke. Oh, and no need for a wig or a cap, dark windows as you can see, and we've done lots of shots with the actor and with the chasing car, so we can splice in close-ups when we edit.'

He makes a cross on his plan and continues without seeming to draw a new breath. 'Anyway, then it's up the short but steep driveway to the garage beside the second to last house on the left - here - straight into the open garage and that's it. There's another couple of scenes we'll be doing next Thursday night, so if you can, please come and do those too. It's on the Remutaka hill road, in the dark and we'll bring a rain maker – should be fun. They're only letting us close the road completely for short sessions and then we have to wait for backed-up traffic to go through, then we can film again – a bloody nuisance, but the best we could get. So, we'd better meet first, go up there together in daylight and have a look – the director of photography will come too so we get it all sorted with you beforehand.'

He folds the plan and starts walking toward the first corner, while he continues talking non-stop over his shoulder without waiting for an answer as he always does, and Lara follows without comment, because she knows better than to interrupt Brian when time is short.

'So, this is my new idea – the script has the car swinging fast up that handy little sloping driveway and just stopping outside the garage with the guy hunching down so the car looks empty, but I think you could do something a bit more spectacular as I said. We'll see what you think. I'd like you to drive fast straight into the empty garage, which we've got permission from the owner to open. Imagine you're trying to get away from someone chasing you and you go into a dead-end street, so you're trapped and then you spot the empty garage standing open. So - instead of simply doing a tight turn at speed to go up that short little slope and stop, you do a snappy handbrake turn. You know the one where you kind of turn at right angles without any drift – I've seen you do it, fuck knows how – but anyway, so you do that, then up the slope, just missing the gatepost and fast as hell into the garage. We've checked the brakes, they're good.'

He glances at her to see her reaction and she grins. 'What if I go straight through the rear wall of the garage?'

'We'll worry about that if it happens – I'm sure it won't.'

They look at each other and laugh, and both think of the occasion last year when she was meant to narrowly avoid a crash with a semi-trailer driven by another stunt driver, and he braked a fraction of a second too late and she had to take evasive action and took out a pedestrian crossing barrier on the median.

By the time they reach the cul-de-sac, Lara feels comfortable with the plan; drifting around these wide corners will be easy at high speed, but at the narrow garage driveway she stops and looks at Brian.

'Do I take out the gatepost? For effect? Or do I just make the turn just in time to miss it? Do you need the car undamaged?'

'Hmm, let me think, take out the gatepost? No, I don't think so - but thanks for the offer! I know you'd do it very neatly, but my idea is that once he leaps out of the car and presses the button for the door to drop down, there's no sign of where the hell he disappeared to, so leaving a broken gatepost wouldn't fit. But that speed bump there - we've laid it down temporarily just for effect – it's just about halfway between the corner and this garage. I want you to hit it really hard – lots of air – so will the handbrake turn work? Do you think there's enough room after you land?'

'I'll have to do a couple of test runs – depends on if I can plant all four wheels on the road when I land, I mean in time to do the turn. Let's do a trial run right away.'

'I've just tested the handbrake,' says one of the technicians, when they get back to the car. 'We've shortened the travel quite a bit, so when you pull hard and fast you get instant action. The release button is very soft, so you'll have no trouble holding it in. Want to try it out?'

Lara takes her jacket off and throws it on a toolbox someone has left beside the car. She moves the seat forward, fastens the seatbelt and says, 'OK, I'll be back in a minute,' and slams the door shut.

Everyone steps away from the car, and she turns the key and revs the engine hard. Maximum speed before the corner, she thinks and starts with high revs in second gear.

She flies down the street, drifts around the corner into the side street with a scream of tyres; a plume of smoke she doesn't see blossoms out from under her wheels. Then another corner and a fast turn into the cul-de-sac, she floors the gas pedal, and a tremendous jolt sends her flying over the speed bump. The car lands with a thump, she has her eyes fixed on the right gatepost, turns the wheel hard at the same time as she pulls the handbrake up, keeps the button pressed in, lets it go and flies up the driveway and into the garage, slams on the brakes and comes to a stop with the nose of the car nearly touching the back wall. A man materialises from an open door at the back corner and gives her a thumbs up, and she realises that he was filming her approach. She waves at him and reverses slowly out and drives back the way she came.

'Jesus - that was fast!' says Brian. 'I was watching the drone camera.' He gestures at an open laptop on the bonnet of the pickup truck beside him. 'Good thing we were filming all the way – you might never be able to do it so fast again.'

Lara does the run three more times, twice a second faster than the first time and once a second slower, and then it's done.

'Brilliant! Roddy would be very proud of you,' says Brian. 'He used to say you were getting to be as good as he was, did you know that? Said you had split-second reactions. I'll text you the time and pick you up on Thursday to go for a recce up the Remutaka road. We've got to move all this stuff now and get the speed bump off the road as fast as. I'll call you!'

The feeling of happiness she first experienced when she parked by the cordon stays with her as she drives back to town and on an impulse, she turns into Evans Bay Parade at the Wind Needle and follows the coastal road past all the little bays, around the point and back towards the city. Her mind is full of images from the past; the first time Roddy took her with him to a film set, so she could see what a stunt driver really does, when they were first going out together. The time he got concussed on location and drove himself back to Hamilton from Auckland seeing double, and how worried she was that he was brain damaged. The many hours spent in the weekends in industrial areas, where there is a lot of space and little weekend traffic, with Roddy teaching her all he knew and the feeling of triumph when she got it right. And the exhilarating day four years ago, when Roddy was in Australia for a week filming and Brian called and asked her to come and do a couple of scenes in a new TV series he was directing in Northland. She remembers how nervous she felt as she drove to the location, how worried she was that she wouldn't be good enough and embarrass both herself and Roddy. And the blissful moment, when she sat in the car ready to go and suddenly realised that she was completely relaxed and knew she could do it easily.

Chapter 30

E arly the next morning a text from Mark arrives and his message seems mysterious at first, but after a moment she gets it: Why did you keep it a secret? You never told me you're famous!

Well, listen who's talking, she thinks. What about your secrets? Obviously, he has found out about the stunt job, so she sits down to check social media and it only takes a minute to find a post shared by Charlotte with a long row of red exclamation marks as a comment instead of words. Someone in the cul-de-sac has filmed the whole thing: there she is walking down the middle of the street with Brian, pausing briefly by the speed bump and continuing to the sloping driveway which ends in the open garage. She watches herself pointing at the gatepost and then they turn and walk back towards the person who must have filmed from a house roughly halfway down the cul-de-sac on the opposite side from the garage she will end up in. Then a good shot from an upstairs window of her coming fast around the last corner in what she must admit is a beautifully controlled drift with smoke billowing away from the car, followed by the flying jump over the speed bump and the sharp handbrake turn into the driveway.

It's very well done, she thinks, top marks to the person who held the phone for running upstairs and catching it from higher up, very effective! I wonder if he or she heard our conversation and knew what we had planned.

After a moment's thought she sends a private Facebook message to Charlotte and less than a minute later she calls.

'I got it from Carina, Gabriella's younger sister. She posted the link on Instagram and asked if that really was you – she said it had to be you or your identical twin. I went and checked it on YouTube and shared it for you to look at. Why on earth did you never tell me about this?'

And why didn't I? thinks Lara. How do I explain it? I think it's just that I've never been good at bringing up things about myself in casual conversations somehow, I'm just a background kind of girl.

'I don't know,' she says. 'I wasn't trying to keep it secret, Charlotte! I just never got around to mentioning it. You know how it is - if nothing leads to it naturally you don't just blurt things out. Or I don't, anyway. It would be attention-seeking, wouldn't it?'

'Well, I'm so damn impressed – I'll have to brag to everyone I know now, if you don't mind. But it's too late for you to mind anyway, it's going to spread from Carina, she has literally hundreds of friends and some of them will recognize you too and spread it further.'

They talk of other things for a while and just before they end the call Charlotte starts laughing. 'Oh my God! I've just gone to YouTube on my laptop while we were talking – the video has been shared more than six hundred times since I called you. And I do love the name of it – You think women can't drive? Watch this!'

'What are you doing sitting in front of your laptop at this time of the morning?'

'I've just fed Thomas and I thought I'd have some me-time before he wakes again, which he will! I think he's a Hobbit – he has two breakfasts most mornings now. Jonas has to be on site very early today to inspect something, he just left.'

Mark can wait, thinks Lara, and I want to consider what to say or if I'm even going to reply at all. And he has no way of knowing if I have read his message yet. She stays where she is, sitting up in bed with the phone in her hand, trying to decide why she never talked about her driving with Mark. Was it because of how he might react? Or was it that she knew he would feel it was a feather in his cap and revel in the reflected fame – because that's how he might have looked at it, food for his ego. He thinks knowing people with money or people who are well-known makes him special. And now he will probably resent finding out about the driving, because he might remember how he snarled at her that night, that he didn't need her to tell him how to drive. The retroactive embarrassment could make him difficult and whatever I say could make him angry.

After thinking about it she replies to Mark's text: Because I'm not famous. Stunt people don't get famous, it's just a job.

Not until she drives to Stafford Street to have dinner with Bridget and Gordon does she realise that she must tell them too. Why they've invited her when they will soon see each other several times over Christmas and New Year, which is practically upon them, she can't imagine. But Bridget was insistent that they wanted to see her tonight, so now she is driving through the city centre, thinking it seems unreal that she has been doing driving jobs on and off for a few years now and never mentioned it to her family, though talking about it never occurred to her until Charlotte pointed out how odd it is.

But if I'm doing another job next week on the Remutaka hill road I must tell them, she thinks. Just so they know where I am – what if something happened and they got this confusing call from Brian or the police and they had no idea what they were talking about? And strangely, the fleeting thought that she might have an accident, doesn't trigger any reaction in her mind; the memory of how Roddy died does not make her need to stop and collect herself, it just makes her feel sad.

Chapter 31

G ordon opens the front door with a copy of The Dominion Post in his hand and gives her a hug. 'I've missed our extra daughter,' he says. 'And why aren't you using your key? You're still a child of the house, you know.'

He leads the way to the kitchen, still talking and folds the paper as he goes. Bridget hands Lara a glass of wine and turns back to something on the stove, and Lara sits down and says casually, 'I did a stunt driving job yesterday – they called me at the last moment when their regular driver let them down.'

'You what? A stunt driving job?' Gordon stares at her across the table. 'When did you start doing this? Did Roddy train you?'

'Oh, years ago, we spent hours and hours in empty streets on Sundays, mostly in the industrial areas – and left a lot of rubber behind. He taught me everything, drifting, sliding, how to keep control on shingle roads at high speed, all kinds of tricks.' She can't help giggling. 'And how to drive on two wheels, but that took a bit longer – it's quite scary having the horizon on a tilt.'

Bridget sits down beside Gordon, still with a dripping spoon in her hand and the look on her face is one of surprise mingled with something like triumph and exclaims, 'Ha! I knew it – I always said you'd surprise us all one day. And you've kept this quiet for some reason, but why?'

Lara looks seriously at her aunt. 'But I haven't – not deliberately. It's not my thing to just come out with things about myself. I talked to Charlotte this morning, she saw it on social media and there's video on YouTube, and I tried to explain why I hadn't told her. I find it hard to mention things unless they come up naturally in conversation. I didn't mean to be secretive or anything.'

Bridget puts the wet wooden spoon on the table, takes a sip of her wine and shakes her head. 'God, you're such a character, Lara! Go get your laptop Gordon, so she can show us and meanwhile I'll put the casserole in the oven.'

They sit in a row along one side of the table and watch the video three times before Bridget and Gordon stop exclaiming and asking questions.

'I'm doing another job for Brian on Thursday evening – or rather, in the middle of the night, on the Remutaka Hill road, and then it's over for now,' says Lara casually, hoping the thought of her driving very fast on a notorious road won't make them worry about her safety. 'It was so nice seeing those guys again, they're nearly like family.'

All through the meal she feels there is something they know that she is unaware of, and it makes her uncomfortable in a way she is not used to in this house. A couple of times she catches a glance exchanged between Bridget and Gordon and finds herself listing possible bad news in her head, as if she must anticipate, be prepared.

. . .

When she leaves at nine, she hugs Bridget, and Gordon goes with her to her car, and just as she is about to get into the driver's seat, he says, 'I've got something to tell you, Lara, and Bridget insists I do it tonight. It's about Mark.'

As they stand there looking at each other across the roof of her car, she understands that what he is about to tell her is serious, but she doesn't feel worried. How odd, she thinks, it feels like whatever it is will be a relief to know, and it will confirm my decision; give the break-up another reason and more substance. Because she still thinks Mark is unlikely to have given up and she might need some extra ammunition to throw at him.

'He's having to resign from his job because he's been having an affair with the wife of one of the partners – it's been going on for months and it came out just recently. Has he told you? No? I'm sorry, Lara – he is bad news all through and he doesn't deserve someone like you.'

Now she feels pity for Gordon and how concerned he is about her, and she walks around the car to where he is standing, puts her hand on his arm and smiles up at his worried face.

'I'll be OK, Gordon – don't worry about me. I've told him it's over and you've just demonstrated I was right to break it off. There were other things that weren't right - and I was never in love with him. Charlotte warned me about something she knew about him too, something she heard from an old uni friend - but I was already a bit wary of continuing with him even before that. How did you find out?'

His relief is obvious and he puts his hand on top of hers. 'Thank God! I've been so worried about how you would react - and Bridget too. I sat next to the senior partner of that firm at a Law Society meeting a couple of weeks ago and we got talking about the changes to the Employment Relations Act and what they might mean long term, particularly regarding this new term 'unprofessional sexual conduct' they've introduced - and he said they had recently had occasion to deal with an employee in unusual circumstances relating to just that.'

'Can you tell me? Or is it confidential?'

The more she knows the better. It will add solid reasons he cannot argue with, if he decides to try and reconcile with her – an affair with a married woman is perfect, and much better than vague reasons like "I don't like you enough" or "you're too temperamental". Not even Mark would expect a prospective fiancée to put up with it, however much he lives in his fantasy world.

Perhaps one of the reasons I felt I had to disentangle myself by degrees, she thinks, was that I wanted to avoid all the arguing and pestering. Because he's after sharing my money, so I'm sure he would try to sway me, and this extra ammunition is very useful.

'I'll tell you, but it's not for public consumption. To avoid a possibly prolonged period of hassle, they decided he had to be the one who made the decision to leave – so they gave him the choice to resign instead of being dismissed. They obviously had to get rid of him, it was an impossible situation, and they gave him two options – he could resign of his own free will, or they would dismiss him with instant effect for non-disclosure of serious issues in his past – things which were not mentioned in his CV or when they originally interviewed him for the job.'

'I know - he stole money when he was a student,' says Lara. 'I hadn't heard about it before, but I suppose some of the student gossip didn't come my way when I was at uni in Waikato. Charlotte told me when she was here - she was worried about me. And was the threat enough to make him resign? I mean, he wasn't charged with theft way back then, so there's no record of it, is there?'

Gordon gives her a wry smile. 'No, they should have charged him, I think, but it's well documented at the university – I mean the reason he wasn't allowed to complete his degree and the fact that he can never enroll as a student at Victoria again. They've got some form of admission signed by him which they drew up when he paid back the money he'd stolen.' He smiles grimly. 'And nobody in their right mind would have someone who's admitted to theft of money in a law firm, And not only that, but they asked very specific questions about any issues in the past when they interviewed him, and they have the right kind of paragraph in the employment agreement. They could have dismissed him, there would have been no come-back possible for him.'

On the way home she acts on a sudden impulse to immediately make it very clear to Mark that she wants no further contact with him at all, to reinforce that she has broken off her friendship with him. Avoiding further random visits or text messages from him has suddenly become urgent.

Maybe he didn't take it seriously when I said it was over in that restaurant, she thinks, and the lure of her money will motivate him to continue, to act as if their friendship is still on. If she can make him accept that she won't under any circumstances go out with him again and that she doesn't want to hear from him either, then she will have finished it once and for all. I'll do it now, she thinks, and then it's done, and I'll be able to sleep tonight.

She pulls over on Boulcott Street and sends an email from her phone telling him she doesn't want to see him again and not to contact her, states her reasons as 'multiple and serious' and adds that there is not the slightest chance she will change her mind. Without reading what she has written, to give herself no opportunity to reword things or maybe delay, she presses Send, starts the car and drives home.

Chapter 32

Feeling as if a weight has been lifted from her shoulders, as if something which has been depleting her inner resources has slipped away, she sits down with a new book she bought a couple of weeks ago and hasn't started yet. There is something about opening a book to the first chapter that is so exciting, she thinks, and it doesn't matter if it's an e-book or a physical book, it's the unknown adventure in your hand and the as yet un-met characters and their lives which will soon be part of yours, their joys and tragedies.

I just don't understand why some people never read fiction, she thinks, what their reasons are, and whether they realise how much richer their lives would be if they did; the innumerable new worlds which would open up for them. Mark wasn't a reader, but that never really surprised her even at the start, even before she knew these latest things about him. He was so focused on the centre of his universe, which was himself, so he probably needed nothing else. Roddy read history and technical books, but he never read fiction. Maybe it is a woman thing – women find other people's lives and motivations interesting and discuss them, and maybe learn from them.

When there is a knock on her door, she is startled. because the outside bell for her apartment has not rung, and nobody can get in through the main front door, so it can only be Weldon. But when she opens the door, it is Mark who stands there, and she feels his anger like a change in the air pressure; a barely contained fury which nearly makes her take a step back. He stares at her with a look of intense dislike, and she looks back without speaking and waits for what is coming, her breathing shallow and fast. This could turn ugly but she knows she must not show her fear.

'Who told you things about me? Someone's been lying! And why did you never tell me about the stunt work? Did you leave me the last to know on purpose - to make me look ridiculous?'

His voice is harsh, the questions are accusations with a question mark at the end, and he hurls them at her like stones, he wants to hurt her and punish her. One thing she has learnt over a lifetime of trying to avoid taking sides or responding to challenges, is that silence is powerful. Since early childhood she has never been able to deal with heated arguments or even intense debates, so staying silent or walking away have become coping responses. Whether faced with a statement or a question, saying nothing nearly inevitably prompts the other person speak again, and it gives her a feeling of control which bolsters her courage, and sometimes it gives her an opportunity to side-track the conversation. And now, facing Mark's aggression, she hopes it will work this time too, as it has many times in the past.

'Well!? Who put you up to this? Someone's been working

behind my back, trying to turn you against me and I want to know who it is!'

His voice is a getting louder, he is nearly shouting, and his face is red. She has never seen him so furious before, and she wonders if he might hit her. Nobody apart from her mother has ever hit her, and she's not sure if she will be able to tell if there is a blow coming now. As a child she learnt to read her mother's increasing fury, she could tell by eye movements and clenched hands when physical violence was about to erupt, but this feels different.

She tries to keep her voice even and calm and makes an effort to stay in place and not take a step backwards, because in the back of her mind she knows that being alone with him inside her flat might be dangerous.

'Nobody put me up to anything, Mark – and I never talk about the driving, not to anyone really.'

'So, what's this email about then?' He holds his phone up and shakes it in her face. 'You write and say you want to end our relationship and for me not to come around! Like I'm some kind of servant you can dismiss without discussion.'

And from somewhere deep inside her a wave of anger gives her the courage she needs, and she tries to keep her voice steady, and her anger helps, makes her feel more in control.

'You didn't tell me you had to resign from your job - or why! You've been sleeping with the wife of one of the partners for the last six months, how is that for a secret? You are a deceitful liar, Mark. I have the right to call it off if I want to, and I can do it any time I like without consulting you - and that time is now. Now, leave my house! I don't want you here.'

Inside her the strength engendered by the wave of anger is receding and she knows she cannot continue this argument. She can't cope with him a moment longer but he might push inside and suddenly the possibility of physical danger seems very real. His face contorted with rage, he shouts, 'You fucking bitch!' and in a split-second flash of warning she knows he is indeed going to hit her, and then his fist slams into her face; she stumbles sideways against the doorframe and cries out with shock and pain.

Rapid steps thunder down the staircase and Weldon appears behind Mark, reaches around to grab his right arm and twists it up hard behind his back. He looks at her over Mark's head. 'Shall I toss him out?' And then, before she replies he looks closely at her. 'Did the little shit hit you in the face?'

She nods and what follows is swift and unexpected. Somehow Weldon spins Mark around and pins him to the wall with a forearm across his throat, lifting his feet off the floor. 'You little bastard - you are leaving, now! And don't come back!'

He lets go and Mark nearly falls, and for a second he looks as if he is going to attack Weldon, but he turns and walks out of the still open front door and down the steps to the driveway. 'Fuck you, you ugly brute,' he shouts over his shoulder as he stalks away.

Chapter 33

Weldon closes the front door, checks the lock and turns to Lara. 'Does he have a key?'

She shakes her head and puts a hand to her face. The pain is spreading now and the whole side of her face throbs. 'No, he doesn't – I can't have pulled the door properly shut when I came in.'

'You need ice,' says Weldon and walks past her into her apartment. 'Come on!'

Still dazed by the rapid escalation of the confrontation, she follows him into the kitchen, leans against the kitchen bench and watches with a sense of detachment as he searches through the freezer, brings out a bag of frozen peas and smashes it hard on the bench to un-clump the peas. He grabs the tea towel, wraps it around the packet of peas and says, 'Stand still.'

Holding her head steady with one hand, he puts the ice pack on the side of her face, and she groans at how the pressure intensifies the pain.

'I know – it hurts, and you're going to have a terrible bruise, but this will help. Sit down and hold on to it.'

Without protesting or saying anything at all, Lara walks through to the living room, sits down in her armchair and waits. She has no idea what she is waiting for, she just sits there and thinks how strange it was that Mark hit her so hard, and with his closed fist, it was brutal, and she never expected him to do anything so fierce. She had thought he might slap her - he was out of control angry, and his hands were twitching. But not that vicious punch! The pain is radiating down her cheek and along her scalp above her ear and the ice seems to be making it worse; she leans her head back and closes her eyes. She hears Weldon moving around in the kitchen, opening cupboards and then the fridge and she wonders vaguely what he is doing, while she tries to imagine what she will say to explain her bruised and possibly swollen face when she does the recce on the Remutaka road, because Brian is sure to comment. Weldon comes towards her and she opens her eyes; he has a glass of wine in each hand and sits down in the chair opposite hers, puts one glass on the little table beside him, leans forward and puts a glass into her hand and holds her wrist for a moment. 'Are you OK? Can you hold it without spilling?'

She nods and takes a sip, and then suddenly she realises she has not said thank you or anything really, apart from telling him she did not close the front door properly.

'Thank you! That's twice now that you've rescued me,' she says and tries to smile. 'God knows what it might have turned into if you hadn't come downstairs. Did you hear it or were you on your way out?'

'My door at the top of the stairs was still open. I went for a late run, and I came in only minutes before you got home and for some reason, I never shut the door, so when he arrived, I heard his raised voice - and I didn't like how angry he sounded, so I opened my door wider. Not that I could hear much, but the tone was alarming, and I had just decided I would intervene when I heard the punch – I actually heard his fist connect with your face. Well, I didn't know it was your face, but I heard the impact of the blow.'

He leans forward and moves her hand holding the frozen peas away from her face and then puts it back again. 'It's going to look bloody spectacular – I'll take a picture of it tomorrow morning, OK? It will be quite amazing by then. You need to be able to prove this happened.'

'Why? He won't come back – he knows he's no match for you.' It nearly makes her laugh to picture Mark trying to tackle Weldon.

'What if you need to take out a protection order against him later on? You need the proof – a photo and the date on your phone.'

She doesn't argue, because he's probably right and there is no point in not doing what seems like a sensible thing. He deserves an explanation, she thinks. Without him here to intervene I might have got badly beaten up. Mark isn't big, but he's stronger than I am, and he was so furious.

'I sent him an email,' she says and sips her wine. Swallowing sends a little dart of pain up to her temple, but she manages to drink some more. 'I told him I was breaking up with him, but he was already angry about something else, and it must have just tipped him over the edge.'

And now she nearly laughs at the thought which just occurred to her. 'I actually stopped on the way home from dinner at my uncle and aunt's place – stopped right there in the middle of town and sent him an email from my phone. I was told something very bad about him tonight, and it kind of added to other things I've found out recently. I broke it off not long ago, but he hadn't accepted it – he didn't take it seriously. He thought he could talk me over or charm me, I suppose. But after what I heard tonight, I couldn't bear not to make sure he really understood I was serious, that I never wanted to see him again. He must have leapt into his car and come racing up here as soon as he read it.'

He makes no comment and seems distracted, so she says nothing more, but suddenly he looks up and grins. 'I've got it! Are you on Facebook or any social media?'

She nods and winces at the pain the movement sets up in her face. 'Facebook and Instagram. I have a Twitter account, but I never use it – or hardly ever.' She drinks some more wine and thinks how nice it is to have someone to do her thinking for her right now, not what she normally likes, but tonight it is a blessing. She can feel her shoulders relaxing, leans her head back and sighs.

'OK, good - you should do a couple of things tonight. I think we can document this without making any obvious statements or accusations. First you unfriend that little shit on Facebook - do it now, tonight. And then in the morning, I'll come down and take a photo of your face with your phone, and you post it without any comments at all, on all your social media accounts.'

He raises his glass as if in a toast and watches her process what he has just suggested until she smiles. 'I learn all these things from my sister-in-law who lives out her life on social media. She tells me strategies for achieving things without apparently saying anything.'

He sees her question before she voices it and smiles grimly. 'I had some problems when my partner left me – it was a little messy for a while – so Manaia taught me ways to deal with the online assault campaign.' He shakes his head, 'My partner was a master manipulator, and Manaia was determined she wasn't going to get away with blackening my reputation - or driving me crazy. So, here's option A - after you unfriend him, you could change your security settings so friends of yours can't share things you post – that way he won't see the photo shared by someone else, if you don't want him to, though he might hear about it and ask someone to show him.'

'Of course,' says Lara slowly. She has listened to him without responding while she pictures how this Facebook strategy would play out. 'If I do things in that order, he doesn't see anything from me after I unfriend him tonight, neither directly nor shared. And what's Option B?'

He gives her a wry smile. 'Option B is what I would choose, for myself. Slightly riskier, because it might make him even angrier, but it has one big advantage. If you unfriend him and leave your Facebook settings as they are, so your friends can share the post, then you achieve two things. They will undoubtedly share it because it implies drama and strife which people can't resist. And it means that even with Facebook's habits of not showing you everything, more of your friends will get to see it, and so will others – friends of your friends. It makes it more widely public and achieves a second benefit – he will see the comments and people will probably ask him questions. Hopefully it will stop him in his tracks if he imagines he can deny he had anything to do with this – because I'm sure people, who know you well, will draw the right conclusions. Particularly if you never respond to any comments – private messages, yes – but not where he can see what you say.' And then he laughs. 'And that's sure to drive him crazy!'

'Excellent - and implying he's capable of physical abuse would be a good thing, so others know, and I won't reply to any comments at all – just ignore what people ask. Oh, no – they'll think it was something which happened in the car today now that damn video is going viral. I'll put a headline above the photo of my face saying, "no, nothing to do with driving and I didn't walk into a door" and leave it at that.'

Weldon laughs, and she can tell he has seen the video, but before he can comment, an alarm clock starts ringing above them and his head snaps up. 'Christ! I didn't realise it would be so loud down here. It must drive you mad - I'll stop using them.'

'No, don't - it doesn't bother me at all. I think it sounds loud just now because both our doors are open, I don't normally notice. I suppose it's your cue to go to bed - it must be eleven o'clock.'

He laughs again and tells her she can put the peas back in the freezer now, reminds her to finish her wine and leaves. She hears him try the door handle on the outer door again before he shuts her front door and bounds up the stairs two at a time as he always does.

Chapter 34

At seven thirty the next morning Weldon takes three photos of Lara's face with her phone and checks she has his phone number, tells her she looks like a prize fighter and leaves for work. When he has left, she stands inside the door and studies the photos and thinks they look worse than what she saw in the bathroom mirror when she got up and maybe the camera intensified the colours, which might be a good thing.

She turns her laptop on and checks that Mark really has disappeared from her list of Facebook friends before she posts one of the photos directly from her phone with a one-line heading, "No, I didn't fall - and no, it was not a stunt driving accident".

Ten minutes later, with a cup of tea and a slice of peanut butter toast beside her, she picks up her book to read over breakfast, but the peace and quiet lasts only about a few minutes before her phone starts emitting social media alert beeps. A quick glance shows her an ever-growing string of notifications, so she checks Facebook on her laptop and studies the questions and comments and emoticons continuing to line up under the photo of her bruised face as she sits there watching. The comments prove that having a heading for her post, as she and Weldon agreed last night as a way of avoiding people jumping to conclusions about a car accident, was a great strategy. With a slight sense of unreality, she waits for Charlotte to call.

As she expected, the call from Charlotte is like unleashing an explosion of questions and exclamations; the mixture of concern, sympathy and curiosity makes it nearly impossible to tell the story in a coherent way.

'Stop!' she exclaims and interrupts Charlotte mid-stream. 'Can I please just tell you the whole saga first before we start on the analysis? And the answer to your last question is yes, I did break up with Mark, and then I sent him an email to reinforce it, because it hadn't registered, and I really didn't want to see him ever again.'

She gets up and walks to the kitchen, with the phone in one hand and her mug in the other. 'Yes, he came around late last night, furious - and this morning I look like this. I had dinner with your parents and Gordon told me the latest about Mark, which you might not have heard, but it's more bad news. And I stopped on the way home and sent off a break-up message to Mark from my phone, pulled over on Boulcott Street - I simply couldn't wait a moment longer. But I can't have closed the front door properly when I got home, the outer door, so he let himself in and knocked on my door, and wham! He was livid, but it was his sense of entitlement and ego which drove the violence, the fact that I had the nerve to firstly break up with him without discussing it – can you believe it? He expected me to discuss it! And the other reason was probably that he thought he was on to a good thing, you know, about the trust money - maybe he thought he was entitled to share it or something – he lives in a fantasy world, I think. And then, snap! - in one moment all he had schemed for was gone and he exploded. And I think even with my exit strategy playing, out he managed to imagine that we had some kind of future – there's something wrong with him, for sure.'

While she listens to Charlotte's reply, which is mostly expressions of disbelief and exclamations about what she thinks of Mark, she makes a fresh mug of tea and puts another slice of bread in the toaster.

'Don't worry about the noise, I'm just making toast – and don't worry about the bruises either, they'll fade. Weldon put a bag of frozen peas on my face last night or it would have been a lot worse – and now I think of it, he might have saved me from an outright beating.'

'Who is Weldon? Don't tell me you had another guy there when Mark came?'

Lara feels as if she has been up all night. It is only eight in the morning, but she has been awake since half past five with her cheekbone and temple aching too much to be able to go back to sleep, but Charlotte's question makes her laugh.

'Weldon, remember? We've talked about him a couple of times, the guy who lives upstairs. He broke it up, he came down the stairs like thunder, he's so big and heavy – and he just twisted Mark's arm up behind his back and sent him packing – and issued some threats. And then he kind of took over, found the frozen peas, found wine and glasses, and sat me down to plan a social media strategy.'

'See, I was right – it's useful to have a man around the house! Have you reported it to the police yet?'

'God, no! I can't think of anything worse than making this into a court case. He's been punished, he knows I will talk about him, even if I won't put his name on social media - and I doubt he'll do it to anyone else now, or I hope not. I'm sure he only did it to me because he had spent so long grooming me and setting me up, and he was prepared to put up with an unspectacular, quiet woman for the sake of the money - he thought he was entitled to the reward.'

Charlotte snorts at the other end. 'It's not right, though, is it? It's not enough! He should be reported and feel the pain and the shame. And you have a witness and photos, so he wouldn't be able to deny it, would he?'

'I know all that – and believe me, if he comes within arm's length of me or tries anything else I'm definitely going to the police. But for now, I think it's unlikely he'll crawl out from whatever rock he's hiding under.'

'I'll do some research and text you when I find out what people are saying, the stuff they aren't putting on social media,' says Charlotte decisively. 'And I won't tell the parents, they'll just worry.'

'Lovely day for a little excursion,' says Brian when he picks her up that afternoon and waits for Lara to do up her seatbelt. 'And what the hell happened to your face? I saw that photo on Facebook – looks like someone punched you. Oh – do you know Terry?' He nods sideways at the man in the passenger seat.

'Of course, I know Terry! We've probably met a dozen times, but not for a while now. And I did say 'hi' to him when I got in.'

Terry swivels around to look at Lara's face, shakes his head and makes no comment. Her face is still throbbing, and she might have taken one lot of Panadol too many, but the main thing now is not to invite any speculation.

'Tripped on a cat and fell against a concrete block retaining wall at a friend's place,' says Lara, and Brian snorts derisively. 'Yeah, right! And pigs might fly - but have it your way.'

She knows without thinking that she has not seen Terry since Roddy was killed, and to avoid condolences she continues without pausing, 'So, tell me how it's going to work – how long do we have? And is it the same car?'

'Fucking frustrating, but the road's ideal – lots of sharp corners, great drop-offs all the way on one side and with the lighting we'll be able to show off a bit of scenery.'

He laughs and says over his shoulder, but thankfully without turning his head. 'Helicopter overhead, big light shining down – it's all part of the script, the chopper isn't there just to light the scene, it's part of the chase. If we want to do it this week it's tonight or never, they said. Apparently from Friday night onwards people head north to Wairarapa and a weekend in the vineyards, Sunday night the big trucks start coming through in both directions, so we have to do it tonight because we have to move north on Monday, and I didn't realise how busy that road is these days.' He pauses to give another driver the finger before he picks up the thread again. 'They're giving us two hours and they'll have those big LED light signs and traffic lights at both ends of where we are filming. They'll open the road every twenty minutes and let anything through that's backed up – and then they close it again, so that eats into the two hours. And men manning barriers, all kinds of shit – it's costing a fortune, but the Americans don't mind.'

Lara realises that she has not asked a single question about the film they are making and is just about to ask when Brian continues, while steering with one hand and gesticulating with the other. 'So, what we'll do today is park in the lay-by closest to where we're filming, and then we walk the route. You are driving downhill, so you'll be overtaking next to the drop-off - you're chasing an SUV, which is in front of a petrol tanker, which is in front of you. You'll overtake the tanker on a corner – great shot from a drone hovering over the ravine just beside you and one overhead.'

'We're not shooting from the chopper,' interrupts Terry, explaining what Brian sketchily touched on. 'We want it in the shots – it's part of the chase.'

'Anyway,' continues Brian. 'You come up alongside the SUV on the next corner – and this is crucial, after the corner you have a very short space to start forcing the SUV towards the side, but we can do it a couple of times and get all the angles and then edit them together.'

He stops talking to swear at a driver who changes lanes without indicating. ''Bloody muppet!'

Terry looks at Lara over his shoulder and rolls his eyes. 'He's like this all the time in the car. Nonstop talking interspersed with abuse hurled at other drivers and driving with one hand on the wheel. I reckon you should be driving - I'd feel a lot safer.'

Brian ignores him. 'So, what we want is the SUV forced into the layby just after the corner and then you and the tanker box him in – you stop, so you block the road and the tanker comes around the corner, brakes hard with a bit of a slide and the SUV is caught – nowhere to go. Let's hope the damn tanker doesn't jack-knife.'

They walk down the road from where Brian parks the car with printouts from Google Earth, stopping now and then to mark things and make notes. Terry has a laser measure and tells Lara the distances from the starting point to the first corner and then the next, but she knows that what will guide her is her visual impression of the distances. Knowing the exact number of metres makes no difference, but she says nothing about this to Terry. A couple of times she says 'wait' and walks back uphill to the last corner, studies the corner and the distance to the next one and makes a mental note.

Before they start back up the hill to where they parked the car, they talk through the script again, and Lara points at the little bay on the side of the road immediately after the final bend.

'So, I physically force the other car into that bay – and it brakes hard to avoid hitting the bank or my car – and then what? Do you want me to slide across the road in front of it?'

'At any angle really – it's not that crucial because the tanker will have slid to a halt alongside it, so the SUV is boxed in. We'll have time to do one run and then return everyone to the starting positions in that big parking bay before twenty minutes is up, and then we have to wait until any normal traffic's been let through.'

Terry tucks his laser measure into his jacket pocket and pulls out his phone. 'I'll take some photos both from this angle and downhill and I'll mark the best positions for the drone operators so they don't get lost in the dark.'

Brian zips his jacket and hunches his shoulders against the wind. 'Amazing how much windier it is up here. The chopper's going to be well out to the side, over the ravine – we'll capture it from the cameras up on the high slope. We scouted out the position for it yesterday and from the drones it should look fantastic.'

Terry looks up from his phone. 'I think you can cancel the watering truck, Brian – it's going to be pouring from midnight. You'll have a lovely wet road, Lara.'

. . .

The afternoon gets more and more frustrating. Lara is exhausted and would love to lie down on her bed for a rest as soon as she gets back, but for some reason her face hurts more when she's horizontal that when she's upright. She spends a couple of hours sitting in the corner of the sofa leaning against the back, which is less painful than lying down, but as soon as she drops off, she wakes up with a jerk that sends tendrils of pain down the side of her head.

'How is your face?' asks the text message from Weldon late in the afternoon, and Lara replies, 'Spectacular and sore. Do you want to come out tonight to see a car chase being filmed? Leaving here half an hour after midnight.'

She is beginning to feel seriously worried about doing that driving on the Remutaka hill road when she's so tired, but eventually the pain subsides, and she goes to sleep on her bed with the alarm set for quarter to midnight.

It is half past four in the morning, when Lara and Weldon finally get back into Lara's car and start down the steep, winding road towards the Hutt Valley, the rain is easing and soon dawn will wash the dark out of the sky and it will be a new day.

Lara turns the heater up high and for a while they don't talk, then Weldon says, 'Thank God you can switch out of stunt mode – I don't think I could handle it after what I've just watched. I don't understand how you can drive like you did up there – in the dark and on a wet road. I was terrified just watching.'

'Oh, it's always worse for those who watch. I used to close my eyes sometimes when I was with Roddy, just couldn't bear to see it going on. I wasn't sure how much you would see from way up that slope, though. Did you see when I passed the petrol tanker and boxed that other guy's car in on that steep double bend? I'm really pleased we got that on the second run, it was quite slippery by then.'

'Bloody horrendous – I did see most of it. I was standing a couple of meters from the guy flying one of the drones,' says Weldon. 'God, the logistics of setting it all up – must cost a small fortune.'

And then he asks the question that hardly anyone dares ask. 'How did your husband die? If you don't mind talking about it?'

This is the first time she tells the story without feeling her insides clench, and after two years it seems like a great step forward to hear her own voice sound normal instead of thin and tense when she responds.

'I wasn't there, I only went with him in the school holidays – he was working in the US, and a tyre blew out at a critical moment during a chase scene. His car hit an Armco barrier nearly side-on at very high speed, and his neck snapped, he died instantly - sideways whiplash, first in one direction and then back, despite the airbags. The impact was extreme due to the speed.'

He says nothing and after a moment, she adds, 'I miss him terribly – he is the only man I've ever truly loved, and he was my best friend too. Sometimes I wake in the night and for a fraction of a second, I think I feel a shadow of warmth, like the body heat left by somebody who hasn't long got out of bed. And then I wake up properly, and I know it's just a dream. My mind conjures up the memory of his warm body next to mine.' She pauses and adds, 'And each time I feel alone.'

For a long moment he doesn't reply, and when he does, he sounds sad. 'I've never known a depth of attachment like that. I never loved my partner deeply enough – or maybe at all. I think I confused lust with love at the very start. And we were utterly different, so after a while she got bored with me being so dull. And then, when she left and realised that we hadn't lived together for long enough for her to claim half of my assets - then she turned into a vengeful monster. I'm sure if she'd known ahead of time, she would have stayed longer, pretended everything was fine - just to make sure she got half of everything.'

Chapter 35

Trying to sound moderately regretful, Lara says, 'I'm so sorry, but I'm not available,' to the headmaster at the high school in the Hutt Valley. Covering for someone who is on parental leave for two terms would be a great temporary job if she needed the income, but the thought of travelling there and back every day puts her off. It's not very far, she thinks, and if I lived in Auckland I'd never think twice about the distance, but I'd rather not commute at all.

She watches the mating dance of a pair of sparrows while she considers what her options really are. Her mother lived comfortably on the income from the trust, but she has no idea what it will amount to now, after a chunk of capital has been spent on the house. She has the money from the house in Hamilton, but it should probably be invested too. She must sit down with Gordon and get the full picture, maybe she should take the next job offer for the new year, just to avoid spending the trust income. Who knows, if interest rates and dividends fall, it might not be enough to live on, so she needs a job for security. And it might be sensible to always leave a portion of the trust income to add to the capital – to earn even more interest.

She runs her fingers gently over the slightly faded bruises on the side of her face and those strange nerve pains still shoot down to her jaw and around her ear like threads of fire. She'll stay away from people who know her for a while longer. Just thinking about having to endlessly talk about it makes her tired, and the longer she stays out of sight, the sooner the issue will die down. But it's the face-to-face interactions she worries most about, much more than the rumours. The thought of someone looking into her eyes and asking, 'Who hit you?' makes her cringe; not because she has any wish to protect Mark's reputation, but every time she replied, she would be reminded that she got herself into this situation and it is very hard to describe the slow and insidious path Mark took her on, right up to the point where he smashed his fist into her face. And, of course, how slow she was to start distancing herself, and how she never thought of what a tempting lure the trust fund is.

'Well, my friend,' says Lara that evening and hands Weldon the glass she has just filled. 'Here we are – for once you are not up there in your ivory tower working away until your alarm clock goes off.'

'Are we friends?' He sounds quite casual, as if it's of no great importance to him if they are friends or not.

She stares at him for a moment in surprise. 'I'm your friend, are you not mine?'

'Of course, I'm your friend,' says Weldon comfortably. 'I wasn't sure if it was mutual, or if I'm just your helpful tenant.'

He doesn't sound as if he is troubled by this, but she is. How could he possibly not realise they are friends, after the things they have not only been through together, but also the things they have told each other? Deeply personal and sad things, which they might never have voiced before.

'You are much more than just an ordinary friend,' she says now and smiles at his face which she can barely make out in the deep dusk and with the light from her living room behind him. 'You saved me from serious harm twice, you've helped me sort out how to deal with Mark, and you made me feel better when I was shocked and hurt after that punch. I can't imagine where I would be now if you hadn't stepped in. And we have also told each other some very personal and private things.'

'Good,' is all he says, and they sit in silence with the sound of a distant piano being played beside an open window somewhere far away floating on the night air. Something by Chopin, thinks Lara, as dusk slides into full darkness and the light under the gnarly tree comes on, as it does every night.

'I love the light shining up into the tree, just love it!' She smiles at the sight of the tree lit from below and thinks how in winter, when the branches are bare, it will look like a sculpture. 'Roddy would have laughed at me - he couldn't abide what he called garden decor.'

'You miss him,' says Weldon quietly, 'I can hear it whenever you say his name. Would you have married that little shit, who punched you? If you hadn't found out everything about him?'

'Oh God, no, never! The idea never entered my mind at any stage. I'd already told him that we were finished, but he decided to persist, and when I told him to get out, he snapped - he is vain and shallow, and I couldn't handle his ego any longer.' She laughs and adds. 'And to top it off, he didn't like my lime green dress, which I love - he said I wasn't glamourous enough to wear a dress like it. And he wouldn't have put frozen peas on my face, either. Will you come to bed with me?'

'I would have liked to,' says Weldon, unperturbed by this sudden invitation. 'But I'm not interested in a relationship, not a romantic one, as they say. I'm just not cut out for it – too focused on my research, happy to be alone doing things I regard as important. But thank you for the offer – I'm very flattered you asked, not what a big, ugly guy expects from someone like you.'

This honest statement makes her feel outraged on his behalf, though he himself said it. She swivels in her chair so she can face him fully, even though she can't see his expression at all now.

'What a ridiculous thing to say! You're not ugly – I like the way you look, and anyway, who cares what people look like. It's what they are like inside that matters, and you are a very, very nice man, and I like you – and I also trust you. And I don't want anything romantic either, I don't know if I'll ever be ready for it again. But for two people on their own, who like each other – as I think we do – perhaps sex now and then isn't such a bad idea.'

'Would it work for you? Just the physical part without the emotional attachment?' He sounds quite casual, as if this is a theoretical discussion, and then she realises this is exactly what this is and it makes her smile. A discussion about a possible joint venture, but they need to sort out the parameters before any decisions are made.

'Yes, I would like it – to be held and touched and feel someone beside me sometimes would be nice, and I like good sex, I miss it. I would never have asked if I didn't like you a lot and totally trust you.'

And out of nowhere comes a comment she hasn't consciously intended, 'And it probably explains why I never went to bed with Mark – I just kept stalling him.'

He reaches out and puts his hand on hers, and the touch of that warm, male hand sends a current of comfort and quiet joy through her. 'Let's go, then,' he says.

'So, what are we now?' Weldon is lying on his side with Lara leaning against his ribcage. The bedroom window is open, and they can still hear the distant piano. 'Sex mates? Fuck-buddies?'

She laughs, 'And thank you, too! That was very nice – and we hadn't even practiced. I think I prefer "friends with benefits" if it's all the same to you.'

She feels his chest vibrate as he laughs quietly in the dark, and he puts his hand on her shoulder and pulls her a bit closer. 'It was nice – extremely nice in fact.'

When he moves her to one side and gets out of bed, she flicks the bedside light on, so he won't trip and watches as he pulls on his jeans and sweatshirt. Neither of them says goodbye or even good night, somehow there is no perfect phrase for this situation; he turns and gives her a little salute in the doorway. They know they will see each other in the normal course of going in and out of their flats, and further arrangements can be left to chance.

When her front door closes behind him, and she hears him try the handle to make sure it is locked, she smiles and turns her light off and listens to him bounding up the stairs as he always does and wonders how this is going to work. Who is going to take the first step? Is it always going to be up to her, is this her role now because she initiated it? Or is it something which can go back and forth between them, bounced from one to the other, not quite taking turns, but as the mood takes one of them?

She doesn't know what she would prefer and perhaps it doesn't matter so long as they are perfectly open about it.

And then she realises that it can only happen if they both feel their relationship is based on total equality, that either of them can ask or say no, and neither must feel rejected. She feels she has stumbled on the single word which makes real sense of this strange and nearly business-like arrangement they have made - equality. Because he is kind and she is kind, and two kind people should be able to make a go of nearly anything together.

Chapter 36

They don't meet the next morning, and when Lara locks her door behind her, she knows he will already be in his lab at the institute. Driving towards the garage which Gordon recommended to get a new Warrant of Fitness for her car, she thinks of how well she slept, and how relieved she is that Weldon got dressed and went upstairs to his own flat last night. But she imagines he is probably as keen as she is to keep their arrangement within boundaries that will make it possible to continue without complications.

The mechanic, who doesn't know her, as this is Lara's first visit, stares at her bruised face and whistles under his breath. 'Yikes – what happened to you?'

She is prepared for this, for people to assume she has been assaulted, but she is not prepared to talk about it with outsiders, so the rehearsed phrase she has already used with Brian and the crew on the Remutaka Hill road comes out without any hesitation. 'I tripped on the damn cat and fell against our concrete retaining wall. Very sore!'

. . .

Sitting in the so-called customer lounge at the garage, which is just a small square room with three rather uncomfortable plastic chairs and a coffee machine, she gets her phone out and unlocks it without turning the sound back on. The phone has been on mute since the morning after Mark punched her, and she only occasionally looks at it. Until the crazy stream of comments and questions finally dies down, she would rather check her social media on her laptop, where they somehow seem less overwhelming. But having forgotten to take her Kindle, and with only the grubby car magazines on the table as options, she opens the Facebook app and sighs when the blue number in the top right corner tells her she has fourteen new comments waiting to be read. She scrolls down half of them and gives up; they mostly say the same thing and use the same emoticons. But halfway through an article about Iceland on the BBC app, a retained, split-second impression from the list of Facebook comments registers properly and makes her go back to look again.

A minute later she knows she did see it right; at 07.04 this morning Anna mentioned Mark in a comment: "Who did this to kind and clever Lara? Did Mark punch her? We know it wasn't a stunt driving accident. And why not a word from Lara since she posted the photo? Has anybody seen her out and about? She is not responding to any of our comments."

She is the first one who has said it openly, and Lara wonders how so many people have managed to comment and speculate, but not mention his name. Or perhaps people are wary of mentioning him, worried about threats of lawsuits or hate mail. Anna might have checked her list of Facebook friends and noticed Mark missing from the list, or perhaps she is just more prepared to come out with it than others are. And for the first time it occurs to her to wonder at the fact that nobody has called her or sent a message asking what happened. Did her statement above the photo of her damaged face somehow send a signal that she does not want to talk about it, for people to stay away from direct contact? How odd that this hasn't occurred to her before now, but perhaps they have talked between themselves in private messages or asked Charlotte, leaving herself out of it to save her trauma or potential embarrassment.

So, thinks Lara and stares unseeing at the out-of-date calendar on the opposite wall, now Anna has posted that explicit comment, will they all be calling each other or maybe messaging Anna, and then? More questions and comments? It makes her tired just to contemplate how much energy a new flood of attention will sap from her, but she knows Weldon was right. This way of documenting the assault has time-stamped it and put it out into the world as a real event, quite unlike what it would sound like, if she never mentioned it in real time and then pulled it out of the box at some later date.

She turns the sound on to listen to a news reading while she waits and then she notices that Anna has sent her a private Facebook message: 'If Mark hit you, I need to tell you something in confidence, but I will only tell you face to face, can't put it in writing.'

Five minutes later another private message, this time from Gabriella, presumably prompted by Anna's mention of Mark. 'Several people have asked me if you are serious about Mark, are you likely to marry him. All v worried, some hint at rumours about past abuse. All certain he hit you, as am I. Be careful! G xx'

Lara replies: 'Yes, private for you: I broke it off and he arrived on my doorstep and punched me. For general consumption: definitely finished. Thanks for worrying about me, see you soon. Lara.'

It is the end of the afternoon and Lara and Anna sit on the deck with glasses of lemon and tonic with sprigs of the mint, which has unexpectedly sprung up beside the deck.

'He's a meth user,' says Anna and looks steadily into Lara's eyes. 'Which, as I'm sure you know, can make people dangerous and occasionally violent, unable to exert self-control and prone to lash out in sudden rage. So even if you have broken up with him, be careful – he's dangerous, not to be trusted.'

'How did you find out? And God, how come I didn't notice? How could he keep that secret for so long – or was I just so ignorant I didn't connect the dots?'

Lara is trying to fit a drug-taking Mark into her picture of him, tries to look back to see if she missed some obvious signs. And why did nobody else warn her? She feels deeply disturbed by Anna's warning, because despite not knowing a lot about drug users and their behaviour, she feels she should have picked it up.

'Believe me, if I'd known earlier, I would have told you,' says Anna. 'I didn't really want to tell you this, but now you must be informed so you can look out for yourself. My cousin's wife is a therapist at a residential clinic where they treat people with addiction issues of various kinds – and they're very careful with visitors. Obviously, they don't want people bringing drugs into the place, so they have pretty robust systems in place. Mark was caught with drugs on their premises, but not to supply someone staying there. He had them on him and he was showing them to the person he visited, but they were for his own use.'

'But why would he show them, why would he bring them into a place like that? It doesn't make sense! Was it cruelty—was he taunting the other guy?'

And Anna gives her a wry smile and says, 'Hard to tell – I don't know him well, so I can't say if it was based on cruelty. The staff there talked to Mark and the other guy separately, and they both said the same thing, so we have to assume it's the truth. Apparently, the patient or whatever they call them, the guy Mark was visiting, said he reckoned he was so strong now he could walk out on the street and if someone offered him drugs, he would be able to say, "no thanks!" and walk away. And at that point Mark pulled a little packet out of his pocket and a staff member saw him do it - and they also noticed that he put it back in his pocket, he didn't give it to his mate. You know, like it was some kind of test or a joke. When he next came, they intercepted him and sat him down for a chat, by which time they had already talked to the other guy, so they knew his side of the story, and Mark admitted that he uses meth. Which makes people unreliable and erratic - and can cause outbursts of violence, even extreme violence. And maybe he uses other drugs as well.'

'Did they report him?'

'Oh, no - it's not what they do, they're not into reporting people. But Lisa, my cousin's wife, she knew that Mark and I had gone to the same high school - and she also knew, of course, that I only returned to New Zealand from the UK quite recently and I'm gradually catching up with old friends from school and university, so she just took me aside and said in confidence that she needed to warn me about someone I might connect with at someone's place who's into hard drugs and has been for some time and to steer clear of him. And he's banned from visiting that facility now.'

Later, when Lara closes the door behind Anna, she stands for a moment and thinks how luck has protected her in more ways than one. She stalled about going to bed with him, and she never really thought of why he didn't protest more about it, but he was playing the long game, of course, his aim was to marry her and get hold of the money. And if she had gone to bed with him, he might have asked for a key and what an added complication that would have been, asking for it back or changing the locks.

After not catching sight of Weldon since the night she invited him into her bed, he texts her from upstairs the next evening, and once again she imagines him standing more or less straight above her head, holding his phone and waiting for her answer. The message reads, 'Want company or too soon?' and she smiles to herself because now she knows she isn't going to be the one who always initiates this process. It can move between them like a tennis ball across a net, from one side to the other, or rather, from upstairs to downstairs, and it doesn't matter who does what. They are equals and have equal rights to invite and to say no. So, she puts the thumbs up emoticon into her reply and presses Send.

'Do you know what?' he says a couple of hours later and runs his hand down her side to her hip. 'This was a really good idea. You know how you said you sometimes need to feel a warm body next to yours and somebody touching you – it's not just about sex. You're totally right – I hadn't realised how physically isolated I had become since she left me, or how I hardly ever touch anyone, and nobody touches me. I mean, those greeting hugs you get in a social context, they're not really touching as such, they're just a kind of formulaic ritual we go through – it doesn't count as personal touching. But this is wonderful, it's human contact, genuine human contact.'

It makes her laugh. 'So, we could forego the sex then and just lie here together and talk?' And he laughs too. 'I suppose we could, but why would we when the sex is so damn good?'

Chapter 37

The very last box that Lara had saved from her mother's massed possessions is so light it might be empty; an old Bata box that once contained a pair of men's boots size 9. When Lara brings it in from the coat cupboard in the front hall, she wonders why she kept it. She puts it on the kitchen bench and lifts the lid, and instantly she remembers finding it under her mother's bed, buried behind shoes and slippers from at least two decades and covered in a thick layer of dust. A small bunch of letters, some of them on old-fashioned airmail forms, others in slightly yellowed envelopes and all addressed to her mother in her father's handwriting. When she and Bridget emptied the house, these were the only letters they found, and Violet's computer was very old and had a password which Lara never worked out, so it was discarded, and any later correspondence is no longer accessible. This is all that remains of her parents' life together, thinks Lara, such a passionate and stormy relationship, now reduced to a couple of dozen letters written after they parted, and no remnant of the initial love story left.

She scoops them out of the box and goes to sit in her favourite armchair with the letters on her lap and opens one at random. It is dated about a month before Lara's eighth birthday and mentions her in the first sentence: "Violet, Please, be reasonable about this – it would be lovely for me to spend a week with Lara, and I could possibly make a visit to coincide with her birthday. If you refuse to agree I might have to come unannounced – I do have the right to see her, she is my daughter, and we signed an agreement saying we have shared custody."

The word 'shared' is underlined and it makes Lara remember his voice, the way he would emphasise something when her mother was creating an argument or being over-emotional.

She checks the dates on the other envelopes and opens the ones with smudged date stamps, hoping to find the next one, wondering what she might find. She knows her father never came for that birthday, and they never had a week's holiday together until she was a teenager and living with Bridget and Gordon. Towards the bottom of the bunch, she finds a letter dated six weeks later and reading it makes her sit as if frozen, caught between crying and wanting to scream with fury. In it her father refers to the reply he must have had from Violet and it's clear he is angry and deeply upset: "I think your threats are cruel to both Lara and myself and misguided, because one day she will find out how you prevented me proper access to her, and she will resent you for it. Please don't poison her mind against me, I can't believe that she really said she doesn't want to see me."

She recalls occasions when she was younger, before she understood more, before she was living with Gordon and Bridget, when her mother said dismissive things about her father, like, 'He's too busy to bother with you – don't nag about it.' And how abandoned it made her feel, with nobody else in the house to protect her from her mother's angry outbursts and random punishments.

'You are coming tonight, aren't you?' says Lara to Gordon, when he calls about something else. 'I mentioned it to Bridget the other day. It's sad that Charlotte isn't here for Christmas this year after all, but she'll see the house later. I've invited you two and a few friends - you might recognise a couple of them who used to come over to see Charlotte and me when we were in high school. Any time from half past five.'

It is the day before Christmas Eve and the housewarming party plan has undergone a major change from when she first thought of it a couple of weeks ago. Then she had thought that inviting people just a couple of days in advance would be clever, so it seemed impromptu and casual, which is the kind of party she likes. And now it's a blessing, because with all the social media attention on her and her bruised face, she's had second thoughts. Her list of guests has been pared down to a half dozen trusted friends, the ones who will stick to the rules if warned not to mention her face or Mark in front of her aunt and uncle.

She sent a group message to them yesterday, 'I would love to see you at my place for a drink to celebrate my move, tomorrow any time from 5.30. But strictly no mention to be made of my face or of Mark or anything related to the recent debacle. My aunt and uncle will be here, and they don't need to know, they would worry.'

She spends half an hour applying foundation and concealer, something she has never before done in order to conceal anything as dark as the bruises, and it turns out to be much harder than she had expected. After a disastrous first attempt she washes it all off and starts again. The result is pretty good, and she knows her friends won't comment, and neither will Weldon. Here's hoping, she thinks, and turns her head this way and that to study the effect in the bathroom mirror, wondering if she will be able to hide the bruises from Bridget. She will make sure not to stand in the sunlight just inside the windows or on the terrace, or she could put on her wide brimmed sunhat if they end up being outside and say she always wears it instead of sunglasses in the slanting evening sun.

At quarter past seven Lara looks around the room and smiles at what she sees; half a dozen old friends, three with partners, two primary school-age children, Bridget, Gordon and Weldon, talking and laughing and seeming to enjoy each other's company. When the doorbell goes, she is ready. An hour ago, she ordered and paid online for a delivery of pizza and garlic bread for half past seven and she returns from the front door with a stack of large pizza boxes, with paper bags piled on top held in place with her chin. But Bridget is there in a moment and takes the bags off the pile and puts then on the island counter.

'Good heavens, Lara – there's enough here to feed twice as many!'

'You just wait,' says Lara. 'If there's more than a third of a pizza left over, I'll give you an extra Christmas present.'

'Plates?' asks Bridget. 'Paper serviettes? I'm not familiar with this kitchen yet, you'll have to direct me.'

'On the bench, far side of the stove.' Lara points. 'I piled it up in the corner there before you came, it's all there, ready to go.'

Very soon her guests have helped themselves and are

scattered inside and outside on the deck with the children's parents giving them strict instructions not to come inside until they have finished their pizza slices and wiped their fingers. Bridget sits down beside Lara on the sofa and asks quietly, 'What on earth happened to your face, did you hurt yourself?'

Lara notices Anna cast a sideways glance in her direction from the armchair beside her and says calmly as she rehearsed it that morning, 'Oh no, it's a rash – I tried a new cream and I had a really nasty allergic reaction, and then it itched, and I scratched it in my sleep. It was very ugly for a couple of days, but it's settling down now. I just put some make-up over it so it wouldn't look so hideous.'

The first guests to leave are Gabriella, Anna and Anna's husband, Paul, who looks like a marathon runner and eats as if he hasn't been fed for several days. She goes outside with them to say goodbye, and as she watches them go down the steps from the veranda, she remembers the day when the drunk stood on the driveway by the open door to her car with a knife in his hand. Looking back on it now. she marvels at how calm Weldon was and feels again the relief she felt when he dealt with the man. I was right about him from the word go, she thinks as she returns inside, he's a rock, my best friend now.

Close to midnight, after tidying up and starting the dishwasher, Weldon takes her face between his hands and tilts her head, looks closely at the covered-up bruises.

'I don't know how you got away with that story you told your aunt - I was waiting for her to say something because it's so obviously bruises.'

Lara smiles fondly and says, 'You never know with Bridget, she's the world's best when it comes to handling situations. She probably didn't believe me, but she wasn't going to say so in front of a dozen people. And I'm prepared to bet she won't mention it to Gordon either. She'll either quietly find out somehow or ask me later.'

'She is a treasure, that woman – I really like her.' Weldon returns her smile. 'Ready for bed or too tired?'

A few weeks later, when Lara is just getting out of the shower her phone buzzes, and she reaches over to the bathroom windowsill and picks up the phone with a wet hand.

'Dreadful news, Lara!' sobs Bridget. 'Jonas has been killed in an accident. Charlotte just called. I'm going to the airport now - the taxi will be here soon, and I'll be in Christchurch by half past eleven. But I can't get hold of Gordon, he's in court and the case has just started, and I don't want to tell him in a text.'

'Oh, God, how awful!' Lara stands naked and dripping and tries to take it in. 'When? And what happened, was it a car crash?'

'No, he was on that big build they've made him project manager for – some huge office building in the middle of town – a steel beam fell from a crane and hit him, he died instantly. Can you go and wait at the court until Gordon comes out and tell him, please? Perhaps try to get a message to him, someone at the courthouse should be able to tell him to come out into the public area, so he doesn't go out the back way, the way he normally would or you'll miss him.'

'Of course. Do you know what the case is about? I'll have to find the right courtroom.' In her head she is trying to imagine the scene: a public place full of people, a shocking message to deliver and not many details.

'It's about someone who tried to bribe a policeman, a detective and then threatened him,' says Bridget and sounds slightly more together. Lara hears a drawer pushed shut with a bang and imagines the bedroom with a case open on the bed and her aunt packing with one hand and holding the phone with the other.

'Gordon was just telling me about it, last night over dinner – it's not his case, but the partner in their firm who was going to do it has just had his gall bladder out. He doesn't do much court work these day – Gordon, I mean. You could call his office and ask, I suppose.'

'OK, leave it with me,' says Lara, thinking ahead even as she finishes the conversation and says goodbye to Bridget. Half an hour later she is dressed and has made three calls, and she sets out with her mind full of half-formed plans. She leaves her car in a parking building and walks to the District Court building in Ballance Street, and twenty minutes later she is talking to a clerk, who directs her to the right court room.

'You can't go closer than the railing in front of the public seating,' he says, 'but you can attract his attention easily. The counsels stay behind their table after the judge has exited – they get their papers and stuff tidied up and so on. So, if you go right up to the closest row behind where they are, you can just call out to him.'

Lara sits as close to the front row as she can, turns her phone off and listens absent-mindedly to what is being said, without taking it in. Her mind is full of disjointed thoughts and speculations. She thinks of Jonas, who was always so cheerful and full of life, and his vital personality that coloured everything he said. And then, on a perfectly ordinary day, he had breakfast, went to work and … died. It seems unbelievable that things can change so quickly, it's a feeling she remembers well from when Roddy died.

After a while she surreptitiously turns her phone back on with the sound off and searches the internet for news of Jonas' accident on her phone, but all she finds is a brief and sketchy paragraph. Frowning, she wonders what she was expecting to find, when all she needs to know is that Jonas is dead.

'Oh, no! Poor Charlotte!' exclaims Gordon two and a half hours later, as they stand in a busy hallway outside the court room they have just emerged from. 'Lucky this case was so quick - it's done, so I can leave. Come with me, we'll go and have lunch somewhere and call Bridget and find out what's happening down there.'

'No, no, we can't talk to Bridget and Charlotte about this in a café or whatever – it's too public. Let's buy lunch and go back to your office and call them from there – I checked the flight, and she should be at Charlotte's just about now if nothing held her up.'

They sit in Gordon's office with their lunch and Gordon's phone in speaker mode between them on the desk.

'You can't talk to Charlotte just now,' says Bridget sounding surprisingly normal. 'She's just started feeding Thomas, but you'll be able to talk to her later. She's had a long phone conversation with his parents, and they're driving over from Westport this afternoon - I've booked them into a motel quite close to here. Charlotte says she can't cope with them in the house, particularly not after the phone call with his mother this morning – it was exhausting for her, his mother was beside herself and couldn't stop asking questions, and poor Charlotte had no answers.'

Gordon reaches for a note pad and a pen. 'I've got to do a few things first, delegate various jobs to others, cancel some client meetings and so on – and then I'll book a flight. I presume the funeral will be at the end of the week?'

'It won't be quite as straight forward as that, I'm afraid – we don't know about a funeral date yet. I think you'll have a few days to organise your work.'

They hear Bridget moving and a door being shut. 'Jonas's parents and brothers want the funeral to be held in Westport which means some extra details to organize. Transport of the coffin of course, and where everyone will stay – they need a few days to set things up, but they wanted to come straight over. I think they were hoping to see Jonas.' When she continues, they hear the hesitation in her voice, she is finding it difficult to find the right words. 'But they can't see him, nobody can - it's very traumatic, his head is destroyed, completely ... demolished. His helmet was no protection against a steel beam falling from a height.'

Gordon and Lara look at each other in dismay; the thought of cheerful Jonas' smiling face 'demolished' is shocking, and Lara can see her uncle is lost for words.

'How awful for Charlotte and his parents,' she manages to say, trying to keep her voice level. 'That just adds to the impact of it all – oh God, sorry, that wasn't a pun, it was just a bad choice of words.'

Gordon picks up the phone and speaks directly at it, as if this will make his words more comforting for Bridget. 'Try not to think of that part, darling. Concentrate on the practical things – you'll have to be the one making dinner and doing the shopping and everything. Let us know when things have been decided, so Lara and I can book flights to wherever we need to go – perhaps we should go to Christchurch first and then all of us together to Westport.'

He ends the call, and they sit there looking at each other, thinking of Charlotte, now a widow with a small baby.

'Isn't it strange,' says Gordon slowly and balls up the brown paper bag his lunch was in and lobs it towards a wastepaper basket in the corner, where it bounces off the wall and falls to the floor. 'First you were widowed so young and now Charlotte – it seems like such an unlikely coincidence.'

'You know what? I hadn't even thought of it – two of us in one family.' Lara feels guilty, as if she should have thought of this as soon as she heard, but all she has been able to think about is how awful this is for Charlotte, and how Thomas will never know his father.

'At least I didn't have a baby,' she adds. 'Though perhaps it's a blessing – it gives Charlotte a focus, she has to look after him. She can't just lie down and not want to get up again, like I did so many times after the first week. Because once the hectic time of making arrangements about everything is over, then the real sadness and grief sets in.'

Gordon reaches over and pats her hand. 'You have coped so well! Like you do everything – low-key and without drama.' Then he smiles and shakes his head. 'Apart from the stunt driving! God, I'll never forget the night when you showed us that video – I couldn't believe what I was seeing. Stunned doesn't come close to describing it.'

She returns his smile and thinks he might be even more surprised if he watches the film when it comes out, because the driving she did on the wet Remutaka road, with the petrol tanker and the other car – that was real drama, the most on-the-edge driving she has ever done.

Gordon gets to his feet and sighs. 'I must get cracking with as much as I can here, probably work late.'

'Come to my place for dinner,' says Lara impulsively. 'Then only one of us needs to cook and if we know by then when to book flights for – and where – then we can do that together. I'll make something that can just sit there until you're done, and we'll heat it up whenever you get away.'

Chapter 39

At eight Gordon arrives with a bottle of wine in his hand, and his phone pings nearly as soon as he walks into Lara's flat. He pulls it out of his pocket as he walks into the living room and stops when he sees who the message is from. 'Bridget,' he says and frowns. 'A long message.'

Lara takes the wine bottle out of his hand and waits until he hands her the phone. 'You can read it for yourself. We can book our flights after dinner.'

"Parents arrived, had dinner here, have gone to motel. Funeral in Westport Monday 11 am, coffin will be driven there Sunday afternoon. A gathering in the church hall after the service. Dinner that night at parents' place. Three brothers and wives etc, so lots of people. Charlotte, I and Thomas drive to the West Coast Sunday morning and stay in Ocean View Motel so we can help with prep if needed. I booked motel units, one for us and one for Charlotte, Thomas and Lara. We can drive back to Christchurch on Tuesday, and everyone fly home when they want to. Love to you both, B."

'Now then,' says Gordon after dinner with a second glass

of wine in his hand. 'We must talk about the trust. We can't just keep putting it off, and you need to know how it works and what to expect.'

Picking up their plates, Lara puts them in the dishwasher and turns to face Gordon, who sometimes has a late change of heart about sweet treats.

'Are you sure you don't want some tiramisu ice cream for dessert? OK, then - and yes, I know, you're right. I was thinking about the trust just the other day and how embarrassing it is that I've never sat down and asked about the details. It's not that I expect you to look after everything forever.'

She sits down at the table again and Gordon picks up the bottle and reaches across the table, but she shakes her head. 'No thanks – it's a lovely wine, but I've had enough.'

'You know how we always say we were surprised when your father left "everything" to Violet in his will? Well, that's not accurate, of course – he set up the trust and left half of his total worth to her, and the rest went to his side of the family. Do you ever hear from them?'

'No, never. They must have been at Dad's funeral, but they didn't make themselves known to me then, there was such a huge crowd. Dad didn't often see them, there was some kind of trouble in his family before I was born. I've only seen them once – when Dad took me to see them on one of his visits. It was after I moved to your place, remember he and I went off for a holiday? I haven't set eyes on them since, and I used to feel it was as if Mum and I had never been part of the family.'

She shakes her head at how strange this seems now that she says it out loud. 'I don't know if Dad's family even knew they never divorced, just separated - but they certainly made no effort that I'm aware of to keep in touch with me. Maybe they didn't realise I was living with you and Mum might have put them off, I wouldn't have known. But surely Dad would have told them where I lived! It's very strange to think I have paternal grandparents who live less than four hours' drive away and I wouldn't recognize them if I met them in the street – or at a funeral. But don't worry, it doesn't upset me, it's their choice. So, tell me about the trust.'

Lifting his glass and holding it up against the light, Gordon sighs. 'A great vintage and a wonderful colour. Did I give you a copy of the trust deed after Violet died?'

'I haven't seen a trust deed in my entire life!' Lara laughs. 'My total knowledge about trusts would fit on a PostIt note, a small one.'

'They're all different – yours is called The Violet Winstanley Trust, as you know. The deed specifies that the income will be paid out to Violet six times per year by set instalments, and when she died you became the beneficiary, on the same terms. And as you also know, the trustees can liquidize investments at their discretion – as we did for the expenses involved in renovating this house. Then, at the end of the financial year we pay you the remainder of the trust income for the year minus taxes and our expenses.'

'And?'

'The trust will be wound up when you turn forty – in what? Two years? All the assets become your property then - for you to spend or invest as you like.'

She waits and thinks she can guess where this is going; Gordon is looking very uncomfortable and sits silent for a moment, so she decides to help him out.

'Are you worried I might patch it up with Mark?'

'Well, I don't know – probably not after all you know about him now, but there will be others who wouldn't mind sharing your fortune. I just want you to be very careful. What I would prefer is for you to come to me if you get serious about anyone, and we'll set up a pre-nup, as they say these days – we usually refer to it as a "contracting out agreement". Which means that you and the other party contract out of the legal acts which regulate how assets are divided in a split-up.'

He smiles wryly and takes a sip of his wine. 'I wouldn't want you to lose half your inheritance. And these days it could happen even after living with someone for three years – whether you're married or not.'

'So, if I had an affair with my tenant for three years, let's say – just for argument's sake. Would it count as cohabiting?'

'Not as long as he was paying rent – affairs are not the same as cohabiting, and the fact that you live under the same roof means nothing, you're in separate flats. Are you having an affair with the guy upstairs?'

He looks quizzically at her, not sure if she just asked out of theoretical interest or if there is something else behind it. Lara smiles and says with no particular emphasis, 'No, we're just very good friends, that's all. And don't panic, he pays his rent like clockwork.'

Gordon looks relieved after this sudden thought that she might be getting into some kind of trouble.

'He's a nice chap, isn't he? I liked him when I met him when we came over for the house-warming drinks. Having a man upstairs is probably a good idea – I know you'll laugh at me for being old-fashioned, but it seems to add a bit of extra safety.' And now he is smiling widely. 'Particularly someone as big as he is – probably very useful.'

In the back of her head Lara has been weighing things up. Her first instinct had been not to worry Gordon and Bridget about Mark's attack on her, and she has never mentioned the incident with the man with the knife. But maybe telling Gordon now will firmly establish why she and Weldon are such good friends and remove any random speculations.

'I'll tell you a couple of things to prove how right you are about the value of having a man in the house,' she says. 'And maybe I'll have another glass of that lovely wine after all.'

To tell both stories, even sketchily, takes fifteen minutes, and responding to Gordon's questions and explaining the details take a further half hour, and at the end of this intense session he lifts his glass in a toast.

'I know you've just explained why you lied about your bruised face,' says Gordon, 'and I do understand you didn't want to worry us, but I wish you had told me! A letter from a legal firm with a warning can be very effective. It's an extraordinary story - I can't wait to tell Bridget. And how lucky you were on both occasions. That guy with the knife – it doesn't sound as if Mark was the slightest use. But I can't help thinking that you should have reported both incidents to the police, not just the knife man that Weldon took care of. I know you've explained why you didn't, I just feel it should be documented.'

'But it is,' says Lara reasonably. 'I'll show you the Facebook post I made after the assault – I think Weldon's idea worked out perfectly, masses of people have seen the photo and shared it with dozens more, maybe hundreds.'

She gets her laptop, opens Facebook and moves around to sit beside Gordon. 'See here? This is the photo Weldon took the next morning and ...'

'Bloody hell!' exclaims Gordon when he sees the photo of her face. 'The bastard - he really punched you hard, like it was a fist fight. You poor thing – and thank God Weldon came down and stopped it.'

'I know – I looked truly awful for a couple of days and then I remembered I had a tube of concealer which I hardly ever use, so I used heaps to cover it up over Christmas. I got quite good at it actually. Never mind, it's all over now.' She points at her laptop screen. 'See what I put with the photo - just that it didn't happen while driving and I didn't fall down. So, I haven't pointed the finger at anyone, I just left people to draw their own conclusions. And look at the comments – I haven't counted, but it's probably over a hundred now if you count people's comments on each other's comments. Incredible!'

He watches amazed as she scrolls slowly down the long list under the photo, and when she gets to Anna's comment she stops and points at the screen. 'There's the only one which mentions him by name – which is remarkable, I think, because nobody else put his name down, but they probably didn't dare in case of repercussions.'

Gordon sits silently staring at the screen, overwhelmed by the responses and Lara moves the cursor to open the private message from Anna. 'Read this – she is the one who mentioned his name, remember you met her here for drinks before Christmas – her husband was the super skinny guy called Paul. She came over the day she sent me this and told me something which explains a lot of stuff, but you mustn't mention it to anyone – apart from Bridget and maybe Charlotte, of course.'

They book their flights to Westport and when Gordon leaves, he hugs her hard at the front door and says to make sure she doesn't go out alone at night. He sounds genuinely disturbed, and she knows he is worried that Mark will return with possible retaliation on his mind.

'Don't worry, Gordon! He's applied for a job in Tauranga and been shortlisted – one of two. Anna and Charlotte have been my spies on social media, and they told me about it last week, so let's hope he gets it.'

'He's got a long list of black marks against his name

now,' is all Gordon says, and Lara locks the door behind him with a sigh.

She feels exhausted and in need of a different kind of conversation and when she hears Weldon's eleven o'clock alarm go off, she picks up her phone and sends him a text message: 'Come down for a glass of wine? Or too late?'

'One minute,' he replies. She opens her door and goes back to the kitchen, puts the dinner dishes in the dishwasher and then suddenly he's there, silently, without her having heard him coming down the stairs.

'God, you gave me a fright! I didn't hear you come downstairs, were you sneaking up on me?'

'Socks.' He points to his feet. 'And not running down like I usually do – my mum trained us all not to run on the stairs in socks. Hey, you look tired, are you OK?'

'I just need to tell someone, it's been a day and a half, as they say.'

They sit in the half-dark living room, with only two low lights on and she starts telling him about the day which started so abruptly with a family tragedy. Before she gets very far, Weldon joins her on the sofa and puts his arm around her shoulders, and she leans against him and continues the long tale, finishing with her final conversation with Gordon. She doesn't mention the bit about having an affair with a tenant, which was never a serious question, just a frivolous diversion for Gordon. She knows as certainly as if it were carved in stone, that Weldon would never trick or cheat her, and she can trust him with her life and her last dollar.

'That accident – shit, it sounds gruesome. I was an early arrival at a head-on accident just outside Palmerston North a few years ago – someone who wasn't wearing his seatbelt in the front passenger seat of one car had been thrown out and landed on his head. The image has stayed with me ever since. I don't know how emergency personnel cope with it, but I hope someone checks on their PTSD status.'

They talk about other things for a while, breaking the spell of sadness and grief, then Lara thinks of something. 'Why did you say you aren't cut out for love – you know when we talked about it ages ago? Not that I'm trying to turn this into romantic love or anything apart from love for a friend, but what did you mean?'

'It was after she left that I realised,' he says thoughtfully. 'I think I mistook lust for love, or maybe I'm not capable of love – don't have the capacity to feel real love. Affection, yes, and interest, yes – and maybe fascination, but not love the way people describe it.'

She turns to look at him and smiles affectionately. 'We are so different – love takes over my life and wraps itself around me, and it makes me feel that whatever I do, it needs to impact on the other person in some good or positive way.'

Then she shakes her head to dispel thoughts of Roddy and what they shared. 'But you must admit it was strange the way we became friends so fast, when we hadn't had time to become real friends, if you know what I mean. We didn't really know each other, but we were friends already.'

'Oh, no – I don't think that's how it works. I don't think time has anything to do with it. It's not a time thing – even if you've known someone for years, it doesn't mean you really know them. You think you know them, but you don't know what goes on in their minds – you only know what they let you see. It's more the immediacy, the intensity that matters.' He smiles into his wineglass. 'Sometimes you've only known someone for two minutes and you realise you know this person, really and truly know them – as I imagine we both did. I think we're very lucky.'

Chapter 40

Lara envelopes Charlotte in a hug with Thomas nestled between them in a cocoon of human bodies. 'Oh, sweetheart,' she says. 'I can't believe it happened to you too!'

They are standing in the open door to the motel unit they are going to share, with Lara's bag at their feet.

'I know, it's so strange. When they came to tell me, I felt as if it wasn't real and I didn't know how to react, I just felt confused – and I thought of you straight away. I still feel as if I should be able to grieve, but I just feel remote – as if it doesn't pertain to me, but I cry a lot. It's all so weird. Did you feel like that?'

Lara drops her arms, picks up her bag and gives Charlotte a gentle nudge. 'Let's go inside, it's freezing out here and Thomas hasn't even got socks on.'

'I was just putting clean clothes on him when you knocked. He had a poo explosion and I had to change every stitch of clothing he had on. I'll have to go and put some things through the laundry, wherever that is. We only got here a couple of hours ago.'

Lara puts her bag in the second little bedroom and after

a quick look at Charlotte's exhausted face, she fills the electric jug.

'Let's make a cup of something before we go to the laundry – Gordon was just going to put his bag in their unit and move the hire car. He parked it in the next-door unit's space by mistake. I brought supplies including quality coffee, teabags, and some biscuits.'

Charlotte's face seems to have aged ten years and she is more like her mother than ever. She has no make-up on, and her eyes are red-rimmed, and Lara remembers how she was after Roddy died, when something suddenly reminded her or when she imagined she heard his voice, or for no apparent reason at all, just instantly devastated. But there is no point in commiserating too deeply right now, and making Charlotte cry, when her parents will turn up at any moment. So instead of doing the in-depth empathy thing she knows will be required later, Lara unpacks her supplies and brings them into the living room.

'Here we are. Wine of various colours, biscuits – both my favourites and yours, tea bags, quality coffee, a couple of nice cheeses and seed crackers, some fruit.' She unloads the shopping bags which have taken up most of the room in her suitcase, sets things out on the kitchen bench and turns the jug on, while Charlotte sits silently watching with Thomas half asleep in her arms.

When Bridget and Gordon come through the door, the bustle of making mugs of tea, sitting down, handing Thomas to Bridget to hold and opening packets of biscuits makes them feel calmer. Gordon hugs Charlotte with tears in his eyes, and then the initial moment is over and they can talk of practical things.

I remember it so well, thinks Lara and helps herself to a shortbread biscuit. The way something would suddenly make me realise, really understand, that I would never see

Roddy again, that he was no longer in this world, didn't exist. It often happened when meeting someone for the first time since he died. I'm glad I know these things from personal experience, or how would I be able to help her?

'I hope we did the right thing saying we'd have a take-out meal here tonight,' says Bridget suddenly. 'I wouldn't want to seem ungrateful after they invited us to the house, but I think Jonas's mum has enough on her plate with so much going on – that meal tomorrow night will be a mega event.'

'Oh God, yes,' says Charlotte tiredly. 'It's not only the brothers plus wives and about a dozen kids, it's the uncles and aunts and cousins, too. Jonas used to say he felt his extended family made up half the population on this part of the West Coast.'

Lara wakes up in the middle of the night and finds Charlotte in the living room feeding Thomas and sits down beside her, not sure if talking will rouse the baby who seems nearly asleep in Charlotte's arms.

'What about tomorrow?' she whispers. 'Who will look after him while we're at the church? I didn't even think of it earlier.'

'Sara, the wife of one of the cousins offered,' says Charlotte in perfectly normal voice. 'She's got a new baby of her own, so she won't go to the service. I'll just drop Thomas off on the way to the church. I can go back and feed him between the service and the after-match function in the church hall, so he'll be fine - he'll probably have a nap.'

The next morning, though having breakfast and getting dressed, they all take turns holding Thomas, who seems to sense the strain and is fretful. Dropping him off with Jonas's cousin takes time with introductions and condolences, and when they arrive at the church just before eleven the whole process starts again. Lara sits with her family at the front and listens as an endless row of Jonas's brothers, cousins and friends reminisce about his life. Charlotte half laughs and half sobs at some of the stories about boating mishaps, sports injuries and embarrassing moment from Jonas's early life, while his mother sobs quietly on the other side of the aisle.

Nearly three hours later, after a very long service, followed by a buffet lunch in the church hall, they pick Thomas up and drive back to the motel for him to be fed and changed, as he is still fractious and unsettled. Lara looks at Bridget and Gordon and thinks they look as if they need a break as much as she does.

'Talking to people you have no idea who they are,' she says to Gordon when they get out at the motel. 'It's not the easiest thing when all the others either know each other or are related. In the end I just resorted to standing silently on the edge of one group after another, listening without contributing anything. They probably thought I was shy.'

'I know,' says Gordon. 'We need a little interlude now before the big gathering tonight.'

'What about Thomas while we have dinner at the parent's house?' she asks Charlotte, while she changes Thomas' nappy. 'If it's a buffet meal you can't carry him around all the time. You might have to eat standing up.'

'Lovely Sandra will look after him again along with her baby – she'll just stay in one of the bedrooms with the two babies. I'll relieve her after a while so she can have dinner. She said she was happy to do it – I think she's shy and she didn't grow up here, so a lot of these relatives are new to her.'

. . .

'Thank goodness this motel unit is so big,' says Gordon and throws his black tie through the door to the bedroom, where it misses the bed and falls to the floor. 'At least we can sit down together and unwind now.'

He turns to Charlotte and pulls her close to his side. 'You poor girl – you must be exhausted.'

'A very long day,' says Lara. 'But at least we had dinner quite early. Sometimes the drinks go on for so long people don't feel like eating when the food finally appears.'

She goes two doors down to her and Charlotte's unit, picks up all she can see that seems like a suitable late evening supper snack and loads it into a shopping bag. She noticed that Charlotte hardly ate anything either at the church hall or at the dinner, so an impromptu supper feels right. She returns to find Charlotte still with Gordon's arm around her shoulders looking as if she doesn't know what to do next.

'Put it all on the table,' says Bridget. 'I've just put Thomas's carrier on the bed and pulled the door shut – good thing he's asleep. A fretting baby is the last thing we need right now.'

Between them, Bridget and Lara find glasses and open wine bottles, locate Gordon's whisky bottle from a half-unpacked carrier bag on the floor and set out the nibbles Lara had brought with her.

'Come on, Charlotte – let's sit down and have a glass of wine. Wasn't it lucky that Lara knew it would be an alcohol-free dinner and brought some?'

'Oh, I had no idea – I just thought we might need a drink at some stage.'

'It's Janta, Jonas's mum,' says Charlotte and pulls a tissue out of the box on the kitchen bench and blows her nose. 'She's a staunch teetotaller and won't tolerate any alcohol in their house. And they all obey her – unless she's not present or can't see them. Jonas used to insist on us two having wine with dinner when they came to visit us – he thought it was crazy how the rest of the family felt they had to fit in with her ideas.'

'A very raucous funeral. All those stories told in the church and all the laughing.' Gordon looks mildly outraged. 'As if it was an after-match function in a rugby club, not a sad occasion. It didn't feel right to me!'

'Oh, Gordon, for God's sake,' says Bridget briskly. 'You say that after nearly every funeral we go to these days. Times have changed – they don't see it as being raucous or out of context. They feel they're celebrating someone's life, but I must admit it's not everyone's cup of tea.'

Bridget sits down beside Charlotte and puts her hand on hers. 'Don't keep on about it, Gordon - let's just relax and have a drink. I like those new crackers made of seeds and ground nuts, Lara. I've seen them in the supermarket, but I never tried them before.'

'They're great with most cheeses,' says Charlotte and reaches for the camembert. 'But don't buy the ones with added spices and things – those don't seem to complement anything very much apart from perhaps cream cheese.'

Gradually, they settle down to intermittent conversation and begin to feel more relaxed, and Lara is pleased to see that Charlotte eats enough to sustain her until morning. Gordon has two shots of whisky in quick succession, and despite Lara shaking her head at him, he insists on telling them how she quelled a rude queue-jumper at the airport.

'She gave her the killer look,' he says. 'That's the look that goes with the stunt driving – very scary, I hadn't seen it before. The rude woman retreated defeated to the end of the line with a red face.'

Chapter 41

A few weeks later, Lara feels that some balance has been restored since Jonas's death and funeral, and she's not wondering quite so often how Charlotte is, and if she should call her or not. The last thing she wants to do it is to make Charlotte feel she has to talk only about her grief, but on the other hand she doesn't want to ignore her either. She remembers the period after Rodddy died, and how hard it was to restore a feeling of normality in her interactions with others.

The evenings are cooling, but on calm evenings Lara and Weldon sometimes still sit on the deck until late, having a second glass of wine after dinner and enjoying the quiet.

'I wish I hadn't bought these chairs!' says Lara. 'Useless damn things!'

Weldon considers her irritated face for a moment and then he laughs. 'God, you look just like an angry five-year-old when you're pissed off about something. Would you explain what this is all about? I think they're great, very comfortable.'

'I should have been able to figure it out, but I didn't

think – I just went in, liked the look of them, sat in one and bought four of them and the table. So stupid! And they are comfortable – it's just that they're cold. Wellington evenings are chilly, or hadn't you noticed? And then you don't want one of these, you want a chair that's like an indoor armchair, which kind of wraps itself around you and protects you from the cold air.'

'Couldn't you wrap a rug around yourself, or put on a jacket?'

'No, it's not the same. It needs to be a kind of wrap-around chair, upholstered. I saw them when I bought these and I thought, who on earth needs to furnish their deck so it looks as if they've moved the living room furniture outside. But now I know why they do it.'

Weldon gets his phone out and hands it over. 'Show me what you mean - I don't spend a lot of time looking at patio furniture.'

'Too small,' says Lara and gets up. 'I'll get my laptop and show you.'

Half an hour later they have passed the laptop back and forth several times, discussed chairs and been side-tracked by barbeques, patio heaters and storage chests for outdoor cushions.

'I'm totally exhausted now, nearly wiped out,' says Weldon suddenly. 'I can't take this amount of online window shopping – it does something physical to me, sucks me dry. Let's do something else.'

'Like?'

'Oh, anything – we could play another game of Scrabble and then go to bed – or perhaps bake something.'

Lara can't believe she heard it right. 'Bake something? For real? But I don't bake – sad but true.'

'I like baking – no, don't look so suspicious. I'm not kidding, I really do like baking and I make fabulous cinnamon buns, those that look like a spiral. They're famous in the family, my nieces and nephews love them. Come upstairs and we'll check out the pantry – I'm sure I have all we need.'

'But it's nearly nine o'clock at night.'

This situation seems unreal to Lara who had no idea that he liked baking. How can you regularly have sex with someone and talk about everything, or practically everything and not know a thing like that? She thought she knew most things about him, but now she wonders what he's going to come out with next.

At half past eleven they sit in Weldon's living room with cups of tea and warm cinnamon buns and Lara smiles. 'You're one out of the box, as Bridget says – you really are. Possibly the most surprising man ever. Cinnamon buns! Who would have thought?'

And Weldon points his bun at her and says with his mouth full, 'And look who's talking! The most surprising woman ever. Stunt driving! Who would have thought?'

'Let's sit on the deck,' says Weldon when he walks in with a bottle of wine in one hand, and a bag of burgers in the other a few days later. 'It might be the last night this season when it's warm enough to eat outside. I got you a new kind of burger instead of your usual – I discovered it on their menu when I was waiting to order, and it seemed like your kind of thing.'

Lara brings plates and glasses outside and dramatizes a shiver as she puts them on the low table. 'Only just warm enough. Let's have a look at the new burger.'

But when she sits down in the padded comfort of one of the new chairs, which were mysteriously delivered the day after her complaints about cold chairs, she feels warmer.

The sun has gone down but there is no dew in the air; she smiles with satisfaction and lifts the top of her burger off.

'Some kind of berry sauce on top of a thick slice of camembert.' She puts her forefinger into the burger and studies what is under a layer of crisp lettuce. 'Aha, smoked chicken! Lovely!' She puts the top of the bun back, licks her finger and takes a bite. 'Gorgeous – thank you.'

'And you couldn't just have tasted it? You had to nearly deconstruct it first?'

'Well, yes – there might have been something horrid in there which I needed to pull out before it got into my mouth. Like beetroot – or Vegemite.'

From somewhere not far away comes the sound of a piano, and they look at each other and smile, remembering that first night. Then a window shuts and they can no longer hear the piano, but having been reminded of how it started, Lara remembers something else she has been thinking of.

'I've been thinking – just a bit, don't get worried.' The corners of his mouth twitch; this lead-in has become a standing joke. 'Don't you think this is better than a love-lust-infatuation relationship? Look at it rationally - there is no need to reassure the other person they're loved, and we won't get jealous – or would we?' She pauses and he waits, his eyes on her face, interested but not yet ready to have an opinion.

'No, I'm wrong,' she says after a moment. 'We would be jealous, but not in the same way as if this were a love affair, don't you think?'

'Exactly.' He smiles. 'Not in the "I've been betrayed" way, more likely we would think "am I going to miss out now" or even "am I not good enough". But I think you're right about the friends-with-benefits arrangement. We know each other, we like each other – we aren't going to fall out of love or discover the aspect we loved has changed, or that we were mistaken, are we?'

Lara raises her glass and laughs out loud. 'Here's to us – I think we've cracked it. I think what we have is better than what all those people are chasing, the perfect love match or romance, whatever they might call it. And it will last until you fall head over heels in love with some gorgeous young thing with legs to her armpits and long blond hair and move in with her.'

The tiny, wicked smile, which she has only lately learnt to watch out for, warns her and she can guess exactly what he is about to say. 'OK, OK, don't say it. I know, you might move *her* in with you, and I'll have to listen to you making love upstairs.'

He picks up one of the paper napkins and wipes his hands before he reaches over and curls his fingers around hers. 'I was going to say that – but only to tease you. I'd never actually do it – I do have a few clues about how to behave. But talking about sex reminded me.'

An hour later they lie as they often do with Weldon on his side and Lara propped on an elbow so she can see his face while they talk.

'This is so comfortable,' she says. 'I'm glad I put central heating in – I bet you couldn't lie like this on an April night in most old Wellington villas. You'd be tucked under the covers, probably with an extra blanket too.'

There is no reply, and she realises that he has fallen asleep, the pattern of his breathing has changed, and she inches her body closer, pulls the covers up and closes her eyes.

Chapter 42

Lara is ironing and wondering if she could make a little business out of her new hobby of doing kintsugi, which is going surprisingly well. Surprisingly, because she has never thought of herself as being good with her hands, and she is enjoying her newfound skill, particularly the patient precision involved in getting it right. When she first became interested in it after watching a BBC documentary about ancient Japanese crafts, she never thought of it as something she could do, but one day she looked at a little grey bowl in a kitchen cupboard and wondered if she had ever used it. The kintsugi idea popped into her head and she decided to break the bowl and glue it together with gold powder from the art shop mixed into the glue. The result of her first effort was not particularly good, with lumpy joins and some glaze splinters missing instead of the delicate gold-coloured veins she had envisaged.

But since then, she has got much better at both the trick of breaking and the skill of gluing, and she's going to enjoy giving her kintsugi bowls away as presents. Not that she needs a job, but if she decides not to apply for any permanent teaching jobs and just sticks to filling in for teachers on sick leave, she might want to do something else as well. What a luxury problem to have, she thinks and hangs her striped shirt on a hanger, not having to work full time is lovely, but she still wants to feel she is occupied and useful. Making kintsugi bowls and selling them would be a nice combination of having an enjoyable occupation and earning some money she doesn't really need. Living on invested money is not something she is totally comfortable with yet; it feels as if she hasn't done anything to earn the right to it. But who knows, she might well get more stunt jobs now that Brian has used her again and is so obviously pleased with her performance and she will find some charities that need volunteers, use her leisure to do some good.

'Time for a coffee in town?' texts Anna and Lara unplugs the iron and replies, 'Meet you at Birdie's at eleven'. This is the first time Anna has contacted her since the revelation about Mark's drug habit and maybe this is about an update; Anna seems to be very careful what she puts in writing and might prefer to talk face to face.

Birdie's is busy and noisy, but Anna is already seated at a table in the far corner where a little half-height wall creates a niche. She mouths 'I got yours' and Lara threads her way between the tables which are too close together and thinks how lucky it is that she is slim.

'This place is so busy,' says Anna. 'I ordered for both of us - or you might have to wait for half an hour for yours. I hope I remembered how you like your coffee from last time – if it's wrong, I'll get you another.'

They make small talk while they wait for their coffee, and then Anna says without any preamble, 'I'm worried about Charlotte – very worried. We're in touch a lot more now, which is lovely, but I talked to her last night, and she said she feels as if living in Christchurch is something temporary, now that Jonas has been buried in Westport. She said, "I can't even just pop out and visit his grave, he's out of my reach, it's like I don't belong here now" - and I felt heartbroken on her account.'

'I know – I was discussing it with her parents the other day and they're going to talk to her about moving back here. It's actually easier to fly to Westport from here than from Christchurch, believe it or not – a direct flight.'

Anna makes a face. 'She'd have to find a place to live, and Wellington is hopeless now with so many Covid refugees who have stayed, like me and Paul – and the prices are horrendous. We were so lucky to get our apartment, central and handy. And she'd have to get a job, but with her skills I imagine it's not going to be hard. Accountants can probably find a job anywhere.'

Lara drinks some coffee while she considers if she should tell Anna the details of Gordon and Bridget's plans. Charlotte hasn't heard them yet and it feels disloyal, but on the other hand she knows how discreet Anna is, so she decides to tell her, so she won't worry about Charlotte.

'Charlotte's parents, who are my uncle and aunt, of course, you met them at my place at Christmas – they're still in the house in Stafford Street. Remember how big it is? The other three cousins are scattered over the globe, so they're going to offer to turn their house into two flats, and let Charlotte and Thomas have one.'

She drinks the last of her coffee and interrupts Anna, who is about to say something. 'To start with they're going to sound her out, so it all depends on whether she's willing to move – and if she is, they'll convert the house.'

Anna's face has gradually relaxed while Lara has been talking, and now she smiles. 'That's such a good idea! Company for Charlotte, built-in babysitting for Thomas and the grandparents get to see him grow up. God, I hope she agrees – I'm being selfish here, but I'd love to have her in Wellington. She used to be my best friend, and I know it's a ridiculous thing to say, but I kind of feel we could be very close friends again after a long time when things just … changed and we drifted apart. A bit like you connected with Belinda.'

'Did I tell you that?' Lara feels confused because she can't recall talking to Anna about Belinda.

'No, she did. She said she probably wasn't very nice to you when you were teenagers, she was a bit arrogant then. We lived next to each other, so I knew her well. But she has changed. She said, "I saw her sitting there at the other end of the table and I remembered how she seemed so self-contained and well-balanced at school, I thought she might be able to help me". And obviously you did. Isn't that wonderful?'

'It's nearly lunchtime.' Lara smiles instead of replying to this final rhetorical question, which she feels unable to cope with right now. She glances at the line at the counter, which has grown quickly over the last few minutes.

'How about we order something to eat and another coffee each? I'll get it if you tell me what you want.'

Returning to the table with a new order-number on a stick she adds, unnecessary she knows, but she has to say it for form's sake. 'But not a word to Charlotte until her parents have talked to her, please. I have betrayed a confidence by telling you and it might upset Charlotte to think we're all trying to re-organize her life for her. I just didn't want you to worry about her.'

'God, no! I won't say a word, I promise. And that reminds me of why I asked you to meet for coffee - we got side-tracked. Two reasons actually. Firstly, could you ask your uncle about the firm where Mark used to work – he was at their office in Tawa, and I have applied for a job at their main office in town. I haven't practiced law in New Zealand for years, and I finally got around to start the process of reviving my practicing certificate – I'm expecting it to come through any day now. I'd just like to know what his opinion is of that firm – I had an interview with two of their people last week and they seemed OK, but I've heard a couple of things about their end-of-year office parties getting sleazy and it didn't sound appealing.'

Lara makes a face. 'I think there's quite a bit of that in law firms for some reason – God knows why. But you're a big girl and can take care of yourself and if anyone gets out of line you just smack them, hard. Preferably some place where it hurts. I had to do it at a leaving party for me at the Hamilton high school where I worked. Someone thought I would welcome some very physical attention – a married guy.'

'And?'

'You'll find it hard to believe, I know, but for once I did something aggressive.' She laughs at herself and the memory of that violent impulse. 'I left the guy standing in the hallway outside the toilets clutching his groin and groaning. But he had been very hands-on, not to say intimately hands-on and took me completely by surprise – I'll save you the exact description.'

They both laugh and then Lara remembers. 'Sorry, I sidetracked you – what was the other thing you wanted to talk about?'

'Oh, yes – Julian emailed me the other day. We've been friends in a long-distance way since he lived in London, years ago. He's heard from Mark – not that he understood why Mark was telling him, because apart from two brief meetings when Julian was here, they haven't had anything to do with each other for a couple of decades. But anyway,

Mark was telling him he's got the job in Tauranga – apparently, it's a very good job and highly paid. He's moving, no, sorry – by now he'll already have moved. Which is a good thing for all concerned, I think.'

'Excellent!' exclaims Lara. 'I wish this place had a liquor licence so I could order champagne – it's the best news I've heard for ages. I was hoping he'd get that earlier job up there, but it seems to have fallen through. I've turned down a couple of invitations lately, just so I won't risk ending up in the same group as him.'

'I should have told you!' exclaims Anna. 'There was no need to worry – I sent a private message to most of the people you know straight after he punched you and asked them not to include him in anything where you might bump into him.'

It's not until they are parting outside Birdie's that the penny drops and Lara starts laughing. 'I know what it was – oh, how funny! You know how you said Julian didn't understand why Mark told him about the new job? Well, I can tell you why.'

She tells the story of Julian's deliberately audible and insulting comment at the café when Mark was walking away from their table, and how obvious it was that Mark heard what he said.

'OK, that makes sense – he was bragging, trying to impress Julian. I must remember to tell him because he was really puzzled.'

Lara has called Bridget to thank her for dinner the previous night, and now she remembers her conversation with Anna a couple of days ago. 'Oh, I know! I was going to ask Gordon something last night, and then I forgot.'

'Anything I can help you with? Or does it have to be Gordon? I can ask him to call you when he gets home tonight.'

Lara explains Anna's hesitation about the law firm which might offer her a job and adds, 'She thought Gordon might have heard things on the grapevine, you know gossip about senior males making women uncomfortable in the workplace – or not necessarily senior men, just men in general.'

'Oh!' says Bridget and then there is an unexpected and quite lengthy silence before she says, 'Perhaps best not to ask Gordon – no, I don't know, perhaps it's OK. Just let me think for a moment.'

Lara is baffled by this very surprising reaction and says, 'OK.' Mentally she trawls through various reasons, but before she makes up her mind what to think, Bridget speaks.

'Listen, I think I must explain why I said not to ask Gordon. You have to keep this in total confidence, and I mean total. It happened quite a few years ago and I don't know if any of it ever reached the ears of you children ... nobody's ever mentioned it. It was kept pretty quiet at the time. I mean within the company – not like recent times when everything is all over the media.'

Then she falls silent again, and Lara stands in her living room, absently looking out the window, thinking that she can't believe this actually means what Bridget seems to be slowly leading up to.

'Of course, I won't say anything – but please, Bridget, if you think that maybe you shouldn't tell me, then don't! I'll just forget about asking Gordon, if you think it would be better.'

'No,' says Bridget, now brisk and decisive again. 'No, I must tell you now so you don't speculate every time you see him. I think you're the sort of person who can do what I did, take it in, consider the bigger picture and decide to put it to one side. He was caught in a so-called compromising situation with his secretary. Very compromising, after hours, in the office.'

'Good lord, I had no idea! In the office, how ... unusual.' Lara's mind conjures up an image of a couple making love on the floor beside a photocopier and she shakes her head to dispel it. She can't possibly imagine her uncle as one of the people in this image.

'Not very unusual at all apparently, quite common in fact. I might as well tell you the really bizarre part of it – it involved the boardroom table.'

Lara finds herself completely unable to think of anything to say and has an insane urge to laugh. She stares out the window at a dandelion in the lawn just beside the deck while her mind frantically searches for something which could serve as an appropriate comment.

'So,' says Bridget after a short pause. 'You can see how asking Gordon that particular question might make him think you knew about his – mistake. And it would probably be better not to.'

'Heavens, yes! Of course, I won't ask him,' says Lara, deeply grateful that Bridget has given her a chance to respond in some reasonably natural way. 'Anna can find out some other way, I'll just tell her he hasn't heard anything in particular. I'll leave the issue about Mark and the partner's wife out of it – I'm sure Anna doesn't know about it and he was in their Tawa office anyway and he's gone now. But how did you cope?'

Bridget sighs. 'This might sound as if I lack passion or pride or something, but I did exactly what I said earlier, I put it to one side. I spent a long weekend in an eye-wateringly expensive exclusive lodge in Taupo and thought through it. I won't pretend it was easy, it wasn't. But there was another woman on her own, a very clever American business woman and we got talking. All the other guests were couples, and after the first evening we decided to have our meals together. She had a graphic way of looking at things, I suppose you can call it. She said she found it helpful in business and she drew it for me on the flyleaf of the book she was reading – she used my case as an example.'

She pauses and Lara stays silent and waits.

'She said I must identify what was the very best outcome and what was the worst and then rank graded version between those two extremes – like by degrees. It kind of clarifies your options and you can cross off the ones which would be intolerable and then decide how far you are prepared to go to achieve the best outcome you can live with. Kind of makes it obvious where the definitive line is.'

'Very analytical,' says Lara and smiles. 'The kind of thing they should teach in school to help kids make decisions about tricky things.'

Bridget chuckles. 'The mind boggles at what the kids might come up with as an example. But anyway, this woman asked me two questions which put it all in perspective, she asked if I loved him and when I said yes, she asked what mattered most – my pride or my love for him. Which clarified my view of what would be the best or worst.'

'It seems unbelievable to me,' says Lara slowly, thinking ahead and trying not to say anything which will upset Bridget. 'I can't get my head around Gordon doing that.'

'Oh well, think of it like this, try to be completely realistic and pragmatic. You have a middle-aged man, very good looking, still in fine physical form and known for his charm, in close proximity every working day to a younger, sexy woman. Call it temptation or a mild flirtation gone crazy, or maybe lust took over from his side, or maybe she offered him sex. Maybe she thought she was on to a good thing? Who knows?'

'Did you ask him?'

'I did not! I came back from my four days away and said there were two ways forward and the choice was his. We could divorce, split everything up and that would be that – I wouldn't fight or make a fuss, but the decision had to be his. Or, if he still loved me, we could continue as before but with a couple of conditions. One would be that if he ever did it again, I would leave him, and another condition was that neither of us would ever mention the subject again – not one single word. I didn't want to know any details and I wouldn't tell you children, who were in your twenties, because it would skew your relationship with him.'

'And it worked?'

'Oh, it did – a bit surprising even to me, I must admit. I had wondered how the reality would match up to the theory, how hard it was going to be to kind of put it to the back of my mind and not let it colour our daily life. But it did work, I suppose we got used to it. The girl had resigned as soon as they were found out – her own choice, and I'm not surprised she did. Gordon was able to stay on as senior partner, much to his surprise. He had expected to have to move on, maybe set up a new law firm on his own, but it seems my stand convinced the other partners to take the same position. And please, Lara, don't let this make any difference to how you feel towards him or how you act with him. It's years ago, and he loves you like one of his own, he really does.'

She thinks of the night Gordon told her about Mark having an affair with a partner's wife and how that would have made him feel, how he would have thought of his own shame.

'I know, Bridget,' she says, suddenly nearly overwhelmed by emotion and close to tears. 'I know he loves me, look how he's always wanting to protect me and help me, just like he does with the others. If you can put it to one side, I'm sure I can too. I'll just have to erase the boardroom table from my mind!'

And Bridget laughs outright and says, 'You won't be able to, but it will kind of fade. If it ever pops up in my mind these days, I put a blanket over them.'

Chapter 44

A text from Bridget seems to have an unstated purpose: 'Have you got time to come for a visit this weekend?' Lara frowns thoughtfully and replies, 'Of course, any particular time?'

'Any time you like on Saturday. Come for lunch?'

'This is a planning meeting,' says Gordon on Saturday. 'You know how we talked about Charlotte maybe moving to Wellington? We've mentioned it in a casual way a couple of times and now when she's had time to think about it, she seems to think it might be a good idea. But before we go any further, we want to sound you out.'

'Have some more soup,' says Bridget. 'And we've got to finish the ciabatta, I baked it yesterday and it will go stale. As you know, we're thinking of dividing the house into two flats.'

They both look at her and she can't imagine what they expect her to say. Isn't this for them to discuss with Charlotte?

'But why are you asking me what I think?' She takes a

piece of bread and reaches for the butter. 'I'm not sure what I can contribute.'

'Oh, I'm sure you can – we have different ideas, Bridget and I,' says Gordon. 'You could say our ideas are at right angles. I thought copying what you did was a great idea, one downstairs and one upstairs, slice the place horizontally – and we'd let Charlotte have the ground floor one, because of Thomas, but Bridget has other ideas.'

'Let me explain it myself,' says Bridget and points her butter knife at him. 'I thought we should divide the house vertically instead of horizontally – two halves, both with two levels.'

She gets up and takes their soup bowls to the bench. 'I'll make coffee while we talk. Why I thought of this idea, is that it would give both flats access directly to the garden – nice for me because I like pottering around outside. And good for Thomas when he's a bit older, he can play outside and we can keep an eye on him from inside, whether it's me looking after him or Charlotte. We'd have to rip out the staircase and re-model the entrance, but I'm sure it could be done.'

'Aha – now I get it. That's a clever plan! So, if you have both flats laid out the same, kitchen and living on the ground floor and bedrooms and bathrooms upstairs, then you could have the kitchens in the middle, with a shared wall which would be rational regarding plumbing and water, and both living areas would have windows or French doors to the garden and windows at the ends as well, so light coming in from both directions. The layout of the flats would be mirrored. And he bathrooms directly above the kitchens, back to back again – more plumbing convenience.'

Gordon chuckles. 'God, Lara – these hidden talents popping out after all these years! I can't get over it, here we were, only thinking of the basic concepts and you've already started working out the floor plans. But you're quite right.

Bridget's idea was that splitting the place vertically would mean nobody has to carry rubbish and groceries or whatever ... boxes of wine maybe, upstairs.'

'And listen,' says Lara, 'and it's not that I want to be depressing but imagine ten or fifteen years from now – if one of you needed a new knee or a hip, you'd be able to temporarily live downstairs just for a few weeks. Best of both worlds.'

'Sorted,' says Bridget. 'We needed this – a more detailed concept to present to Charlotte for her to think about, with a variety of good reasons. And it'll be like two houses side by side, rather than two flats in some funny way, don't you think? Feel more independent, perhaps, like those semi-detached houses in England.'

On a rainy Wednesday morning Lara sits in her living room, where she has sat since she got up to make breakfast an hour ago with a cooling mug of tea in her hand. She is still in her PJs and stares without focus out the French doors, as she once again goes over every single word she has exchanged with Weldon over the last couple of weeks. That something is wrong is becoming increasingly clear every day, but she can't put her finger on what it is. They've had sex twice, she thinks, or maybe three times, but it's been kind of low key. Their conversations have been a bit less engaged than usual and a couple of times she's caught him looking at her in a new way, kind of detached or as if he's re-assessing her and she's not meeting expectations.

The feeling that he is holding something back has been gradually growing in her mind, and over the last couple of days she has become convinced that she is right; he has formed a plan or knows something he is not sharing with her.

They met in the hall last night when she was putting her umbrella away and he was coming in from work, and the way he said "Hi, what a wet day" and more or less straight away went upstairs confirmed her suspicion. It could be one of several things; maybe he has simply grown tired of her, or perhaps she is taking up too much of his time, or he has become attracted to someone else and now he's wondering how to end their arrangement. Of all the explanations she can come up with, the most likely one is that he is simply bored and can't decide how to end it without drama. Because they are going to keep on meeting in the hall or outside, and unless he moves, she will have to learn not to mind so much, but it is affecting her deeply. She knew she was taking a risk when she asked him to come to bed with her, and now, thinking of that night, she cringes at the thought that she brought this dilemma on herself. But then I didn't know, she thinks sadly, I had no idea it would become anything else but a friendly and convenient arrangement for two lonely people.

She has become very fond of Weldon and she feels a strong connection now, a risk she didn't count on at the outset. The worst thing is that she can't make up her mind if she should tackle him head-on and ask what is on his mind, saying she has noticed that something is wrong. I'm a coward, she thinks, I don't know what I would do it if he says he wants it to end, or that he's moving out. Just thinking about it makes her want to cry, and if she cried in front of him, it would ruin everything; she would become an object of pity and embarrassment in his eyes, and she can't bear the thought.

When she finally gets up and puts the mug on the kitchen bench, she has reached no decision. I'll wait, she tells herself, it might be something at work. She'll leave it for a week or two and see what happens. The thought of living with this uncertainty is stressful, but it's better than bringing it to a point of no return by asking him and finding out the worst, the thought of which now makes tears pool in her eyes. She wipes her eyes on the edge of her PJ top and goes to get dressed, avoids looking at herself in the mirror and gets the vacuum cleaner out.

'Charlotte is coming to live here! Isn't it lovely?' says Bridget excitedly over the phone, and then she continues without waiting for an answer. 'And she thinks all of us sharing our house is a great idea! I can't tell you how happy we are – so now I must get ready for stage one.'

Lara can tell there's more to come, so she abandons emptying the washing machine and sits down in her favourite corner of the sofa. 'So, what's stage one - is she just going to bring clothes and things and you'll all live together while you sort out the details? How is it going to work? You can't possibly radically remodel the house and live in it at the same time.'

'No, I know – but trust Gordon to have thought of all possible options to fit in with how she would react.' Bridget laughs. 'I accused him of being way ahead of himself when he started planning, but now it turns out to be a blessing. He's renting a three-bedroom apartment from a client who has an apartment in one of those unit buildings, or whatever they're called – you know, where everyone owns their apartment and then they pay a corporate entity to do the building maintenance and whatever. Some people own an apartment there and live in a house somewhere else and let the apartment – like an investment. Some are for short-term hire, like when people come to Wellington for a holiday, and some just live there.'

'Where is it?'

'Somewhere in Taranaki Street, I don't think he told me the number – he said it's only a ten minute walk to the waterfront too, so it's lovely for Charlotte. She'll be able to go for walks with the stroller down there. It's modern, has a big balcony, whatever that means, three bedrooms and it's on the fourth floor. That's all I can tell you – I've been so busy I've forgotten to ask for any more details and it doesn't matter anyway.'

'And available right now? I can't believe your luck! With so many people trying to find good accommodation and despairing of ever getting anything – it seems uncanny.'

'Not available for a month, but then we can have it as long as we want on a month-by-month lease. And as always, it's not what you know, it's who you know. Gordon acts for the woman who owns the apartment and she usually lets long-term – at least two years, but her tenant is leaving and she's making an exception for us, as a favour, she feels a connection because it turns out she owns one of Charlotte's paintings – can you imagine?'

Chapter 45

A week later, Lara drives across town to Stafford Street at quarter past seven in the morning, hoping to avoid the early rush hour but very surprised at the amount of early traffic. And as she usually does, she pauses after parking to look up at the bush clad slope of Mt Victoria and thinks how wonderful it is to be able to live so close to real untamed nature and still only have a fifteen-minute walk to the edge of the CBD, perhaps less.

Gordon will have left a few minutes ago, if he still sticks to the routine of a half hour walk to his office downtown, unless it's raining when he leaves twenty minutes later and takes his car. But today the sun is shining, the autumn air is crisp and fresh, and it's going to be a perfect day.

'Did you talk to Charlotte this week?' asks Bridget when she opens the front door. 'Have you heard the latest news?'

'I don't know – we talked on Sunday, I think, or maybe Saturday. She said she thought she had a tenant for the house, but I know nothing after that.'

'OK – she does have a tenant now; they move in next week. It's just incredible how fast this is moving, nearly too fast. Come and sit down for a few minutes before we start and I'll tell you, Did you have breakfast?'

'Right,' says Bridget ten minutes later and puts a mug of coffee in front of Lara. 'This is the latest. She's decided that moving sooner rather than later is a good idea. So, as I said on the phone the other day – clearing out those bedrooms is the first big task at this end.'

She gets up and returns with a packet of chocolate macaroons. 'Have a biscuit even if you did have breakfast.' She pushes the packet of chocolate macaroons toward Lara. 'Someone Jonas knew is going to live in the house until it's sold. Some real estate agent told Charlotte it will sell better in the spring and this guy doesn't mind – he's still looking for something he can afford to buy. Apparently houses in Christchurch don't sell well in autumn or winter.'

She smiles at Lara's hesitation about the biscuits. 'For goodness' sake, take one! It's not going to make you fat. Anyway, the owner of the apartment is prepared to let us have it for as long as we need it – I think I told you she owns one of Charlotte's paintings – isn't it funny? She never told Gordon that she went online and found Charlotte's website and bought one after she saw the one Gordon has in his office.'

'I asked her once a couple of years ago why she's not painting now,' says Lara. 'She said she didn't have time, what with working full time and being married. Did she ever talk to you about it?'

'Oh, that was Jonas,' says Bridget calmly and bites into a macaroon. 'I found out on a visit down there when they were first married. I asked where she painted, because I couldn't see her stuff anywhere, like in the spare room – and Jonas said they had decided to have their evenings and weekends together.'

'But he played golf, every weekend. How did that fit?

And he played squash during the week too. This is incredible – I never thought he would have been like that.'

'Well, he was,' says Bridget and it's easy to see that she too found it hard to accept. 'And when I said to Charlotte later how she could paint while he was at golf and then put it away, she said it wouldn't have worked for her. It isn't something you do at a set time and then stop to suit someone else, she would never be happy with that, so she kind of gave it up.'

They look at each other in silence for a long moment, then Lara shakes her head and gets up. 'Let's go upstairs and get started.'

'OK, this is what we need to do. First the clearing stage, which is today's job and maybe tomorrow. I'll get a skip tomorrow, when we get an idea of what the volume is going to be. And then what's left can go to the apartment when it's ready for us, and then come back here, or at least some of it, when the changes to the house are done. We're only going to have two bedrooms in our flat here, so we'll get rid of the excess furniture now – battered old armchairs in the kids' rooms, student desks that haven't been used for a decade or more, not since Linda left, anyway. And there's a lot of rubbish in the wardrobes and cupboards. I don't want to have to do this in a rush later on.'

At five Bridget calls it a day, and they review what they have done. 'I know it looks like all we've done is create a giant mess, but now I know exactly what needs to be taken downstairs to go in the skip, and I'll get boxes to put smaller things in.'

'I'll be back at the same time tomorrow. Pity we can't get a skip right up to the house, but with two of us we'll do it easily.'

. . .

At half past nine Lara has had dinner, tidied up and on a sudden impulse cleaned the fridge and despite having spent the whole day helping Bridget move and carry things, she feels energetic. She nearly laughs at herself: coming home from a day like this, part physical and part emotional, and then tackling the fridge seems a bit mad.

Without giving herself time to consider and maybe decide not to, she sends a text message to Weldon: Just finished housework, time for wine and cheese?

This is only the second time she has done this in the last couple of weeks, and she holds her breath and stands with the phone in her hand until the thumbs-up emoticon pops up a minute later. She must ask him, she thinks, because she can't stand this any longer. It's on her mind the whole time, and it's driving her crazy. She knows she said "no ties" but she can't bear the thought of losing him – if you can lose someone who never belonged to you.

'Do you really think that's wise?' asks Weldon a few minutes later and Lara pauses in the act of pouring two glasses of wine and looks quizzically at him.

'I'm not planning on driving anywhere.'

He looks thoughtfully at her for an unnervingly long moment before he speaks, with that assessing look that has so disturbed her lately.

'You do know you're pregnant, don't you?'

'What?!' Lara stands as if frozen, her mind a blank and the wine bottle still half tilted in her hand.

Weldon reaches over and takes the bottle from her unresisting fingers. 'You really didn't know?'

She can't take it in, it can't be true, everyone knows she can't have children. She was married to Roddy for nine years and never used contraception and never got pregnant.

'But I can't be,' she says slowly while conflicting emotions tumble through her mind. 'I can't have children.

Not that we didn't want them, but I never conceived.' She thinks for a moment and adds detail, as if this makes it an indisputable fact. 'And we were so content just on our own, we never did anything about it – like fertility treatment or anything. We just never got around to it, I guess. People expected us to fret and agonise, but somehow we didn't.'

And then another thought strikes her, and she looks at him. 'Why do you think I'm pregnant?'

He studies her face carefully before he replies, but when he does, he is factual and unemotional. 'You haven't had a period for two months.'

'I haven't? I didn't realise – how do you know?'

Now he smiles. 'Of course, I know – obviously better than you do yourself. You had one a couple of months ago, maybe three, and you haven't had one since. And I also noticed tiny changes, body changes. Are you upset?'

She stares absently at the two cheeses she got out of the fridge a few minutes and also an eon ago, and tries to work out how she feels. She is suddenly certain that he is right, but how does she feel? She is aware of Weldon's eyes never leaving her face and to reassure him she pulls her thoughts together and says decisively, 'Of course, I'm not upset! I think I'd like to have a baby.'

'You might want me to leave.' Weldon face betrays no emotion, his voice is calm and neutral, and Lara is instantly overwhelmed by a feeling of impending loss.

'What? Are you crazy? Of course, I don't want you to leave – it's your baby too. Oh no, no – I'm sorry - do you want to leave? Do you want me to say you're free to go? Of course - this isn't what you thought you were letting yourself in for.'

Her voice is starting to break, and she struggles to hold back tears. Weldon takes hold of her shoulders and pulls her close. 'I'm the one who's been worried – don't you start now.

I thought you knew and were waiting to tell me, so I've been wondering why you were waiting, if you were getting up the courage to ask me to move out.'

'God, no! How could you possibly think that?' Lara looks up at him, desperate for him to understand she means it. 'Please don't leave!'

'Of course, I'm not going to leave – don't be silly,' says Weldon and gives her a little shake. 'There is nowhere else I'd rather be. Let's sit down.'

They sit opposite each other at the table, Weldon with a glass of wine and Lara with a glass of water and for a long time they don't speak, it feels as if there is no need to say anything just now. Eventually Lara cuts a slice of Havarti, adds a dab of fig paste and looks at Weldon in a considering way.

'You know what? I do want a baby. And this might be the cleverest set-up for raising a child ever invented. Don't you think?'

'In what way?'

'The way we live, I mean – in the same house but independently, we have our own spaces and use them as we like, and we don't even have to go outside to see each other. We can share the baby between us – which is what I presume you would like to do? God, I'm so relieved – you can't imagine how scary that was! I'm sure my heart stopped for a second when I thought you were about to say you were leaving.'

'Of course, we're going to share the baby, half of it is mine after all and bags I get the top half. But seriously, I'm great with babies,' says Weldon surprisingly and pours himself some more wine. 'Both my sisters and my brother have children, six all up, nearly seven – they range from three to fourteen, no fifteen, in age. And I have babysat and changed nappies, and I know how to heat a bottle and get a restless baby to go to sleep. Pretty much a baby expert.'

It makes her laugh, partly with relief and partly at the image which popped into her head, of Weldon's big hands dealing with a tiny baby.

'I'm definitely not a baby expert – I haven't really had anything much to do with babies. Most of my Hamilton friends have children, of course, but I've not been hands-on involved. I've watched Charlotte change Thomas's poopy nappy - pretty gross, I must admit, but perhaps it's OK when it's your own baby.'

'You'll learn,' says Weldon comfortably. 'And think how convenient when he or she is three or four. You say 'no' to something they want, and they'll just go upstairs and I might say 'yes'. Endless opportunities for a smart kid to develop negotiating skills.'

'Please don't go back upstairs, or not yet,' says Lara an hour later. 'I want you to stay close.'

She wakes in the early hours of the morning, and he is still there beside her, and she pokes him in the ribs to wake him up and says, 'Do you know what? I'd rather have your baby than anybody else's in the whole world.'

Chapter 46

Lara holds the door open for Bridget, Gordon, and Charlotte, who is carrying a sleepy Thomas wrapped in a rug. 'I'm so glad you could come - it was just a sudden idea that maybe some wine and cheese after your event might be nice, and we've all been so busy lately, we haven't seen enough of each other.'

'I'll put him down in your bed if you don't mind,' says Charlotte. 'He's exhausted after this mad afternoon of crawling around trying to keep up with all the other kids, and he didn't have his usual afternoon nap. He'll drop off to sleep in two minutes.'

Lara watches as Charlotte tucks Thomas into her bed and makes sure the top sheet is tightly tucked in under the mattress. 'There! Look at him, his eyes are closing already. He loves to be tucked in tight and it stops him rolling off the bed accidentally in his sleep.'

They leave the door open, and Lara turns the passage light on. 'What was this strange event you went to? I thought it was an auction, but I must have got it wrong.'

'No, it was an auction - a family event according to the

couple who organized it, to raise funds for new outside play equipment for the play centre that Thomas will be going to next year. Everyone turned up with their kids, and they auctioned donated things – all kinds, art and kitchen stuff, a few bits of furniture, a box of wine. Very successful, I think. Dad bought the wine, of course.'

They look at each other and grin and Gordon says, 'I think I raised my hand by mistake, and they thought it was a bid.'

'I'll ask Weldon to join us,' says Lara casually, and picking up her phone from the kitchen bench she sends a text to him before she turns to Charlotte. 'You didn't meet him last time, did you?'

'No, but I'm very keen to – I need to thank him for saving you from evil predators.'

Lara hears Weldon's steps on the stairs and turns as he comes in the door from the hall. 'Here's Weldon - you met Gordon and Bridget when they came for a house-warming drink, and this is my cousin, Charlotte.'

While they are greeting each other, she gets wine out of the fridge and carries the tray of nibbles to the table at the sitting room end. Weldon looks across, their eyes meet, and she nearly giggles, any minute now the fun will start.

Then Gordon comes towards her with a wine bottle in each hand, and Lara notices Bridget studying Weldon, who is talking to Charlotte while he gets glasses from the cupboard and puts them on a tray. Now, why is she looking at him like that? she thinks, but then Gordon blocks her view and asks her something, and she switches her attention to him.

As they seat themselves around the coffee table, Charlotte says, "What a pity it's too cold to sit outside on your lovely deck now" at exactly the same moment that Gordon picks up one of the wine bottles and holds it up exclaiming, 'I've never heard of it before – Zero, what a terrible name for a wine.'

Lara knows this very moment is when they start acting out their script; Gordon's comment provided the perfect cue.

'Oh, not so mad,' she says lightly. 'It's alcohol free and I'm drinking it because I'm pregnant. I'm having a baby in November – or maybe early December.'

For all of one second you could hear a pin drop, then Charlotte jumps up, delighted and pink-cheeked with excitement. 'Oh, my God – I didn't think you could have children, how lovely!'

She hauls Lara to her feet, and they hug each other tight. Bridget has a funny little smile on her face, but Gordon is staring at her with a frown creasing his face.

'Yes, isn't it lovely?' says Lara and untangles herself from Charlotte's arms. 'Another baby in the family and at close quarters.'

'And what about Mark?' asks Gordon, still frowning. 'Does this mean we have to have him in the family too?'

'I sincerely hope not,' says Weldon calmly, having to improvise now, as neither he nor Lara had thought of this angle. 'The baby is Lara's and mine, and I can't see why Mark should have anything to do with it.'

He looks innocently at Gordon, who stares as if he can't believe his eyes. 'You are the father of the baby?'

'I am.'

Gordon seems to have lost his voice and Bridget steps in, as she often does. 'And you

fell in love after you saved Lara from being beaten up, I suppose.'

Weldon flashes her a smile. 'Not really – but she is my best friend, I'm *very* fond of her.'

Lara moves closer to Weldon, who puts his arm over her shoulders as she smiles at her family and says, 'Oh no, we're not in love – we just decided to have a baby together. Weldon's my best friend - and I'm very fond of him, too.'

'But, how …' starts Gordon and Charlotte bends down and puts her hand over his mouth. 'Oh, for God's sake, Dad - don't ask how it happened. You have four children of your own and I'm sure we all know exactly how it happened.'

She pats his cheek and grins. 'And I for one think this is wonderful - the best news for a long time. Great for Lara, and Weldon looks pleased too, I must say - I hope he is! And living here, perfect! One parent downstairs and one upstairs.'

Having side-tracked Gordon's possible interrogation, she raises her glass. 'Here's to best friends having babies together and another little squiggle in the family – I'm so happy!'

Gradually they settle down again, and Weldon responds to Bridget's questions about his family, and she laughs when she hears how experienced he is with babies.

'Just as well,' says Lara from across the coffee table when she catches the phrase 'baby expert'. 'I don't have a clue, but Weldon will show me how it's done, he has looked after so many nieces and nephews since they were tiny, he really is an expert.'

Gordon looks at Lara, still slightly confused. 'But what do I say? You know, if someone hears you're having a baby. Are you partners, or engaged or what?'

Weldon laughs. 'Lara tells me we are "friends with benefits", but that phrase might not sit well with you - just say we're partners for the sake of simplicity. Then you don't have to answer lots of questions and there is no need to mention I'm the tenant.'

'It's nearly time for dinner – let's order pizza or something to be delivered,' says Charlotte quietly to Lara at the kitchen bench, where they are replenishing the tray. 'We're so settled in now and the parents are getting to know

Weldon. And so am I, of course. And Thomas will probably sleep right though after this afternoon's exertions.'

Lara puts another bottle of wine in the fridge and says, 'You suggest it, and I'll order it. Make sure you find out what Gordon and Bridget want – I don't think I've ever bought pizza specifically for them before.'

Much later, after pizza, more wine, and tiramisu ice cream, when Lara and Weldon are finally alone, she pats the sofa cushion beside her. 'Come and sit down and leave the mess, I'll tidy it up in the morning. I want to lie down, but I want you somewhere close.'

'And?' Weldon picks up her legs and rests them across his thighs, as she slides down to put her head on a cushion. 'What's this about?'

'Oh, nothing much, just a few thoughts that popped into my head while they were here. I've noticed that your eleven o'clock alarm hasn't gone off for ages – so you don't have to rush upstairs and turn it off when we're in bed, I suppose. And when I introduced you to Charlotte I had a thought - why are you called Weldon? Was it your mother's maiden name, or something? Your brother is called Michael, your sisters have perfectly ordinary names, and you are called Weldon?'

'Fay,' says Weldon and she can see he's trying to keep a straight face. 'It's true, and you're allowed to laugh.'

'You're named after Fay Weldon, the feminist writer? Really?'

'You can ask my mum if you like – you'll meet her soon. We must tell my side of the family about the baby too, you know. We can't spring a fully formed baby on them, all of a sudden. But the bit about Fay Weldon is true. My mum was a fanatical admirer of her books and ideas, she thought she was the best thing since ... whatever was really great before that. And she was convinced she was having a girl – who would be called Fay.'

'Didn't she have the ultrasound scan? Oh, wait, perhaps they didn't do it then. I don't know when they started.'

'Neither do I.' Weldon sits thinking for a moment and then he shakes his head. 'I'll look it up later – but anyway, I turned out to be a boy so she just switched to Weldon. And then my dad put his foot down and said, no more fancy-schmancy names, the next one gets a regular Christian name - and that was that.'

He puts his hand on Lara's stomach and says, 'Hello, baby! How are you in there? Shall we call you Fay?' and Lara's eyes fill with tears which overflow and run down her temples, and she sniffs and smiles at the same time.

Chapter 47

Lara is sitting at the dining table holding a shard of ceramic firmly against the edge of the broken bowl which rests on a piece of cardboard in front of her when a ping announces a text message. Ignoring it, she concentrates on holding the shard in precise alignment for five minutes until the glue is dry enough, then she gently lets it go and picks up her phone.

It's from Tobias, who hasn't been in touch for some weeks. 'Can I come for a visit after work – about six? I have something to tell you.'

Lara considers for a moment, makes up her mind not to ask any questions and replies, 'Of course.'

He wants to tell her something in person, but what could it be? Trying to stop herself from speculating is useless and every now and then for the rest of the afternoon her thoughts revert to the message. When Weldon comes home, she calls him as soon as his footsteps have reached the top of the stairs.

'Are you working tonight or would you like to come

down at six and meet Tobias? He's coming on some mysterious errand, and I'd like you to be here.'

'Why, is he dangerous?'

'Don't be silly, of course he's not dangerous. But I got a funny feeling when he said he has something to tell me. It could be something about Mark, though I can't imagine what it would be after all this time – or why he would think it concerns me.'

'OK, I'll be down shortly.'

'Yes, please, a beer would be nice' says Tobias after he's been introduced to Weldon.

For some reason they sit on the stools at the free-standing counter, something Lara hasn't done since she moved in. Sometimes when she cleans the floor, she wonders why she ever bought them, she never sits there to eat and all they do is look modern and nice, but until now without practical function.

But here they are, and Weldon moves one stool so he sits at right angles to Lara and they both look expectantly at Tobias, who says without further ado. 'People say you're pregnant. Is it true?'

'Yes, I'm pregnant – it's no secret. Why?'

'Apparently the consensus among those who trade in gossip is that I'm the father. Possibly because we made such an excellent job of faking being in love in various public places - and maybe because I already have five kids, so I'm supposedly good stud material.'

'We were such good actors,' says Lara and she can't help smiling at the memory. 'Particularly you – all those little romantic glances and touches. But you've had a lot more practice than I have.'

'Touché!' Tobias grins. 'So – is it Mark's baby?'

Swivelling on her stool to face Tobias full-on she says calmly. 'No, it's *not* Mark's baby, it's mine and Weldon's – we made it together.'

'Ah!' says Tobias and starts laughing. 'You two … well! I had no idea and obviously neither does anyone else. And it's not that I have anything against being presumed to be the father, not at all – but I was worried when I thought it was Mark's. In case he took it into his drug fuelled brain to do something dramatic, I mean.'

'So, you knew about the drug habit?' Lara wonders if he knew when they first went out for dinner, when Tobias told her he'd asked around to find out more about Mark.

'I heard about it just recently. There's a lot of gossip going around about how he assaulted you and how dangerous he might be. No point in telling you, because you already knew by then. One of my ex-wives showed me the Facebook photo of your face.'

They have pasta and meatballs and spend a pleasant evening, surprisingly pleasant, thinks Lara and looks at the two large men now sitting opposite each other at the table with empty plates and glasses of red wine in front of them, deep in a debate about sea level rise and the moral obligation to take in climate refugees from Pacific islands that are slowly disappearing under water. She listens sleepily and wishes she could go to bed, and suddenly she yawns twice in succession, and they stop talking and look at her.

'Bedtime,' says Tobias and gets up. 'Trust me, I know all about pregnant women. Thanks for dinner – very enjoyable. And don't forget to somehow make it public that it's not my baby – I don't mind another baby, but I think Weldon should get the credit for this one.'

'What's your job?' asks Lara when they stand talking in the hall. 'I never asked and nobody has mentioned it.'

'I'm an orthodontist. Why?'

'Really? I thought you'd be something slightly risky, like a hedge fund manager or a bitcoin trader or whatever.'

'Definitely time you went to bed!' Tobias kisses her cheek, shakes hands with Weldon and leaves.

Chapter 48

On a warm and blustery late October day Lara turns into Stafford Street and takes one look at the congestion, does a three-point turn in a neighbour's driveway and drives back the way she came. Five minutes later she threads her way between a pick-up truck, a van and a giant skip, steps carefully around a toilet and a hand basin which block the path and climbs the steps to the front door. The first person she sees is Warren, who looks her over with obvious surprise.

'You're pregnant!' he says, and then he collects his wits. 'Congratulations!'

'You're very observant,' says Lara, and Warren grins.

'Not really – it's hard to miss when you're nearly as wide as you're tall. I was just surprised.'

She refrains from asking why he is surprised and looks around, feeling slightly dislocated. 'My God, I can hardly imagine what was here before – it's unrecognizable.'

'Pretty radical, all right. But now that we've ripped it apart and fixed all the plumbing and wiring issues, it's just easy stuff left. We'll have it done in no time.'

A man appears behind Warren with a roll of cabling in his hand, ignores Lara and says, 'I'm done for today – I'll be off now, let me know when you need me for the next stage.'

'How come you were available for this at such short notice?' Pregnancy brain thinks Lara, she didn't even think of that when she first heard Craig and Warren were doing this job so soon. 'I thought there was a waiting list a mile long.'

'It's about two miles long now, gets worse all the time. But we were lucky – we managed to hire two more men, both experienced and now we've split into two teams, Craig and a guy he's known for years are doing one job while I and the other guy we hired do this job.'

'I'm meeting Bridget and Charlotte here for a little tour – I hope we won't be too much in your way,' says Lara and raises her voice when a nail gun starts up on the other side of the wall behind her. 'Just a quick tour because I haven't seen the place since you started. They should be here any minute.'

'No problem – just watch out where you walk, there are holes in the floors here and there.' Warren points to the framing to their right. 'Go in there and have a look at the plans while you wait – I've got to go and talk to my off-sider.'

When Bridget arrives without Charlotte, Lara is standing beside a saw table set up in the space which used to be the dining room, studying the plans with a frown.

'Oh, hi – I didn't hear you. What a racket!' She points at the plans and looks at Bridget. 'I think the plan has changed since you showed me a couple of months ago. Isn't this bit there where the linen cupboard is going to be?'

Bridget looks at the place on the plan where Lara's forefinger is and then up at the ceiling as if she can see the walls up there, and then returns to the plan. 'Yes, I think we decided to move it a bit to the left, I can't remember the reason – something to do with the wardrobe in the room behind that wall.'

'Hi,' says Charlotte, who has come in behind them and takes Lara by the shoulders, looking her up and down. 'My God, it's not twins, is it?'

'If it is, nobody's told me. The midwife says people who are short and slim often end up looking like pumpkins – nowhere to hide the baby. But not long now and I'll hopefully be back to normal.'

Bridget interrupts, still looking at the plan. 'But Lara, tell me what it is you can see that I can't, because it seems perfectly straight-forward to me.' She points at the plan again. 'About a meter of wall, then the linen cupboard door, then another bit of wall.'

'Let's get Warren in here,' says Lara and walks over to what was the front hall. 'Warren!' she yells and puts her thumb and forefinger in her mouth and wolf-whistles, which makes Charlotte and her mother look at each other and laugh.

'I never knew you could do that,' says Charlotte, impressed. 'What a useful talent!'

'Was that you wolf-whistling at me, Lara?' Warren emerges from behind a half finished wall and points a hammer at her. 'It's been a while since anyone did that – I'm flattered.'

She reaches for the pencil that sticks up out of his breast pocket and points at the plan. 'Sorry to disappoint you, Warren, it was actually more of a summons, but never mind. Look at this please - if someone's got this door open and someone else comes out of the bathroom the doors will crash into each other.'

It takes Warren two seconds to see what she means. 'Of course, you're right. The linen cupboard door should be hinged on the other side and open away – well spotted. We decided not to have the bathroom door opening inwards, to make it seem more spacious, perhaps a bad decision.'

And Bridget, who has looked at the plan while Warren and Lara have been talking, says, 'It's my fault entirely, Warren. You told me it was a bad idea to have a door opening out into a passage and see where it's landed us! Thanks Lara, we'll change it back to how it was – the bathroom door I mean, so it opens into the bathroom.'

Warren grins, 'OK, I didn't want to blame you, but there's a good reason for a lot of the standard ways of doing things.'

'And where is Thomas,' asks Lara as they start their tour. 'Why didn't you bring him? I haven't seen him for a whole week.'

'Can you imagine him here, wanting to get down, running around and falling over things. He seems to have decided that walking is boring and runs everywhere - so he's like a little demon set on self-destruction, no common sense and no fear, but fully mobile. I either spend all my waking hours watching him, or I'd have to tie him to his high chair. I left him with one of the mothers in the toddler playgroup – we do a lot of baby swapping.'

They part on the street outside with promises to get together for coffee or a meal soon, and Lara sits in her car and texts Gordon. "Need to talk legal stuff with you some time in the next two weeks. Please don't mention to anyone, this needs to stay between you and me. Lara xx"

Chapter 49

Gordon frowns, half concerned and half puzzled. 'What do you mean? I don't get it.'

'What don't you understand? What getting married means? Or what changing a will means?'

Lara is teasing and hopes he'll relax, because she could sense his legal protector role slipping into gear before she had finished her fist sentence. If this turns into the kind of battle she has worried it might, then she will have to haul out plan B, which is so awful that she can't imagine how she would even get the words out.

'But it makes no sense — you said at the start that you're just best friends. Why marriage? I know he's a very nice guy, but what if he's after your money?'

Lara leans over the desk and puts her hand on Gordon's and smiles. 'It's not his idea, it's mine and he doesn't even know about it yet. And he might well turn me down. Actually, he probably will.'

'What? You're going to do the asking?'

'Let me tell you a story,' says Lara, lets his hand go and leans back, because leaning forward over the pumpkin bump is very uncomfortable and makes it impossible to take a deep breath.

'I specially asked your secretary for a long appointment because I had a feeling this might take some time. And I'd appreciate it if you would let me tell the whole thing without interrupting, because it's really important to me that you understand what this is about.'

His face is a mixture of suspicion and grumpiness, but he nods and says, 'OK, then.'

'So here it is – it started after he first dealt with the knife man and then saved me from being totally beaten up by Mark. The way he dealt with the aftermath then made me realise what a lovely, kind and clever man he is. The funny thing is I had already decided, after our very first meeting in a café, that I had never met anyone that I so instantly felt I trusted, as if I'd know him forever.'

She studies Gordon's face for a moment and tries to imagine what he's thinking, takes a sip of water from the paper mug she got from the water cooler in reception, and continues, well aware that she already told him this on the day Jonas died, but wanting to make sure he remembers.

'He didn't just send Mark on his way, he also really scared him – had him up against the wall with his arm across Mark's throat and his feet off the floor. And then he let him go and told him to bugger off and took charge of me, because I was – well, I don't know what I was, perhaps immobilised is the word. So, Weldon marched me into my kitchen, found a bag of peas in the freezer, wrapped it in a tea towel, put in on my face and told me to sit down. He found wine and glasses and sat down with me to plan a social media campaign of such cleverness that I could never have done it without him. So now you know the first instalment.'

Gordon nods. He's got control of his face again, and she

has no idea what he's thinking, so she carries on. 'And over a very short space of time we became what must be called best friends, though it sounds a bit teenage. But whatever – one night when we were sitting on the deck quite late in the evening, I asked him if he would like to come to bed with me. And he said, thank you very much, it's very flattering to be asked, but no thanks.'

Gordon lets out a chuckle and his eyes twinkle, so Lara says, 'Yes? Your reaction?'

'What a bloody fool! Fancy turning you down – what's wrong with the man?'

Lara blesses the instinct that made her ask for a double length appointment and tells Gordon every single detail she can remember of Weldon's reasons for not going to bed with her, and then the conclusion to their discussion. At the end of this monologue Gordon looks slightly less concerned, but she knows this isn't the end of it.

'So, you're going to ask him to marry you? Why? And what if he turns you down, as you say he's likely to do, what then? Will it ruin your friendship?'

It's not that she hasn't thought of this herself, but hearing someone else say it makes it a more threatening prospect, something so cataclysmic that she shudders at the thought. Perhaps this is the stupidest idea she's ever had, something which might break a precious relationship. And for what? There is nothing to be gained from being married to Weldon compared to what they have now. She knows Gordon is right but somewhere in her heart she has come to feel that marrying Weldon would be the ideal outcome.

'I don't know – I really don't,' she says now, suddenly hesitant and prepared to walk away and reconsider. 'No, you're probably right, it might be a disaster. I must re-think this and work out why I have this urge to marry him. Maybe it's pregnancy hormones or something. So, let's put it aside for now, you're probably right. But could we still talk about what else I want done?'

'Of course, it can't do any harm and I'd like to hear what you've come up with.'

He looks relieved that she is amenable to his suggestions, and she can guess what his concerns are. Not that Weldon isn't honest or that he is scheming, but just that sometimes good marriages end in a break-up and the consequences can be hard to live with.

'Right – I know I get control of the capital when I'm forty and it's not far away – but things happen. And I want to set things up, so if I were to die before I'm forty the trust money goes where I want it to go. I made a will at your request after Roddy died, but things have changed since then.'

Gordon says nothing, but he picks up his pencil and pulls his pad towards him. Lara continues, hoping what she is going to say will make sense to him, because she wants these things changed now, whatever might happen with her and Weldon's relationship.

'When Violet died you said the trust would be wound up if I die, and that my will would determine who gets the money. There's presumably no need to change the trust deed, but I want to change my will, so my new wishes and provisions are in place whether I die before I get control of the capital or after.'

She knows Gordon put the traditional clause into her will about any potential future children – but it is no longer good enough.

'I want my will to say that the house goes to Weldon and also one fifth of the capital, another fifth to Charlotte – outright and with no conditions. And the rest sits in a trust for my child, with you, Charlotte and Weldon as trustees.'

There is a long moment of waiting while Gordon makes

notes on his pad and then he looks up. 'Perfectly doable – and it won't take long to do. We can have the paperwork ready for you to sign in a couple of days.'

She can't believe her ears; this seems to have been far too easy. Is he not going to protest, suggest some tweak or another or try to talk her out of it? But no, he looks as if her suggestion is reasonable and nothing out of the ordinary, and the relief makes her grin.

'You have no idea how worried I've been that you would say no, you won't do it,' she says. 'And I'd have to go to someone else to get it done – it would have been so awful!'

'But - and I'm sure you were expecting a "but". Point one, Charlotte doesn't need your money – Jonas's company had him well insured and the Accident Compensation Commission has also paid out. There's no need to give her money and - point two, giving money to Charlotte and not the others would be hard to conceal and would appear unfair, don't you think?'

'My brain isn't working well, is it? I didn't even think of how it would look – I just wanted to make sure Charlotte is OK. So how about I leave a set amount to each of the cousins then? Now that I know what the total is, I know there will be plenty for Weldon and the baby. Let's give them a decent chunk each.'

Chapter 50

On a Friday afternoon in November a message from Tobias arrives, unexpected and with a slightly mysterious undercurrent. "Would you and the big guy like to come on a little excursion tomorrow am, for about an hour. I'll pick you up at ten if that suits you."

Lara reads it twice with a puzzled frown and forwards it to Weldon with a question mark, and he calls her two minutes later.

'Do you know what he's talking about? It seems very mysterious, don't you think?'

'I know – it has that tang of mischief I associate with Tobias, like he's up to something. What do you think?'

'Well, I wouldn't ask him for any details, if I were you. He's sure to be waiting for you to do just that, so leave it and just say we'd love to come. A mystery outing – sounds good to me.'

Tobias and Weldon get on extremely well and seem to understand each other, so she takes his advice and replies saying they would be delighted and will be ready at ten.

· · ·

'Hello, pumpkin,' says Tobias the next morning. 'You look ready to burst. Hi, Weldon. Hop in and we'll go on the mystery tour.'

During the drive the men discuss the new All Black assistant coach and speculate on what caused the sudden change, while Lara sits silent and tries to make deductions from the route. When they pass the ferry terminal and take the extreme left and swing into the old Hutt Road alongside the motorway she gives up and resigns herself to just wait and see, because this is an area she is totally unfamiliar with. Tobias parks outside the giant orange Kennards Storage building, turns the engine off and leads the way to a door on the side of the building.

'We're just looking today, so no need to drive in,' he says over his shoulder and heads down a long corridor with numbered, locked doors on both sides. 'Right, here we are.'

Weldon glances at Lara and she can see he is trying not to laugh, because finding themselves in a storage facility is the last thing they would have guessed as a likely destination.

Tobias unlocks the big padlock, pulls the door open and reaches in to switch the light on and stands back.

'My God!' Lara starts laughing at the sight of three large and brightly painted carousel horses. 'What a surprise!'

'Gorgeous, aren't they? I bought them about ten years ago.' Tobias puts an affectionate hand on the rump of the nearest horse. 'I got them when a travelling circus was getting rid of their large carousel – there were eight of them to start with and I've just finished restoring the last one.' He picks up the leather reins which are looped over the ears of the horse and runs them through his fingers. 'I had to learn leatherwork and a lot of other stuff, but I must say I'm proud of the result.'

'And you've sold five – they must be a collector's item,'

says Weldon and walks around the horses, looking at them from all sides. 'You've done a great job!'

'Oh, I'm not selling them – I've given each of my ex-households, if you can call them that, one each. For the kids, so that's three horses gone and two have been christening presents for godchildren I've acquired along the way. And now I want you to pick one for the pumpkin seed – if you don't mind having one in the house.'

'I can't believe it,' says Lara, still staring as if mesmerised at the gaudy horses tossing their carved manes with a foreleg lifted high. 'They're magnificent. And imagine a child sitting in the saddle on one of these – what a lucky child! Thank you!'

'We need to decide on installation techniques, though. Seeing you two are probably permanently fixed in Orchard Street, I thought it would be lovely to have it the way it was on the carousel, with the pole fixed to the floor and the ceiling. But it's up to you – none of the others have been set up like that. They've removed the bottom end of the pole and had various types of bases made up, but it's not the same as the pole.'

Weldon studies the heavy wooden block under the nearest horse with the pole set in it and then he looks up. 'You had those mountings in the ceiling made especially – very clever. So, if we did it the original way the horse would be on its pole a way off the floor, sort of floating. I think it sounds great. We'd just have to decide on the perfect place – your flat or mine?'

Lara looks thoughtfully at the red, black, and gold horse. 'I love this one, it's so festive and colourful. And don't you think the front hall would be perfect? I'm sure it's big enough and it's shared territory and what a gorgeous sight for visitors and us – open the front door and there it is in all its glory.'

. . .

Back at the Orchard Street house they pause in the front hall to discuss where to place the horse to best advantage without impeding access to doors before going upstairs to Weldon's flat to have lunch. When Tobias leaves it is late afternoon and Lara hugs him as well as she can with the pumpkin bump between them and says, 'You're such a lovely man, Tobias! I'm so glad I accosted you in that restaurant or I would never have known what a treasure you are. Thank you!'

'Pumpkin seed!' says Weldon when Tobias has gone. 'He's a card, that one. Now that I've heard the whole story about how you got to know him, I wish I could have seen you cross the floor and ask him to kiss you in the restaurant. I doubt you could have picked anyone more up to the job than Tobias. And what a magnificent present – what a lucky pumpkin seed! But let's move on to the next problem.'

'Do we have a problem?'

'Names,' says Weldon with a determined look. 'We still haven't decided and I don't think it's a good idea to leave it until she's arrived or we might make some silly choice that the poor kid will resent for the rest of her life – or it will get abbreviated to something silly. Let's sit down and have a serious talk about it when I've tidied up here. You look tired – why don't you go and lie down on your comfortable sofa and I'll come down in a few minutes?'

She knows he's right and she has three names in her head, but for some reason she has held back on telling him what they are, though constantly delaying it isn't going to make it any easier.

'So, names - your surname, of course, as we already

discussed. Winstanley beats Blythe hands down,' he says half an hour later. 'And I veto your suggestion to call her Fay, just to please my mother – I think we should please ourselves, and hopefully the pumpkin seed.'

Lara pushes a cushion behind her back to make herself more comfortable, studies what she can see of her body and sighs. 'I'm like a new species of whale. My three favourite names are Cordelia, Juliet, Isadora and Daisy.'

'Which is actually four – not that it matters,' says Weldon. 'Or did you just add Daisy at the end to kind of provide a contrast?'

'True – I just flicked it in as a total opposite, a diversion, but what do you think?'

'Explain them to me please. They're all very serious names, except Daisy. I know Juliet is in a Shakespeare play, but the others?'

'So is Cordelia – the youngest of King Lear's daughters, the good one. And the most famous Isadora was Isadora Duncan, the scandalous dancer. I just like the sound of the names, nothing to do with who had them earlier.'

Weldon gets his phone out and says, 'Let's do some research – we're not leaving anything to chance when it comes to this naming issue.'

Half an hour later Lara wakes up when Weldon taps her nose. 'Listen to this – your choice of names is very interesting – doom and gloom. In the original version of King Lear, Cordelia ended up in prison and was eventually hanged. Juliet was mistaken for dead by Romeo, who killed himself – then Juliet came to, discovered him dead and stabbed herself and died. So, both of those suffer terrible deaths. Isadora is a lovely name – the original spent her life in the early decades of the nineteen hundreds in France, often drunk, had a lot of lovers, had three children who died in childhood and finally perished herself at the age of fifty, when her long scarf got entangled in a wheel of a sportscar which broke her neck. But I think Daisy is a great name, and it seems to have no dreadful connotations.'

Lara yawns and sits up straight. 'Really? You like it? I'm surprised – but then I was surprised when you had walnut cake too, the first time we met. OK, Daisy is sweet, but it's not so cute you can't imagine an adult woman called Daisy, and Daisy Winstanley is a nice name, I like that both end in a "y" – OK, let's call her Daisy.'

They go to bed in Lara's flat and just before midnight Lara pokes Weldon in the ribs and says, 'I think Daisy wants to come out early.'

Lara opens her eyes and nothing makes sense for a few seconds. She is on her back looking at a white ceiling, but not a familiar one, definitely not her house. And then suddenly, she knows where she is and in a fraction of a second her mind plays back every detail: the hours of contractions at home, the trip to the hospital in Weldon's car, a wheelchair ride and later a trip on a gurney along a corridor with fluorescent light fittings rolling past above her like the white lines in the middle of the road. And then what? Lara frowns and it's not until she suddenly remembers Weldon holding her hand and saying something about "go to sleep" that she puts a hand on her stomach and knows she has had the baby, and she turns her head toward the light.

The window is covered with a curtain, but it is daylight outside, not early morning, later than that. In a large chair with a fold-out foot-rest Weldon reclines with a tiny shape resting on the slope of his chest.

'Weldon,' says Lara and he turns his head and gets up very carefully, with Daisy supported with one hand against his chest.

'There you are! Daisy's been waiting for you to wake up.'

He reaches for the remote with his free hand and raises the head end of Lara's bed slightly before he hands her the baby, and the moment her hands touch her baby's skin Lara falls in love, and she knows it is forever, nothing can change this feeling. The emotion is so strong and so true it brings tears to her eyes, and she looks up at Weldon and sees he is not far off crying either.

'She's perfect,' he says. 'Absolutely perfect. I have inspected every single centimetre of her, and she is the most flawless infant ever created. I think I'm in love.'

Two hours later, when Lara has discovered that having stitches makes going to the toilet a very unpleasant experience and limped back to her bed groaning, Weldon takes her hand.

'Never again! I couldn't bear watching you go through that again, it was too much - brutal,' he says seriously. 'I don't think you're built for it, so let's stop at one – she's got lots of cousins to play with, she doesn't need a sibling.'

Somehow his tone of voice and the way he looks at her seems to signify something, a change which she can't quite define.

'To tell you the truth I never even considered a sibling – it never entered my head. I mean, think of my age - in the risk zone for sure, so no protests from me about being a one-child family.'

'And it will avoid any future crises with my blood pressure, my anxiety levels and the risk of collapsing in a heap on the floor.' Weldon smiles but behind the smile he is serious, and he wants her to know it. 'All of which nearly happened when the worst drama was going on. I really thought you might die when they had such trouble getting her out – and your blood pressure was doing something crazy that worried them, but I never registered the details, I was too busy panicking. Quite frankly, I thought I was seeing my life crumbling in front of me.'

Chapter 52

Lara opens the door and stands to one side as Charlotte enters trying to maintain a steady grip on Thomas's hand, while he struggles to pull her fingers away. 'Where's Daisy? Thomas wants to kiss her. It has to be a supervised kiss if you allow it, because he's developed a new kissing technique that's more like a head butt than a caress – he nearly gave Dad a nosebleed yesterday.'

Lara looks down at Thomas, who is tugging on Charlotte's hand and making growling noises. 'Have you turned into a kissing monster?' She pats his head but he ignores her and continues to struggle. 'But you can't kiss Daisy right now because she isn't here - she's upstairs having a nap with Weldon. He'll bring her down when she wakes up.'

'I thought he was going back to work after two weeks – couldn't he tear himself away?' Charlotte looks back to make sure Lara's font door is closed and releases Thomas's hand.

Lara glances at the ceiling as if she could see the scene in Weldon's living room; she knows, as surely as if she were standing in the door watching them, that Weldon will be sitting in his new reclining armchair with the footrest up, reading something complicated on his tablet with Daisy sprawled like a starfish on his chest, sound asleep.

'He's taken another week – well, he's working part time from home. She seems to love hearing his heartbeat – she goes to sleep on his chest, it settles her down in seconds. Not what the textbooks would recommend, perhaps, but we never read any of the books, so who cares? What is it you wanted to tell me in person? You said you had some news that would interest me.'

They sit on the deck with iced lemonade so they can watch Thomas investigating the garden and digging holes with a soup spoon, and Charlotte brushes shortbread crumbs from her skirt and says quite casually, 'Mark's been arrested and I think the police will want to talk to you.'

'What? Did he attack someone else?'

'No, he got engaged and they went to some house or shop where you can buy drugs – for Mark to get new supplies I suppose but it might have been for him to distribute. And believe it or not, they happened to be there just when the cops did a raid on the place. But anyway, they were caught coming out and he had quite a lot on him when he got arrested, so the charge is dealing a class A drug. You know how there's a kind of legal line drawn between how much is possession for own use before it becomes the sort of quantity that means you're a dealer? Apparently, this was way over the line.'

Frown lines have appeared between Lara's eyebrows while she has listened to this, and now she says impatiently, 'So how am I of interest? He never used drugs here, he was only here twice after I moved in and for very short visits. God! I hope I'm not going to be suspected of drug use.'

'No, of course you won't – but someone's told the cops

how he assaulted you and since then they've seen the photo you put on Facebook. Anna followed up on the rumour she heard and discovered there was a mention somewhere of how he might get a warning or something – because of his otherwise impeccable character and work history! Which is why someone has told them about him assaulting you. And then the cops got hold of Anna after they read the stream of comments on your post with the photo. She was the only one who had named him, so they've talked to her to confirm it's the same "Mark". And she called an hour ago and asked me to give you advance warning because you weren't answering her text messages or calls this morning.'

And as they sit there staring at each other, at a loss about what to say, the doorbell rings and Lara thinks, it simply can't be the police, not when we've just talked about them – it would be a ridiculous coincidence, the sort of thing that would only happen in a TV drama.

She opens the door and finds two police officers on the doorstep and nearly laughs out loud, because suddenly the situation seems farcical rather than serious and it changes her mood.

'Oh no,' she says, smiling cheerfully, when they ask if there is a space where they can talk to her in private. 'There's no need for that. This is my cousin Charlotte, who knows all about it, and Thomas is too young to understand what we're talking about. Come out on the deck so we can watch Thomas eat dirt while we talk. Would you like a glass of home-made lemonade? We're just having some – no? Well, just go ahead with the questions then.'

They have barely started when Weldon comes through the French doors from the living room with a sleeping Daisy draped over his shoulder.

'Hi - I thought I heard Mark's name mentioned from upstairs,' he says and sits down beside Lara. 'I'm Lara's partner and this is Daisy. If you want to know what Mark did to Lara, I can tell you, because I was upstairs when she opened the door for him and I heard the whole thing, including the thump when he punched her in the face. I tossed him out, of course, and I can sign a witness statement or whatever is required.'

It's over in a surprisingly short time and the police officers leave after asking Lara and Weldon to come in and sign formal statements the next day.

'Remember to bring your phone so we can sight the photos with the date,' says the older of the two on the doorstep. 'Just so it all fits together timewise. And please reconsider if you want to press charges personally – it will add weight to the prosecution's case. Your friend Anna mentioned rumours about other incidents in the past and we're looking into those as well. Having a drug user with violent tendencies out there menacing women is not a good thing.'

'I'll think about it,' is all Lara says before she closes the door behind them and turns to Weldon. 'What do you think?'

But before he has time to answer she hears a muted buzz and realises it's coming from the pocket of her jacket which hangs on a hook just inside the door. Pulling the phone out she looks at the screen and sees that it's Anna calling and thinks, another ridiculous coincidence, today is a day of surprises. She turns the phone to speaker mode. 'Hi Anna - the cops have just been. I didn't hear my phone before – I'd left it in my jacket pocket.'

'How did it go? Was Weldon there as well?'

'Yes, it was a very social interview, practically a family event.' Lara laughs as she walks through the living room to the deck. 'Charlotte and Thomas are here – then Weldon came down from upstairs with Daisy, and we conducted the interview on the deck, so it was very domesticated. And now we're on speaker and we can have a group discussion about whether I should press charges or just let the cops do whatever they do.'

'Oh, you should,' says Anna seriously. 'You absolutely should! It's important now, because I've heard about a couple of other incidents, and it all adds up. I've been sleuthing around on social media, and I've got the names of two girls who ended up with injuries after encounters with Mark, one with bruising around her neck, photos available. Because I now work at the same law firm where Mark was at, I've found out a few things from the girls here. So, it's got to get done – he's a menace to women and needs to be stopped. I've been in touch with both of those women, but just briefly so far.'

'OK, I will,' says Lara, who has been thinking hard while Anna was speaking. 'Are the others going to do it too? Press charges I mean - tell them I'll pay for you to represent all the women you can find who're willing to lay complaints – just in case it makes them more willing to come forward.'

'Oh, great!' says Anna. 'Thank you! I think it might make a difference to at least one of them, the one whose neck was bruised. She never reported it at the time because she was scared of Mark retaliating. When I finally identified her and called her, she said "he was getting so weird, it was the drugs he was taking, and I thought he'd get to me before the cops could do anything if I reported him". And she might have been right.'

Weldon puts his hand on Lara's shoulder and says, 'Anna, we'll fund anyone who needs it – or even if they don't need it but who come forward.'

'You can put them in touch with me if that's any help.' Lara pauses and thinks for a moment. 'Unless it puts the situation into the realm of conspiracy? But they might need some emotional support?'

By the time Charlotte leaves it is late afternoon and Weldon has put Daisy in her Moses basket and gone back upstairs to do some work, while Lara makes a meal.

'Fridge dinner!' she says when he comes back down a couple of hours later. 'We have enough leftovers for a kind of multi-component meal - let's eat now before she wakes up. I checked on her a few minutes ago and she's sound asleep.'

'I've got a present for you.' He hands her a plain white box with no markings. 'Let's see if you can guess what it is.'

Inside the box is a small rectangular plastic object the size of a matchbox and Lara turns it in her hands and sees a USB port on one side.

'One of those backup things? Or some security gizmo? I've no idea, really − it could be anything. There's a little slide thing on the side, does it open? Maybe it's a tracker for my car in case Daisy and I get hijacked, so you can find us?'

'Your imagination is doing well but not quite well enough.' He takes the device out of her hand, moves the slider to the right and hands it back. 'Listen − and don't hold it too far away.'

She holds it close to her head and stares at him, overwhelmed. 'A heart beating! Oh my God, you've recorded your heartbeat for Daisy.'

'For when I go back to work on Monday − it might be a good thing to have if she frets and my chest isn't available. I bought two − the other one is under her mattress in the Moses basket right now, but one here and one upstairs seemed a good idea.'

'Brilliant! How long does the recording last before you have to restart it?'

'It goes forever – when you turn it on, it plays in an endless loop. But after a few hours of use – about ten I think – you need to plug it into a USB port somewhere, your laptop for example, and recharge it.'

Then he laughs. 'God, I hope we're not creating an addict and end up having to wean her off it when she goes on sleep-overs – or when she gets a boyfriend.'

And Lara turns back to the oven and thinks, here's this man I got to know more or less by chance, and he's a bit overweight and not at all handsome, certainly not anyone's idea of a romantic hero. A man, who is often happier being silent than talking, but he can bake cinnamon scroll buns and a better father would be hard to find - my best friend. Serendipity is the only word for it.

Chapter 53

Lara has just put Daisy to bed in the cot they bought when she turned four months, with an identical one upstairs in Weldon's flat, when she hears his footsteps thundering down the stairs.

'I don't know what's going on with your bank,' he says frowning as he walks in looking down at his phone. 'Look at this! I can't believe you hadn't noticed - it's been going on for months!'

She takes the phone and glances at the screen before she hands it back, goes to the fridge and gets a bottle of chardonnay out, hands it to Weldon and turns back for glasses.

'Pour us a drink – we might need it! I can't believe you hadn't noticed earlier,' she smiles at his concerned face, but she knows this might go wrong very quickly and she will have to be prepared to back down and admit defeat. 'I set up an automatic thing which just returns your fortnightly rent payments to your account. I decided I don't want to be your landlady any longer.'

'Now listen,' says Weldon and his voice has taken on the serious tone he only uses when he is worried about something. 'You can't do this – I know we live in separate flats, but it might turn into one of those situations where I can claim half your assets, like my former partner nearly managed to do with mine. And think what Gordon would say – he would be horrified if he found out.'

Lara points towards the living room, tries to make her voice calm and unconcerned. 'Please sit down and listen, and I'll tell you why.'

She sits in the chair beside his and smiles into his serious face, hoping he will understand and accept and not become insistent. 'Point one – I am an independent adult. Point two – Gordon has nothing to do with what goes on in my bank account.'

She takes a sip and puts the glass on the coffee table and counts her points off on her fingers. 'Point three – I don't want to be your landlady because I'd rather be your partner and your lover and the mother of your child. Point four – there's so much damn money in the trust it doesn't even matter if you walk away with half of it – it's an obscene amount which I never did anything to earn. I just had a very famous and successful father who never spent any of his loot on himself.'

'Ah – the trust!' he says. 'Of course, the trust can't be shared, so that's safe. Good! But even so, the house ...'

'Weldon, please don't be difficult about this! If I die you get this house unconditionally and a large chunk of money, and you become a trustee along with Charlotte and Gordon – if the trust is still operational. It gets wound up or whatever it's called in fifteen months when I turn forty, so chances are I'll survive until then. And paying rent is silly when we both know our friends-with-benefits arrangement is as good as a marriage anyway – I presume you feel this too? Can't we just forget about the damn rent? It doesn't sit well with me, it feels wrong – and it's so silly when we share a lot of expenses and buy the things we both need or use.'

He makes no response to this, so she continues, trying to sound calm and reasonable, as if they were talking about who is paying for a meal out or something minor.

'This is how I think about the money bouncing back to you – you can feel you're paying rent if that's what you want to do, and I can then gift it back to you because I don't need it or want it. And if anyone wants to check the answer is clear – you are paying rent. How's that?'

He sits silent for a long while looking out into the garden where dusk is just about to trigger the light which illuminates the tree, and she watches his face and thinks that this is one of the many things she likes about him. This ability to quietly consider and weigh things up, no knee-jerk reactions and no outbursts of emotional debate, and at the end of the process he will say something which makes perfect sense. And now his attention swings back to her and he nods.

'OK – I won't argue, I can see it would upset you. And as you said, if I'm in your will then you obviously mean it. When did you make the will?'

Her relief is immense, and she reaches out and curls her fingers around his, grateful for his lack of emotional arguing or protests for form's sake, and also for the lack of effusive thanks.

'Oh, ages ago – when I was pregnant. I wanted to make sure you'd never need to move or lack for anything – I think the main thing in my mind was that if I died in childbirth, you would be so well provided for that you could look after Daisy, stay at home and be a full-time parent if that's what you wanted, or hire a live-in nanny. It felt urgent at the time and then after she was born, I wanted the safeguard for you and for Daisy forever.'

He lifts her hand off his and kissed her knuckles. 'I would never leave you, Lara.'

And she believes him, he is truly hers.

Many Thanks

We hope you've enjoyed reading this story and would consider leaving a review on your favourite review site, or with the retailer you purchased from.

These are not only much appreciated, they also help other readers discover new authors.

For more in this ongoing series, plus other titles, please read on.

Letters from the Past

Letters from the Past is a series of stand-alone novels where a letter from or about the past reveals something that changes a woman's perceptions of herself or of her family, and that affects her outlook on life.

These books are such fun to write, and I am always working on the next title in this series. I hope you will enjoy reading them as much as I enjoy writing them!

Tina

Having had nobody in her life since her husband died, Lara unexpectedly finds herself involved with three men. One is planning to use her, one she plans to use for her own ends, and one becomes a "friend-with-benefits" with surprising results. Sometimes a quiet schoolteacher is not all she seems at first glance.

Callista experiences an event of apparent ESP at the Okehampton Castle ruins and becomes a media sensation, but the effect it has on her life is dramatic. How do two people, one calm. one seriously claustrophobic, who feel they are poles apart, cope for an hour and a half in total darkness in a stalled lift? And can they handle the consequences?

Sofia's life is in turmoil: a difficult diva mother, a letter with a confession about a family killing and having to accept help from a man she loathes when she is injured. Can reluctant attraction turn into love?

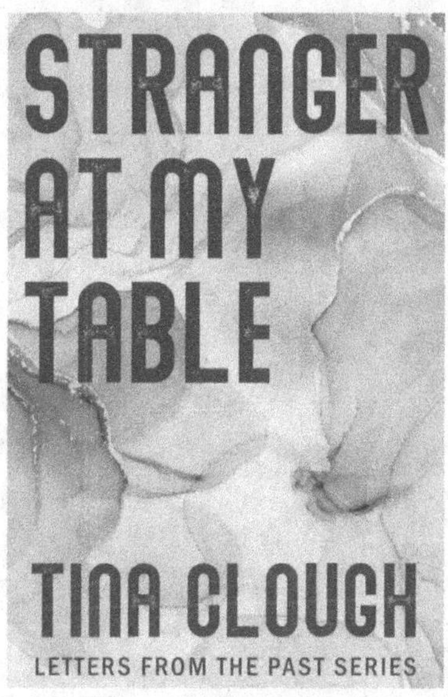

Who is the stranger living in the empty house Miranda inherited from her grandmother? Why is he living like a secretive recluse in someone else's house? Reckless Miranda decides to confront him, and what she discovers prompts her to set out on a fearless quest to bring justice to a man who has given up hope. But is the gamble too great or a risk worth taking?

When Emma finds an old letter in a library book she is instantly intrigued, but by researching the origin of the letter she unwittingly opens the door to danger and becomes the target for threats and harassment. Nearly desperate, she takes a leap of blind faith into the unknown and accepts an offer of help from a stranger - but can she trust him?

Jamie, an ardent protester against the gigantic Vista Resort development and Leo Masters, the high-powered developer, seem unlikely to ever agree on anything. But unexpected coincidences and chance brings them together in a fragile state of mutual respect. Will courage and kindness resolve the situation, or do they need help?

After a bizarre accident with ESP overtones, the media haunt Arapera. But can she trust an offer of help from a man she has only met once? Or will she regret it for the rest of her life if she doesn't take the chance? Sometimes life is a knife-edge balance between staying safe and taking risks, and there is no way of predicting if the gamble is worth it.

Also by Tina Clough

THE GIRL WHO LIVED TWICE

What would you do if you woke up one morning and found that time had rewound exactly a year? Would you revisit your past mistakes and try to do better? Would you try to get revenge on those who had wronged you? Or would you use what you knew to get rich? When Mia finds herself in her own past, she must decide how best to use her pre-knowledge of one year's worth of events and personal issues.

RUNNING TOWARDS DANGER

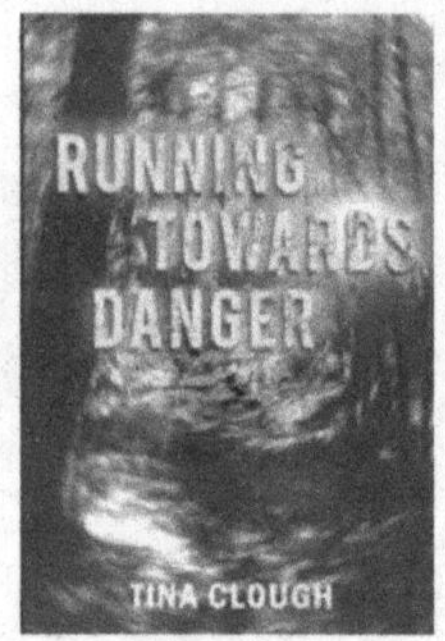

When Karen's flat-mate Nick is gunned down in front of her in the street her life is turned upside-down. Everything she thought she knew about him turns out to be a lie. She becomes a suspect in the police investigation and drug bosses think she knows where Nick has hidden a large sum of money. When her life is threatened, she decides to leave town and disappear.

Karen becomes Cara and creates an anonymous existence, severs all links to her past and adopts a cash-based way of life that leaves no electronic traces. But despite her careful planning danger still stalks her and she is forced to make dramatic choices in the face of threats and brutal violence.

Can she trust the man she is attracted to, or has he been sent by the killers to gain her confidence and find the money they believe she has?

THE CHINESE PROVERB

Book 1 - Hunter Grant Series

Army veteran Hunter Grant thought he had left war behind in Afghanistan – a conflict that left him with physical and psychological scars.

But finding an unconscious girl in the Northland bush and gradually untangling her story involves him in warfare of a different kind in his own country.

Hunter sets out to find and punish the man Dao calls Master, but he soon finds there is more to this story than enslavement. Before long he himself is being hunted by the overlord of a drug empire whose sole objective is to kill Dao because she knows too much.

Protecting her and waging war while trying to keep the police from stifling his enterprise takes all Hunter's ingenuity and determination and puts him in deadly jeopardy.

ONE SINGLE THING

Book 2 - Hunter Grant Series

Journalist Hope Barber disappears two weeks after returning to New Zealand from an assignment in Pakistan, leaving her front door open and her bag and phone inside. The police are tight-lipped about their reluctance to act, and Hunter Grant and Dao agree to help Hope's brother Noah find her. Details about Hope's time in Pakistan gradually emerge but only raise more questions.

Was Hope under surveillance?

Was she linked to terrorists?

And who is the man Hope called 'my stalker'?

FOLDED

Book 3 - Hunter Grant Series

First notes asking for help and folded into tiny origami shapes are found outside a city apartment building, then a physics textbook with tiny writing between the lines and then the woman who found them abruptly resigns and disappears. Are the notes asking for help real or is it a game? Hunter Grant, ex-army and with a pragmatic view of justice, reluctantly agrees to help find the missing woman.

Things get complicated when a high-powered lawyer arrives form the US, and shortly after his meeting with Hunter and Dao, a "cease and desist" letter arrives from the Cayman Islands. Inspector Bakker - a woman, who in Hunter's words "looks as if she would be useful in a brawl, provided she was on your side" - takes instant exception to his involvement and threatens to arrest him for interfering in an investigation.

Dao sets out alone on a dangerous mission, driven by a compulsive need to find out what has happened to the girl who wrote the notes, and Hunter looks death in the face when he decides to risk everything to put an end to the Darknet forces that threaten their lives.

THE SHADOW BROKER

It is 2026 and individual freedoms are severely curtailed, with state surveillance everywhere. State Security has a Watch List, and being on it means that nothing you do or say escapes the authorities, but does the Kill List really exist? And if it does, how would you know if you were on it?

Coded messages on a found burner phone, top-level government corruption and a shadowy mastermind who calls himself The Broker. In this climate of state control, three unlikely friends start quietly looking for connections and set in motion a deadly game of hide and seek that will change their lives forever.

Trying to uncover the truth means risking your life, and nothing is more dangerous than searching for evidence of government corruption.

About the Author

Tina Clough grew up in Sweden and now lives in New Zealand; dividing her time between writing fiction and translating and editing medical research papers.

Between working and writing she looks after an acre of fruit trees, vegetable gardens and roaming hens.

Apart from reading her interests include photography, wine, growing organic vegetables, making jam and kayaking.

https://lightpoolpublishing.com